Deadly Secrets

By Hilda Stahl

Victory House, Inc.
Tulsa, OK

Published by
Victory House, Inc.
P.O. Box 700238
Tulsa, Oklahoma 74170
(918-747-5009)

Dedicated To

My Son

BRADLEY ALLEN STAHL

"Mighty Warrior"
(number three of seven)

About the Author

Hilda Stahl was born and raised in the Nebraska Sandhills with sand between her toes and wind in her hair. She walked the prairie, enjoying the vastness, and never once thought about writing or being a writer.

After accepting Christ into her life as a young teen she felt a great call from God to help others.

As a young wife and mother living in Michigan, Hilda knew she couldn't leave her family to be a missionary or an evangelist. One day she saw an ad for a correspondence course in writing and took it. Some days she'd only have minutes to write, but she wrote during those minutes. She studied books on how to write every opportunity she had. She wrote when the babies were in bed or in school. She wrote even when rejection slips piled high around her. She wrote when she was too tired to see. She wrote and she wrote, and then she began selling almost everything that she wrote. That's how this award-winning author of nearly 100 books and hundreds of short stories began touching hearts with God's love. She belongs to the Society of Children's Book Writers and is listed in many publications including *Foremost Women of the 20th Century, International Authors* and *Writer's Who's Who,* and *The World's Who's Who of Women.* Her books are published in several languages.

Hilda Stahl — one of America's best loved authors. Her stories combine mystery, adventure, romance and real-life conflicts. Her books help readers to handle situations in their own lives as well as show that God is always the answer.

Hilda Stahl had a dream that she would be a famous writer; the dream came true. Even though she went home to be with the Lord in early 1993, Hilda's books continue to minister to people around the world. *Deadly Secrets* was published posthumously.

Chapter 1

With the blare of country music from a nearby music store following her, Carolynn Burgess eased open the back door that led directly into Dud Dumars' office in downtown Middle Lake. He'd called her practically the minute he'd gotten back from his vacation and asked her to meet him at noon without letting anyone know — not even Jay Sommers, the only person in the office who knew she was not just a part-time secretary for Dumars' Investigative Services, but an undercover investigator.

Excitement trickled down her spine. She'd thought about retiring since she was nearing the age of retirement, but she couldn't handle the thought of staying home all day without the excitement of working for Dud. She smiled at the man sitting behind the wide desk. The smell of peppermint candy tickled her nose. "You're looking good, Dud."

Grinning, he pushed himself up, hiked up his gray slacks and rubbed a veined hand over the pink spot on his bald head. He was short and wiry with a mind like a steel trap. "Meg's better."

"Praise God!" Carolynn brushed a tear off her dark lashes. It had been touch and go with Meg for the past few months.

"I appreciate your prayers." Dud blushed slightly. He wasn't used to talking openly about anything religious.

Carolynn sat on the folding chair across the desk

from Dud. He had his visitors use the uncomfortable chair on purpose to keep them from staying too long. She crossed her legs and dropped her purse on the floor beside her. She wore aqua slacks and a cotton blouse with splashes of pink and aqua. She studied Dud thoughtfully. "So, did you call me to tell me Meg's better?"

"I wanted you to know, but I need something else." He settled in his high-back leather chair, then with his arms on his desk, leaned toward her. "It's not often that Meg asks me to help someone, so when she does I jump to it."

Carolynn lifted a brow and waited.

"Meg met the young man at the grocery store yesterday. He struck up a conversation." Dud rolled his eyes. "I know it's not like Meg to talk to strangers, but she said this one really touched her heart."

Carolynn chuckled. "Why's it so hard for you to get to the bottom line, Dud?"

He shrugged. "It's not the normal way I do business."

"Tell me anyway."

"Gil Oakes is the stranger's name. He's in his mid-twenties and he's looking for his birth mother. He said he knows she's in the area, but he can't trace her. He's been here almost a year and still nothing."

Dud looked out the window to the right of his desk, then across at a water color of flying ducks on the far wall, then finally back at Carolynn. "Meg told him I'd find his birth mother for him." Dud cleared his throat. "For free!"

Carolynn saw the color creep up Dud's wrinkled,

scrawny neck and she chuckled. "So, you're embarrassed that you agreed after all these years of saying you run a business, not a charity."

"Something like that."

"And you want me to find this Gil Oakes's birth mother?"

Dud nodded.

Carolynn studied him closely. "Do you want me to do it for free?"

Dud barely moved his head.

She laughed again and waved a hand. "Sure. I'll do it."

He brushed his hand over his face. "You know you don't have to."

"I know. I finished the case at the Provincial House — it turned out to be nothing — and the cantata is over, so I have time." Carolynn pulled her notebook and pencil out of her purse. "I wish you could've heard the cantata. It was inspiring!"

"And you sang the lead?"

She nodded. Once she'd dreamed of being a professional singer, but it had been impossible for her to do so because of her family obligations, so she sang at church, weddings and other functions. She sang wherever she was welcome and always did so with her whole heart.

She opened her notebook. "What've you got?"

"Gil Oakes was born in Flint to an unwed mother, Melanie Reeve, and she put him up for adoption through Children's Services. His search led him to Grand Rapids, then here to Middle Lake. But he hit a dead end."

Carolynn quickly wrote the name and info. "She could've changed her name. Married." Carolynn looked up, her pencil still over her pad. "Or be dead!"

Dud nodded. "Meg said Gil Oakes was afraid she might be dead. Got tears in his eyes, Meg said."

"What about the birth father?"

"He didn't mention him. I don't know if he knows his name."

"How am I supposed to handle this?"

Dud ran a finger around his collar. "I'm a suspicious man, Carolynn. We all know that."

She grinned and nodded.

"Why would this stranger talk to my wife in the grocery store and spill his guts to her?"

"Why indeed?"

"I want you to check him out, but also find his birth mother. I don't want him to know you're working for me."

"Fine by me. You got an address, phone number and place of employment for this Gil Oakes?"

"Right here." Dud handed a piece of paper to Carolynn. "Meg trusts him. Who knows? Maybe she has every right to. This business made me cynical." Dud grinned. "If my own mother was alive, I wouldn't even trust her!"

"Are you thinking Gil Oakes played up to Meg just to get her to get you to help him for free?"

"You cut right to the chase, don't you?"

"Sure do." Carolynn tucked the paper and the notebook back in her purse. "That's why you hired me to do undercover work for you all these years."

"You're right about that, lady!"

Carolynn glanced toward the door. "I'm changing the subject on you, Dud."

"Shoot."

"What's Lavery up to?" Her name was Christine Lavery, but she insisted on being called Lavery. She was Dud's only woman detective. For the past several years she'd taken it on herself to prove Carolynn was more than a secretary. So far, she hadn't succeeded. "Lately she's been dogging my tracks, getting a little too close for comfort."

Dud slowly walked around his desk and leaned back against it. "I noticed she's been real short-tempered since I got back from vacation. Maybe she needs time off. Maybe it's a woman thing. PMS or whatever."

Carolynn laughed and shook her head. "Or maybe she's pregnant. My girls all got crabby when they were."

"She says she doesn't want kids. Too much work. Too hard on the figure." Dud picked up the photo of his three daughters. "I'm sure glad Meg never felt that way."

"Children and grandchildren are a special blessing all right. Lavery doesn't think so." Carolynn slowly stood and hooked her purse strap over her shoulder. "Keep an eye on Lavery for me, Dud. I don't want her learning about me. She'd spread it around town and especially to my family."

"Don't give her a thought, Carolynn. You're smarter than she is. But I will watch her." He walked to the back door with Carolynn. "Lavery's still licking her wounds over that case she fumbled. She'll get over it in time. She's a lady full of pride. And her pride was hurt."

"Everybody messes up once in a while. Jay Sommers and I did over that Provincial House deal. How can Lavery think she'll always win?"

"That's her nature, I guess. I'll give her a few days off. Tell her to go away with her husband for a while."

"Good idea." Carolynn opened the door, checked to make sure Lavery wasn't in sight, said goodbye and hurried to her car.

She glanced at her watch and groaned. She'd promised Christa she'd pick Adrial up from the airport. Christa and Ian were both too busy, so they'd asked her yesterday. Christa was her second daughter and Adrial was Ian's niece. Adrial was going to spend part of the summer with Jeanna, Christa and Ian's only child.

Carolynn sighed and started the car. She'd promised to pick up Adrial, so she'd do it, then she'd get down to business with the detective work she'd been hired to do. "This time without pay," she said with a chuckle.

★   ★   ★

He parked his car several spaces back from hers in the almost-empty parking lot of Middle Lake Christian Center and rolled his window down. Warm wind blew against him and he closed his eyes for a minute, enjoying it. This was a good time of year. Red, pink and blue flowers were blooming along the sidewalks and the trees along the street were full of leaves. It had been another long Michigan winter. Spring had flirted with them last month, but finally it had arrived to stay. He chuckled under his breath, then muttered, " 'Flirted with them.' I like that. I'll have to remember it."

He leaned out the window to get a better look at the woman as she slipped from her car. He frowned. He should've killed her yesterday when he'd had the chance outside of Wendy's. Could he follow her into the church and do it? It seemed almost — irreverent.

The smell of exhaust fumes from the traffic on the street filled the air. A small, long-haired brown dog yapped, ran across the parking lot and disappeared around the corner of the church.

The church reminded him of the one his mother had sent him to when he was thirteen. It sprawled out across the well-kept green lawn. Broad sidewalks ran from each door to the vast paved parking area. The giant sanctuary with a tall white cross splitting the sky was flanked with huge wings, probably Sunday school rooms and a fellowship hall. It was bigger than the church he'd attended when he was thirteen, but it was painted the same white with the same copper-colored roof. He'd hated the church but he'd had to go anyway. He pressed his lips tightly together and his stomach rolled. People had stared at him and whispered behind their hands about him. He'd burned with embarrassment but never said a word to let on. Finally he'd wised up. He'd get off the church bus, sneak away to a nearby park, then slip back when it was time for the Sunday school bus to take him home again.

Impatiently he pushed thoughts of his past aside and watched the woman lock her car door, hesitate, then

look around. Her face was almost as white as the clouds
in the sky, making her red lips stand out boldly. The
wind tugged at her purple skirt and tousled her long
brown hair. A wide purple belt that circled her narrow
waist held her multi-colored blouse tucked in. She was
pretty.

His grip tightened on the steering wheel. She might
be pretty on the outside, but inside she was as ugly as
sin!

With a toss of her head she walked to the side door
of the church and disappeared inside.

With a slow, deliberate movement he opened the car
door to follow her. Another car pulled into the parking
lot and stopped with a screech near the doorway the
woman had walked through. He growled low in his
throat. Sweat beaded his forehead and he quickly pulled
the door closed. He watched the driver get out of the
car. She was about the same age as the woman he'd
followed. She wore jeans and a pink, pull-over top with
flowers around the neckline. Her long, light-brown
hair was held back in a ponytail with a wide pink stretch
band. She opened her tan purse and pulled out a tissue.
She bit her lip and dabbed at her eyes and cheeks. He
frowned. Was she crying? His heart went out to her
and he wanted to make her feel better, but he sat still
and watched her run into the church. Had she come
to see the woman he'd followed?

He slapped the steering wheel. Once again he'd lost
an opportunity to kill her. He knew her name just as
he'd known the names of the other women, but he
never used their names even in his thoughts. It was

better that way. He served justice as he should without being swayed by a pretty face or a nice name.

★   ★   ★

Inside the church, Silver Rawlings stopped, took a deep, shuddering breath, and dabbed at her moist face again. "I won't cry again," she whispered even as tears filled her eyes. She looked down the wide hall toward Tim's office. He wasn't expecting her, but she knew he was expecting Gwen Nichols. Was the woman she'd followed into the building Gwen Nichols? Silver bit back an anguished moan. Pain like a million needles jabbed her heart. If so, were they together right this minute? Surely Tim wouldn't agree to let Gwen even see Brittany! But he was kind-hearted. As the assisant pastor of Middle Lake Christian Center he was expected to be kind.

Silver ran down the tiled hall to Tim's office and burst through the door. It was empty. Her breast rose and fell. "Tim?" Her voice was barely above a whisper. She stepped back out in the hall and listened for voices. With the office doors closed it was impossible to hear anything. She ran back down the hall to the secretary's office. May DeBoor wasn't at her desk, but the custodian, Sherard Roscoe, was dusting the plants that hung around a wide window. He turned, the rag dangling from his wide hand. Wide red suspenders held up his dark-green pants and kept his matching shirt tucked in at his wide hips. Shadows of the plant leaves covered his bald head. He narrowed his blue eyes.

"Something wrong, Mrs. Rawlings?" No matter how

many times she'd asked him to call her Silver, he wouldn't.

"I'm — looking for my husband."

"I saw Tim about an hour ago in his office."

"He's not there now." Silver looked toward May's desk. "Where's May?"

"Took a break since I was in here. She'll be back in a couple of minutes." Sherard tucked the corner of the rag in his back pocket. "You look upset. Anything I can do?"

Silver shook her head. What could anyone do except maybe Gwen Nichols? "I must speak with Tim."

"Check the nursery. He told me earlier he'd forgotten his daughter's jacket Sunday."

Silver nodded. Tim had gotten Brittany from the toddler nursery on Sunday and had forgotten her jacket. "Thanks, Sherard." Silver hurried away without even a proper goodbye.

The nurseries were on either side of the vestibule, making it easier for parents to drop off babies and toddlers on their way into church.

Silver stopped in the vestibule, her heart thundering. Was Tim talking with Gwen about Brittany in the toddler nursery? Silver leaned weakly against the wide oak table that held two tall silver candlesticks with white candles on either side of a basket of silk flowers that looked real — bright yellow daffodils, vibrant pink hyacinths, delicate baby's breath and feathery green fern. She looked down at the spotlessly clean white tile floor, then at the empty coat rack along the wall. Slowly she walked toward the closed door of the toddler's nursery. Would Tim and Gwen be inside?

Silver opened the door, then gasped. Tears streaming down her face, the woman Silver had followed into church knelt on the floor. Tim wasn't there. "Is there something I can do?" Silver asked in a low voice.

The woman jumped up and brushed frantically at her tears. "I thought I was alone. I didn't mean to trespass."

Silver frowned. "Were you here to see someone? Are you — Gwen Nichols?"

The woman brushed past Silver and ran out the door.

Silver stood uncertainly, then hurried to find Tim before he gave Gwen Nichols permission to see baby Brittany.

★   ★   ★

Jeanna Shaneck forced a bright smile as she walked across the patio to Mick. "Just wait 'til you meet Adrial, Mick! She's my favorite cousin and I know you'll love her."

Mick caught Jeanna's hand and pulled her to the bench beside him. "I wanted us to have time for each other this summer, Jae. With you working three days a week at your mom's store and doing volunteer work twice a week at the Provincial House and me working the hours I do, we won't see much of each other. I don't want your cousin to come between us."

Jeanna forced back a shiver as she leaned against Mick and touched his strong arm that was warm from the hot sun. "I've decided not to work at the Provincial House any more." A band tightened around her heart and she turned her head away from Mick's surprised look. She couldn't talk about the Provincial House with him or with anyone. No one must ever learn the terrible secret that was ruining her life.

"Does Kip know this?"

"Why should your brother know what I do or don't do?" Her voice cracked and she flushed.

"You two have been going there together for months now. I thought you enjoyed it as much as he does."

She turned to Mick and forced a smile. "Hey, I want to think about Adrial coming. She should be here soon."

"You're sure she won't take up all your time?"

"I always have time for you, Mick. Who helped you build up those gorgeous muscles when you started your weight-lifting program when we were thirteen?" She wrinkled her small nose, then grinned. "I won't let anything get in the way of our being together this summer." She glanced across her yard to his and the smile froze on her face. Kip stood beside his car looking at them, at her. He lifted his hand in a wave and she quickly turned away. She would not let him know that she'd seen the wave, nor would she wave back!

Mick tugged a short, brown curl. "Why the scowl, Jeanna?"

She wiped it away with a quick smile. Mick didn't need to know that his brother made her feel very strange. "What is keeping Grandma? She should be here from the airport soon. I wish I could've gone with her to pick up Adrial." Jeanna rubbed her hand down her shorts, then flicked an ant off her bare leg. "I haven't seen Adrial for four years. We used to have so much fun together and so much in common. Did I tell you that we both loved to read and that we could talk for hours about a book that we'd both liked?"

Mick laughed and tapped the end of Jeanna's straight nose. "I think you've told me all about Adrial Shaneck. My interest is in the curly, brown-headed beauty, Jeanna Marie Shaneck. You know the one? She's the girl with brown eyes and a great body, plus a brain that equals Kip's."

She raised her eyes in mock despair and tried to ignore the prickle of awareness that she felt just hearing Kip's name linked with hers. She glanced next door again just as Kip backed out of the short driveway in his silver Toyota and drove away. Now, she could breathe again. She forced a laugh and squeezed Mick's hand. "Your brain is just as good as Kip's and you know it."

Mick flexed his muscles and his blue eyes sparkled with laughter. "Muscles and brains. Who can resist that combination? Now, if I had talent to write like you and to paint like Kip, I'd have it made. I wouldn't be your average, but handsome boy planning to be a gym teacher."

She thumped his broad chest that was covered with a tan tank top. "Well, average, but handsome boy, I think you're wonderful and so will Adrial."

"Oh, sure. I'll knock her off her feet!" He jumped up and swung Jeanna around with a loud whoop. She squealed and laughed and almost kicked the black cockapoo that lay in the grass beside the patio. The dog lifted his head and peeked through his hair and barked two short yaps. Jeanna pulled free from Mick and dropped down beside the dog and hugged him.

"It's all right, Blacky. The big brute didn't hurt me. But he seems to forget that I'm not twelve."

"Your grandma's driving in, Jeanna."

Jeanna leaped up with Blacky beside her as a small, blue car stopped outside the garage door and Carolynn Burgess slipped out. Her light-brown hair was cut short and waved around her head. Her blue eyes crinkled into a smile as Jeanna called to her, then ran around to the passenger side of the car.

"Adrial?" Jeanna stopped dead as the tall girl slid out of the car. Could this gorgeous creature be the plain girl she'd seen before? Her strawberry-blonde hair curled and fluffed around her beautiful face. She was dressed in a soft lime-colored dress that showed off her narrow waist and left her long legs bare from the knees down. She had a figure that matched Miss America as well as Miss Universe. "Is it really you, Adrial?"

She laughed a silvery laugh and flung her arms around Jeanna. "Of course it's me. I got tired of being ugly and decided that I could be as beautiful as you if I worked at it. You know, the right clothes and makeup and hair style."

"I am overwhelmed! You are absolutely gorgeous!" Jeanna turned to introduce Mick to Adrial but her voice stuck in her throat at the look on his face. If she didn't know better she'd think he'd fallen in love.

Adrial stepped forward with her hand out. "Hello, I'm Adrial Shaneck."

"Mick. Mick Jennings. I live just next door so we'll be seeing a lot of each other." He took her hand in his.

Jeanna looked from Mick to Adrial with a frown.

"I'm glad." Adrial finally pulled her hand free and turned to Jeanna. "It's great being here! I think it'll be a better summer than I thought."

Jeanna moistened her suddenly dry lips with the tip of her tongue, then reached in the back seat to lift out the travel bag.

"I'll open the trunk," said Carolynn. "Mick, how about helping with that stuff?"

"Sure, Mrs. Burgess." He ran around to the back of the car and eagerly lifted out the bag while Adrial followed him. Her skirt swished around her shapely legs and Mick took it all in as if he'd never seen beautiful legs before.

Jeanna suddenly felt too thin and ugly. She stood helplessly beside the car. If Mick went this crazy over Adrial, what would Kip do? He was older than Mick and he'd dated girls longer. Abruptly Jeanna pushed thoughts of Kip away.

"A guitar!" exclaimed Mick as Carolynn lifted it out. "Do you play guitar, Adrial?"

"I'm quite good and I love it!" Adrial turned to Carolynn. "I'm really looking forward to hearing you sing again."

"Thanks." Carolynn closed the trunk with a click.

Jeanna walked slowly toward the back door, a case in each hand, as she remembered the hours she'd listened to beginning guitar lessons when she'd stayed with Adrial four years ago. Jeanna frowned. Maybe this summer wasn't going to be as great as she'd thought.

Mick opened the back door and waited while the

others walked inside. "I'll carry the things upstairs if
you want."

Carolynn nodded as she set the guitar down. "That
would be nice, Mick. I have to get going, kids." She
hugged Jeanna and Adrial. "Have fun."

"We will. Thanks for your help, Grandma."

"Anytime." Carolynn hurried to her car, already
making plans for her next stop.

Inside the house Jeanna watched Mick load himself
down with cases and she frowned. He certainly was
showing off for Adrial. It would serve him right if he
tripped on the stairs and tumbled down.

"You're so strong, Mick!" Adrial laughed breathlessly
as she followed Mick up the wide stairs.

Jeanna wrinkled her nose and followed. "Just set the
stuff inside the door and we'll take care of it. Don't you
have to go to work, Mick?"

"Not today," he said as he dropped everything on
the thick carpet.

"Your room is beautiful, Jae!" Adrial spun around
with a laugh. She stopped beside the twin bed closest
to the chest. "Is this one mine?"

Jeanna nodded.

"This is going to be fun! We'll gossip all night long."

Jeanna grinned. "Just like old times. I've missed you,
cousin." The jealousy faded away and she hugged
Adrial. "It is so good to see you!"

Mick stood beside the cases, his hands resting lightly
on his lean hips. "Girls, how about coming over for
a swim when you finish unpacking?"

"Not today, Mick," Jeanna snapped.

"Oh, I'd like to," said Adrial.

Jeanna shrugged. "I guess we could." She'd have to have a long, serious talk with Mick about his interest in Adrial.

"See you later." Mick tugged Jeanna's curl and smiled at Adrial, then strode out, whistling happily.

"He is beautiful, Jeanna! Is he yours?"

Jeanna frowned. "Of course not!" She didn't want to explain her wonderful relationship with Mick to Adrial. Their love was understood and Adrial would realize that soon enough, if not on her own, then Mick would tell her. Other girls had tried to come between them, but Mick had never let it happen. He wouldn't this time either. "We'll get your things put away and then you can rest a bit."

"I'm not at all tired." Adrial kicked off her shoes and padded across the room in her stocking feet. She stopped beside Jeanna's desk and touched her typewriter. "Have you heard anything about your short story?"

"Not yet." Jeanna's stomach tightened. "I want it to sell! It took me a long time to write it and I can't take a rejection!"

"At least you're starting a career, Jae. I don't even know what I want to do after high school. I get so upset at times when I don't know what I want to do with my life."

"What happened to your plans to travel and see the world?" Jeanna sat cross-legged on her bed and pulled a stuffed rabbit onto her lap.

"That takes money, Jae, and right now I don't have

any." Adrial sighed and flipped back her silky hair. "I'm glad your mom said I could have a summer job at her store. It'll help pay for my senior year, but after that I don't know. Dad said he'd help me with college, but I don't know if I want to go."

"A lot of kids I know feel the same way. I'm going and I'm glad I learned that I have a special talent for writing."

"Do you still have the job at the medical facility? Provincial House, isn't it?"

Jeanna jumped up and picked up a case. "I quit that job." She couldn't talk about it, not even to Adrial. Jeanna unsnapped the case and lifted out a handful of clothing. "We'd better get your things put away." Maybe some day she could tell Adrial what had happened, but not yet, not when it was so new and terrifying.

"I guess we should." Adrial listlessly opened a bag. "Once I thought about being a nurse. Maybe I should work at the medical facility just to see if I'd like that kind of thing."

A shiver ran down Jeanna's back. "Maybe. But let's not talk about it now. Mick's expecting us to swim with him."

"And I brought just the thing!" Adrial laughed as she lifted out a skimpy, yellow-and-black swimsuit.

Jeanna groaned under her breath as she pushed a pile of clothes into a drawer.

Several minutes later they walked into the warm sunshine and across the yard where Mick was already swimming in his pool. He called and waved, then pushed himself out with a rush of water. His muscles rippled as he stepped toward them. He was dressed in navy-and-white trunks and his entire body was bronzed and glistening. Jeanna wanted to push him back into the pool, out of sight of Adrial.

"Hello, girls!" Mick whistled and raised his brows. "This is really my lucky day!"

Adrial laughed with pleasure as Jeanna impatiently dropped her white, terry wrap onto a lounge chair. She had always felt beautiful in her bright-blue suit, but suddenly beside Adrial she felt drab and ugly. She dove in without a splash and swam underwater to the far side. She surfaced and water ran down her face and neck onto her tanned shoulders. The sun burned down on her and she blinked against the glare.

"Hello, Jeanna."

Her heart jerked and she looked up at bare legs covered with dark hair, up past red trunks, a lean torso, tanned to a teak-brown, then to Kip's smiling, too-handsome face. "Hi," she said without a smile.

He stepped off the edge of the pool and water closed over his dark head, then he bobbed up. He was too close and she could hardly breathe. She wanted to swim away, but suddenly she couldn't move, couldn't make her body obey the command her brain was giving.

"I met your cousin. She's a beautiful child."

"Child? Hardly that. We're the same age." Jeanna caught the teasing light in Kip's dark eyes and a smile tugged at her wide mouth. For years he'd teased her about being a child even though she was just a little younger than he.

"I thought you had to work today." He caught hold of the edge of the pool to keep himself next to her.

"I didn't know you kept up with my schedule."

"I always know what you're doing, Jeanna."

The words wrapped around her heart and made her weak all over, then anger rushed through her. "Don't use your sweet talk on me, Kip Jennings. I know you too well to fall for that!"

"What's wrong with you, Jeanna?"

"I've heard you talk to other girls in that tone and I've seen the way they fall all over you. Well, it won't work with me!"

He laughed softly. "Won't it?"

Shivers ran down her spine. She heard water splashing and Mick and Adrial laughing and playing together, but every nerve was aware of Kip next to her. "Go find yourself another playmate."

"What if I don't want to?"

"Then it'll be a first!" She started to swim away, but he caught her arm and fire burned where his hard fingers and palm touched. The sounds in the pool faded away and her heart thudded against her rib cage. "Let me go," she whispered hoarsely.

"First, tell me why you refuse to go with me to the Provincial House."

"I already told you. It takes up too much of my time." Could he see the fear in her eyes? Did the panic sound in her voice?

"I know better than that." His grip tightened. "Mabel Pranger has been asking for you. I told her that you'd be there tomorrow."

"How could you tell her that?"

"She misses you. She said you always make the days easier for her. The least you could do is visit her."

Jeanna shook her head, her face ashen. "I don't have time!"

With a frown he released her arm only to clamp his hands around her narrow waist. He pulled her hard against himself and her heart jerked, then raced as he pulled her under. Water closed over her head and she struggled weakly. Abruptly he released her and swam away. Every nerve in her body tingled as she slowly surfaced, then swam to the edge of the pool. Weakly she leaned against the cool tiles, her heart hammering. Slowly she pushed herself out of the pool and stood dripping on the tile, then cautiously peeked around for Kip. She couldn't see him and she breathed a sigh of relief, then slipped on her terry robe and held it snugly around her wet body, shivering even in the warmth of the afternoon.

"I'm going in, Mick. Adrial." Jeanna waited, then spoke again but they were too involved with each other and didn't hear. With a sigh she walked to the house. She could drive herself to work in the pickup and Mick could stay to entertain Adrial.

Much later Jeanna walked outdoors dressed in a yellow tee shirt with a scoop neck and yellow slacks. From the sound still coming from the pool she knew that Mick had totally forgotten that he was to drive her to work. A hand touched her arm and she gasped, then stared up at Kip. He had changed into jeans and a light-blue, pullover shirt. A weakness spread through her that she couldn't understand.

"I'm taking you to work." He smiled and she pulled away, shaking her head.

"That's not necessary."

"I know Mick said he would, but he's busy." Kip caught her hand and tugged her toward his silver Toyota.

Reluctantly she slipped into the passenger seat, then waited with her hands locked over her purse for him to get in. He seemed to fill the car and she could smell a faint odor of the soap he'd used when he'd showered. Her stomach tightened and she clutched her purse in her lap.

He was silent as he drove down Hickory Street toward Madison. The traffic was heavy on Madison and she was glad that she hadn't driven herself.

"What did you hear about your story, Jeanna?"

Her brows shot up in surprise. "I didn't think you'd be interested."

"Of course I am."

"You never were before."

He shot a look at her, then laughed. "Before what?"

She looked away in confusion. What did she mean? "I haven't heard from the publisher yet."

"Let me know when you do."

She was silent for several seconds. "I can't really believe you want to know, or that you care."

He pulled into the large parking lot and stopped the car beside the tall brick building with the huge sign that said Maxi's. He turned to her, his arm over the seat, his head tilted. "I care."

Her eyes widened. "Why? You never did before!"

He leaned forward with a soft laugh and his breath fanned her flushed cheek. "Before what?"

"Stop that!"

"You look beautiful today, Jae."

Her pulse leaped and she fumbled for the door handle. "I'll ride home with Mom. Tell Mick."

Kip shrugged.

"Thanks for the ride." She sounded breathless and she hoped he wouldn't notice.

"My pleasure. I'll talk to you soon."

She hurried toward the side door of her mom's store, as her heart jumped funny, little jumps. What was wrong with her? Why should Kip affect her this way when she was in love with Mick?

She stopped just inside the air-conditioned entrance of the store, then glanced out just in time to see the silver Toyota pulling away. She caught a glimpse of strong shoulders and a dark head and she wanted to run out and wave so that he would smile at her one more time. She frowned in irritation, then hurried to the escalator and to the second floor where she worked in the children's department. She would keep very busy and she would not think about Kip Jennings.

Just then she looked across the store and saw Nurse Wilder in the linen department. Fear pricked Jeanna's skin and she jumped out of sight behind a floor display, her hand over her racing heart and her eyes wide in alarm.

Had Nurse Wilder come to spy on her? Jeanna bit back an anguished moan. Maybe Nurse Wilder wanted to double-check on her to make sure she kept her word and stayed away from the Provincial House.

Finally Jeanna peeked around the display, her heart in her mouth. Nurse Wilder was walking away and Jeanna dashed toward the children's department to safety.

Chapter 2

Slightly frowning, Carolynn Burgess stopped just outside the front door of Provincial House. If she was right, Gil Oakes's mother, Melanie Reeve, was Nurse Bess Wilder. Carolynn rested her hand on the heavy glass door, but didn't push it open. A warm breeze ruffled her hair. A lawn mower roared in the yard across the street. If she'd found Bess Wilder so easily why hadn't Gil Oakes? Something about this smelled worse than the potatoes she'd burned last night.

She'd been deep in thought about Gil Oakes and hadn't realized the potatoes had boiled dry. Robert hadn't said anything about the potatoes, but she had seen in his face he'd wondered where her mind had been. She hadn't burned much of what she cooked all the years they'd been married, but when she did, it was usually pretty bad. Over dinner she'd told Robert about Gil Oakes.

"Did you talk to him yet?" Robert had asked as he poured a glass of diet Pepsi.

Carolynn shook her head. "I'll see him tomorrow after I see if Bess Wilder really is his birth mother." Carolynn absently pushed the green beans around on her plate. "It's strange that I worked on a case at Provincial House — only to learn the patients were dying of natural causes, not being murdered as Jay Sommers had thought. And now, I'm back there."

"Is that where Jeanna works?"

25

"She did, but for some reason she doesn't now. I meant to ask her about it, but Adrial's staying with her and they're wrapped up in having fun for the summer."

They'd talked about Jeanna a few more minutes, then Robert told her about Raeleen Ost being strong enough to walk again without a cane.

Now Carolynn pushed open the heavy door and stepped inside the reception area of Provincial House. Sue Gaylord, dressed in yellow, sat behind the long counter. Sue had gone to school with Eleena, Carolynn's oldest daughter. A huge vase of flowers stood on a small table to the right of the counter near the door leading back to the patients' rooms. "Morning, Sue."

"Mrs. Burgess! What brings you here again?" Sue darted a look around. "Is your granddaughter with you?"

Carolynn frowned as she stepped to the counter. "Jeanna? No. Why?"

"Nurse Wilder said not to let her even come in here."

"Why not?"

Sue shrugged. "I have no idea. And Jeanna had such a wonderful way with the people, especially Mabel Pranger."

"Jeanna hasn't mentioned a word about it to me."

"She was really upset. I could tell. Kip Jennings said he'd get her to come back. He doesn't know Nurse Wilder forbade her to come back, and I sure wasn't going to tell him."

"I'll talk to Jeanna. But now, I came to speak to Nurse Wilder."

Sue gasped. "Don't tell her what I said, will you?"

"Of course not." Carolynn smiled reassuringly. "I came to see her about a personal matter."

Sue picked up the phone. "She should be in her office. Let me tell her you're here." Sue listened, then frowned. "That's funny. She's not there. Do you want to wait here for her or make an appointment and come another day?"

"I'll wait."

"How's Eleena?"

"Just fine. She and Kail are in Idaho on vacation for a couple of weeks. Tad and Lucy really didn't want to go, but Eleena knew they'd feel differently once they were there."

"Teenagers!" Sue shook her head. "They're something else."

"But I love 'em!" Carolynn chuckled. "I couldn't always say that when my four were teens. But teen grandchildren are fun."

They talked a few minutes longer, then Sue tried Nurse Wilder again.

"Maybe she went out the back way and is gone already." Sue lowered her voice. "She sometimes does that. Dr. Browne gets a little upset with her."

"Oh?" Carolynn knew just the tone of voice to use to get more information.

"She's so moody! I don't know what her problem is, but something's bothering her."

"Is she married?"

"Yes, but her husband left her last year." Sue grinned.

"I guess he got tired of her mood swings."

"Any children?"

"No."

Carolynn thought of Gil Oakes. Nurse Wilder had a son — unless she wasn't Gil's mother after all. "Make an appointment for me to see Nurse Wilder tomorrow, will you, Sue?"

Sue looked at her book. "She's free at eleven, then again in the middle of the afternoon."

"Eleven's a good time." Carolynn glanced at her watch. "I have to meet someone in a few minutes. Say hello to your family, Sue."

"I will. Tell Eleena to call me when she gets home. It's been awhile."

Carolynn nodded, said goodbye, and hurried out. A few minutes later she sat in the cafe where she'd agreed to meet Gil Oakes under the pretense of getting preliminary information for the agent who'd be helping him. She'd called him last night and explained who she was, set up the meeting and described herself to him. She said she'd be wearing a pink blouse. She glanced around the room. She was the only woman in the cafe wearing a pink blouse, so he was sure to find her.

Just then a man at a nearby table pushed back his chair and walked toward her. He was younger than Stan, her youngest son, was nice-looking with short brown hair, brown eyes and a medium build. He wore gray dress pants and a white shirt with thin green stripes. "Carolynn Burgess?"

She smiled and nodded. "Gil Oakes?"

He nodded and sat down. "Thanks for seeing me."

"I hope the agency can help you find your mother."

He closed his eyes for a minute, swallowed hard, then looked intently at Carolynn. "I need to know who she is, Mrs. Burgess."

The waitress brought glasses of water and left menus. "I'm Karen and I'll be your server."

"We only want something to drink, Karen," Gil said, smiling. "I'll take coffee. Mrs. Burgess?"

"Iced tea, please. With lemon."

Karen nodded, took back the menus and hurried away. Sounds of rattling silverware drifted out from the kitchen over the voices of the other customers.

Carolynn pulled her notebook and pencil from her purse. "Now, Gil, suppose you tell me what you know about your birth mother."

He rubbed his hand along his jaw. "She is here in Middle Lake, but I don't know where. She's younger than you. I don't know what she looks like, but maybe she has brown hair and eyes like mine. She might be gray, though. Her name is — or was — Melanie Reeve. She had me out of wedlock and put me up for adoption."

"Does that bother you?"

Gil ran his finger around his collar. "I suppose she did it because she couldn't take care of me."

"It takes a mother's love to part with her baby when she knows it's for his good."

He took a drink of water, set his glass down and rubbed his finger on the condensation. "You're probably right. I want to tell her how thankful I am for loving me so much."

Karen brought the iced tea and coffee, then walked away again to wait on two women who'd just sat down.

Carolynn sipped her tea. She liked the taste a touch of lemon gave it. The cold liquid felt good against her dry throat. She set her glass down. "What about your natural father?"

Gil shrugged as he set his cup of steaming coffee on the saucer. "He wasn't listed on the birth certificate. But I'll ask my birth mother about him. If I ever find her."

"I'm sure Dud Dumars will be able to help you. He knows his business."

"So I've heard."

"How did you trace your mother to Middle Lake?"

"Someone in Flint knew her and said she'd talked about moving here. So, I came here."

"What's her occupation?"

"She's a nurse."

"Did you check the hospital?"

"Yes. She wasn't there. She could be in private practice."

"What about a medical facility?" Carolynn kept her voice light. She felt strongly that something fishy was going on.

"I couldn't get any information. I tried all three of them."

Carolynn sipped her tea as her brain whirled with thoughts. Should she tell Gil she'd already found his birth mother? No, she'd leave that up to Dud. She flipped her notebook closed. "I'll give this information to Dud Dumars and he'll give you a call when he knows anything."

"You're all being very helpful and I appreciate it." Gil smiled and his eyes filled with tears. "I don't meet many kind people."

How would he feel when he learned his birth mother wasn't kind either? Carolynn bit back a sigh, said goodbye and walked away. She sat in her car and waited for Gil to come out. She'd follow him and see what she could see. She waited a long time, but he never came out. Frowning, she hurried back inside the cafe. He wasn't there either. Had he gone out the back door to avoid her? Or maybe his car was parked out back. With a groan she hurried to her car and drove to Dumars.

★   ★   ★

Silver faced Tim across their living room. "Did you talk to her?" Silver asked sharply.

Tim nodded. "I said she could see Brittany."

Silver's legs gave way and she sank to the edge of the couch. "How could you? What if she wants Brittany back?"

"We adopted her legally. Gwen Nichols has no claim to Brittany."

"But she gave birth to her! That must give her some rights!"

Tim sat beside Silver and took her hand. "It doesn't. And she doesn't want to make any claims on her. She just wants to see that she's okay. She wants to hold her, then she'll go away and never see her again."

"How do we know that, Tim? How do we know

Gwen Nichols won't steal Brittany and run away with her?"

"She's not that kind of woman."

Silver looked at him sharply. "How do you know?"

Tim spread his hands wide. "I talked to her."

Silver lifted her chin high. "Tim, I won't let her see Brittany or touch her or speak to her! I mean it!"

Tim slowly stood. He seemed to tower over Silver. "I gave her my word. I'm sorry, Silver. Gwen is going to meet me at the church in a few minutes. I'll take Brittany with me. You can come too, if you want."

Tears streamed down Silver's cheeks. "Brittany's asleep. You can't just wake her up to take her to meet her — her birth mother."

Tim shrugged. His nerves were stretched almost to the breaking point, but he didn't let Silver see. He kept his voice calm. "I'll wait until she wakes up."

Silver jumped up with a cry. "Gwen Nichols will never see *my* baby! Never!"

★   ★   ★

He once again parked outside the church and watched her slip from her car. Just why had she come here again? Was she getting *religious?* Was she *sorry* for her sin? He shook his head and frowned. She should be! She had no right to give up her precious baby! She gave birth to her — she should keep her! It wasn't fair for babies to be given to strangers! Well, she'd pay for giving her baby away. She'd pay just like the others had.

He glanced around. No one else was in sight. Was anyone watching out a window? His nerves tingled.

This time it'd work. This time he'd kill her, then he could go on with other things in his life. He might even ask Dena to marry him. She'd hinted at it over dinner the other night. He smiled as he reached for the tire iron.

Slowly he walked toward her car with the tire iron at his side. He reached the side of the car just as she opened the door and started to get out. She saw him and frowned. He lifted the tire iron and struck her hard across the head. She fell in a crumpled heap — half in and half out of the car. "You got just what you deserved," he said softly.

He nonchalantly walked to his car and drove away. Later he'd clean up the tire iron and put it where it belonged.

★   ★   ★

Jeanna looked around furtively for Kip, then walked into the Jennings' yard. A robin stood in the driveway, then flew away. A large white cat ambled across the grass, its tail high in the air. No silver Toyota stood outside the garage. Jeanna knew Kip was gone and she could safely go next door to get the ice rings Mrs. Jennings had made for the party for Adrial.

Blacky wriggled at Jeanna's feet as she pressed the back doorbell. She frowned down at the hairy black dog. "Go home, Blacky. Laura Jennings doesn't want you in her kitchen."

The door opened and Kip stood there in his bare feet wearing just a pair of white running shorts. Jeanna gasped and jumped back, almost tripping over Blacky.

"Your car is gone!" It sounded like an accusation.

"Mick borrowed it to run errands for the party." Kip motioned her in and she finally stepped into the large kitchen and he closed the door, leaving Blacky outdoors. "Mick's car is in the shop, as usual, getting a new fuel pump." Kip stood with his bare feet apart and his hands resting lightly on his lean hips and Jeanna had to look away to gather her thoughts so she could remember why she'd come.

She looked around helplessly, then spied the refrigerator and remembered. "Your mother fixed two ice rings for me. I came to get them."

"I didn't think you came to see me. You've been hiding, haven't you?"

"Don't be ridiculous!" But she had been "hiding" so that she wouldn't have to talk to him about the Provincial House or anything else. She stepped toward the refrigerator, but he moved with panther grace and blocked her way. She was forced to look up at him and her hands curled into fists and her breast rose and fell as his eyes traveled from her curly brown head down to her blue tee shirt and down her long, shapely legs to her sandaled feet and her red toenails, then all the way back up, finally to rest on her full lips that were slightly parted. She wanted to turn and run for her life, but she couldn't move.

"Am I invited to your party?" he asked in a low, husky voice.

She panicked. "You? You don't like little-kid parties! You've said that every time I ever asked you in the past." Oh, he just couldn't come to the party tonight!

How would it look to have her walking around in a daze?

He looked her up and down again. "You aren't a little kid any more, Jeanna. I've noticed."

She flushed painfully, but lifted her chin high. "Stop it! You can't flirt with me the way you do with other girls! I know you too well. I came for the ice rings. Let me get them and leave. Please!"

"I'm not stopping you." He trailed a long finger down her face, sending sparks shooting along the trail. "You are as much aware of me as I am of you."

"Never! I love Mick!" She looked helplessly toward the back door.

"That's not love!" His voice was like a stinging whip. "You and Mick have been friends all of your life. You love him as a friend and brother."

Her eyes blazed. "You mind your own business, Kip Jennings."

He stepped closer to her so that she saw the gold flecks in his brown eyes. "I'm making you my business, Jeanna Shaneck."

Helplessly she turned her head and stared at the plants hanging at the window above the sink. Her heartbeats almost deafened her.

"Am I scaring you, Jae?" He chuckled softly as he cupped her face with his large, sun-browned hands.

She lifted startled eyes to his as she struggled against the desire to touch her lips to his palm. "Let me go, Kip," she whispered hoarsely. "I have a party to get ready for."

"Am I stopping you?" His breath fanned her face. "I'm

sorry if I seem to be rushing you, but I've been patient long enough."

"Patient? What do you mean?"

"What big eyes you have." He laughed softly. "Could it be that you're too immature to know what's happening to us?"

"Nothing's happening!" Her voice came out weak and she flushed and looked away.

He laughed again, then dropped his hands to his sides.

With a strangled cry she ran to the door and jerked it open.

He was after her in a flash and caught her arm. She struck out at him in panic, but he caught her flying hand with easy grace and held it against his chest. She felt the thudding of his heart and it sent tremors through her body.

"You forgot your ice rings, honey."

Honey! Her ears rang and she stood very still as he released her and walked to the refrigerator. He carried the ice rings back to her with a grin on his face.

"Here you go. Enjoy your party but tell those boys to keep their hands off you or they'll have me to answer to."

She grabbed the ice rings and fled. Blacky barked at her heels. At her back door she stopped, her breast heaving and her cheeks flushed bright red. Why had Kip said what he'd said? Was he only teasing her? She bit her lip and shivered, then rushed inside and slipped the ice rings into the freezer in the utility room. With her cold hands locked together she leaned weakly against the dryer and closed her eyes. She would not allow Kip to ruin her evening!

With a deep breath she walked into the kitchen where her mother was making tacos for the party. "Need any help, Mom?"

"I thought you got lost." Christa looked up from grating colby cheese onto the wooden counter top. "Is everything all right? You look flushed."

"Everything's under control, Mom." Jeanna forced a bright smile. "We'll eat on our patio and swim in the Jennings' pool." She slipped an arm around her mom's slender waist. "Thanks for helping me. I couldn't do it without you."

"You're welcome." She kissed Jeanna's cheek, then picked up the pile of cheese and dropped it into a glass bowl. "Sarah called and said that she and Jimmy will be here early to help."

"Great." Sarah was Jeanna's best friend and she was looking forward to meeting Adrial. "I'll go see if Adrial is ready. I can't believe that she's nervous about tonight."

"She knows there'll be at least twelve people here and they'll all be looking at her. That would make me nervous too."

Jeanna laughed. "Mom, you're like Grandma Burgess — nothing makes you nervous." Jeanna ran upstairs to her bedroom.

Adrial sat on her bed with her head in her hands.

"What's wrong, Addie?"

Adrial sat up straight and forced a smile. "I don't know if I can handle tonight, Jae."

"Sure you can!" Jeanna dropped to the bed beside her cousin. "What's wrong with you all at once? Everyone will love you." She'd almost added, like Mick had, but she forced the words back and the thought. Mick was only being extra nice. Wasn't he?

Adrial sniffed back tears and dabbed her eyes with a tissue. "I'm not used to my new self yet and I still need pep talks. I wish I could be as sure of myself as you are."

"Just talk about what interests the other guy. It always works. Find out their interests and then talk about them and you'll have it made."

"You make it sound so easy."

"It is. You'll see."

"I might feel left out."

"You won't." Jeanna jumped up. "Are you going to wear your swimsuit under your clothes?"

"Yes, but not the bikini. I don't know why I bought such a tiny scrap of suit. I could never let anyone see me in it!" She laughed and rolled her eyes. "I was trying out my new image when I bought it. Some days I have all the confidence in the world, and the next day I want to crawl into a closet and never show my face."

"Oh, Addie! Don't feel that way! You have everything that any girl would want."

"Do I?" Adrial looked hopefully at Jeanna with wide eyes.

Jeanna tossed the swimsuit to Adrial. "Put that on, be nice to everyone, play your guitar and you'll be a sure hit."

"I hope so. And Mick will be there."

Jeanna grabbed her suit and slammed out of the bedroom to the bathroom. Why didn't Mick set Adrial straight? He was spending too much time with her and she was getting the wrong idea.

Just as Jeanna finished dressing, the doorbell rang and she ran lightly down the stairs and swung open the door. "Hi, Sarah. Hi, Jimmy." Sarah wore baggy shorts and an orange tee shirt. Jimmy's long, thin legs were covered with faded jeans and he wore a tee shirt like Sarah's. Sarah's long, blonde hair was braided and hung down her slender shoulders. She smiled, but her blue eyes looked a little worried. Jimmy was tall and lean and resembled the pole he used in high school to make his famous pole vaults.

Adrial stopped beside Jeanna with a hesitant smile.

"Adrial, this is Sarah and Jimmy. The short one is Sarah."

A laugh burst out of Adrial and she said, "Hello. I'm glad to meet you both. Let's go to the patio, shall we?"

Jeanna wrinkled her nose as she followed them. Her pep talk had worked wonders. Maybe she needed someone to give her one.

"Whose guitar?" asked Jimmy as he picked it up and awkwardly strummed a C chord with his foot on the bench and the guitar resting on his leg.

"It's mine," said Adrial. "Do you play?"

"A little. I don't have even one callous yet."

"You'll get them."

Sarah pushed Jeanna to the far side of the patio. the smell of roses filled the air. Sarah peeked back at Adrial. "Does she eat boys alive?"

Jeanna laughed. "I don't think so. But if I didn't trust Mick, I'd be very nervous."

"Does she flirt with him?"

Jeanna shrugged. "Maybe. Yes, I guess she does. I try not to let it bother me." Jeanna popped open a bag of potato chips and poured them into a large plastic bowl on the table. Maybe she should break up the cozy scene between Jimmy and Adrial before Sarah got too upset over it. Adrial was showing him how to place his fingers for a G chord and he seemed to be enjoying it too much. Jeanna turned to ask Sarah if she minded what was going on, but the question died in her throat at the sight of tears in Sarah's wide blue eyes. "Are you worried about them?" asked Jeanna softly, motioning toward Adrial and Jimmy.

Sarah shook her head and sniffed, then frantically rubbed away any sign of tears. "I'll be all right."

"What's wrong, Sarah? It's not just Jimmy and my cousin, is it?"

Sarah shook her head and sniffed. "It's Meg."

"What has your sister got herself into this time?"

"I can't talk about it."

"Why doesn't your mother do something?"

Sarah twisted her braid around her thin hand. "She's too tied up with herself and she doesn't see that Meg's in real trouble. She doesn't care, but I do, and I want to help Meg if I can."

"But what can you do? Meg's fifteen and won't listen to you."

Sarah nodded. "I know, but I have to try. She needs attention from someone who cares, and I care. I care so much I ache inside."

Jeanna bit her bottom lip, then caught Sarah's hand and squeezed it. "Look, Sarah, you can't do anything for Meg tonight, can you? Put her out of your mind enough to enjoy yourself. Can you do that?" Jeanna knew all about pushing important, terrible things to the back of her mind, and if she could do it, then so could Sarah.

"I'll try, Jae."

Jeanna leaned close and whispered, "You might have to try a little harder when you see Adrial in a swimsuit."

Sarah giggled and looked down at her almost boy-thin body. "Thanks for the warning."

Just then Mick walked to the patio and called a hello to Jeanna and Sarah, then joined Adrial and Jimmy. Jeanna forced a laugh and set Sarah to work helping her.

By seven all the guests had arrived and were swimming in the pool as Jeanna stood on the edge watching. She opened her mouth to call to Mick, then snapped it closed. He wouldn't hear her over the noise. With a sigh she walked down the steps into the cool water and swam as if she was alone. Everyone seemed to be having a good time, but something was missing for her and she couldn't figure out what.

Later she climbed out of the water and reached to slip on her terry robe. It caught on one sleeve and she tugged, then a soft chuckle beside her sent her pulse leaping. Kip held the end of her sleeve and his brown eyes twinkled with mischief. "What are you doing here, Kip?"

"I live here. Remember?"

"At my party, I mean."

He shrugged his broad shoulders. "I thought I'd crash it. No one will care, and I see that you need another guy to make it equal. I'm your man."

The way he said it made it sound very personal and she twisted her robe in agitation. "I suppose you can stay. We're just ready to go have tacos at my place."

"Tacos! My favorite."

"Oh? Mine too."

"That must mean something." He grinned and she smiled. "Adrial seems to be having a good time."

Jeanna nodded.

"Has Mick left her side?"

"What do you mean by that?" Jeanna's voice was sharp.

Kip turned away from the pool back to her, his brow lifted. "Did I strike a nerve?"

"Of course not!"

He took her hand. "We're a team tonight and we'll stick together. Adrial and Mick are welcome to each other." Kip's smile zoomed to her heart and she didn't want to pull away from him.

"Mick's only being nice to Adrial," Jeanna said stiffly.

Kip squeezed her hand. "Save that story for someone who will believe it."

"I think I know Mick a lot better than you do even though he is your brother."

"Let's stop the discussion and get to the tacos." Kip lifted his voice and called, "Tacos! Tacos, everyone. At Jeanna's."

The rush from the pool made Jeanna laugh with

pleasure. She turned to Kip. "Let's go before they devour all the tacos!"

He tugged and she ran with him across the soft grass to the patio where the others were already fixing their plates. The smell of spicy hamburger filled the air.

"And to think I might have missed all this!" Kip waved his hand toward the people thronged around the food.

"I am glad you came."

Kip looked down at her, his eyes searching her face. "You are?"

Panic seized her because of something she saw in his face and she forced a bright laugh. "Of course. With you beside me we can fight our way through the crowd for a taco. On my own I wouldn't stand a chance."

"Well, all right then, let's go."

She picked up a paper plate and a tortilla and piled it high with hamburger, onions, lettuce, tomatoes and plenty of yellow cheese.

"Let's sit over there." Kip motioned to an empty bench and she followed him to it, balancing a plate in one hand and a glass of red pop in the other.

Music from a neighbor's house blended together with the chatter and laughter. Tommy spilled his taco and Blacky ran to it and wolfed it down, then sank to the patio to watch for another chance to eat.

Jeanna bit into her taco and juice ran down her hand and wrist and she laughed and wiped it off with the yellow paper napkin. She looked up at Kip with a soft laugh and the look in his eyes took her breath way. Her appetite fled as he leaned down and rubbed his forehead against hers. Inside she felt softer than a melted marshmallow.

"Eat your taco," he whispered as he dabbed the sauce off the corner of her mouth. His leg brushed hers and she jerked away as if she'd been stung. He chuckled softly, knowingly, and she glared at him, then turned away to watch Adrial pick up her guitar and strum it.

"Sing for us, Addie," said Mick.

Adrial glanced at Jeanna and she nodded, so Adrial sang in her pleasant voice and others grew quiet and listened.

"That was beautiful," said Mick. "Hey, Kip, sing with her, will you? Your voices will blend perfectly."

"Come on, Kip," said Jimmy, then several others joined in.

"Go ahead," Jeanna encouraged, nudging him.

Kip pressed his knee against Jeanna's, then stood up and walked to Adrial's side while everyone cheered. Adrial smiled at Kip and Jeanna's stomach tightened into a cold, hard knot.

"I'll sing the lead," Adrial said as she picked the notes of a Sandi Patti song that Jeanna especially liked.

Kip nodded and they sang together and their voices blended in a beautiful harmony that brought tears to Jeanna's eyes.

Just then Jeanna thought of Mabel Pranger at Provincial House and how much she liked the song. A desire to see Mabel again rose in Jeanna, then she forced it away. Not even Mabel could get her to go back to that place!

Chapter 3

Silver slowed as she pulled into the church parking lot. The only other car in the lot belonged to the woman she now knew was Gwen Nichols. The car was empty, yet the driver's door was open. Silver's heart jerked. Was Gwen looking for an open door to the church? Tim had the key and he'd planned to admit Gwen when he arrived so she could see Brittany.

Silver pressed her lips together as she parked on the far side of the other car and turned off the key. She'd taken the key to Tim's car when he was changing Brittany's diaper. By now he'd know she had it and would be very angry. "No way will she see my baby!"

Perspiration dotted Silver's face as she stood beside her car and looked toward the church. The sun had set, but the pavement was still warm. Had someone inside let Gwen in? Maybe Sherard, the janitor? Her sandals slapping the pavement, Silver ran to the side door and tried it. It was locked. So were the other doors. Impatiently she looked at Gwen's car. Why was her door open and where was she?

Silver walked slowly toward the car. The hairs on the back of her neck stood out. Shivers ran up and down her spine. Something was wrong. She stepped around the back of the car. Gwen lay half in and half out of the car. Had she tripped and fallen?

"Gwen?" Silver called in a faint voice. She stepped closer. She saw Gwen sprawled across the seat, her head bashed in and blood all over. Silver gagged and almost vomited. With a cry she turned away from the horrifying sight. The world seemed to spin and turn black. She sank to her knees, whimpering. Someone had struck Gwen Nichols and killed her! But why? Maybe the killer was still nearby.

Silver staggered to her feet, her head spinning. With one hand to her stomach and the other over her mouth, she stumbled to her car. She had to get away before she was killed. Her hand trembled as she started her car. Could she drive the few blocks to her house? She had to tell Tim. He'd know what to do.

A few minutes later she raced into her house screaming, "Tim! Tim! She's dead!"

Tim ran downstairs, Brittany in his arms. He sat her on the floor near the couch and caught Silver to him. "What's wrong?"

Trembling, Silver clung to Tim and sobbed against his shoulder. After a long time she told him what she'd seen. "I know she's dead, Tim. I could tell!"

Tim's heart stood still. "Did — did you hit her, Silver?"

She shook her head hard. "No! No! No, of course not! I could never *kill* someone, not even Gwen Nichols!"

Tim believed her and held her close again. With his face against her hair he said, "We'll have to call the police."

Silver jerked away and stared in horror at Tim. "The police? Will they question me? What if they think I did it?"

"We have to call them, Silver."

"No! Wait! Holly Loudan told me what great support Carolynn Burgess was to her when she and her aunt were suspected of murder. Holly said Carolynn knows the police and she was able to make things easier for them." Silver gripped Tim's hand. "Let's call Carolynn and see if she'd come help us. Like she did for Holly."

Tim thought about it and nodded. "I'll give her a call. I feel terrible calling her after nine at night."

"She won't mind."

Tim ran to the phone and soon had Carolynn on the line. "I know it's late and I know you can't really do anything, but you gave Holly support during her hard time; now we need you."

"What's wrong, Tim?"

He told her, stumbling over his words.

"I'll be right there." Carolynn hung up and turned to Robert who was watching TV. "Something terrible has happened." She told him as quickly as she could.

"I'll follow you over and watch Brittany while you deal with the — other." Robert couldn't bring himself to say 'murder' or even 'the police.' It was still hard to imagine his wife was involved in such things.

Carolynn gave Robert a quick hug. "Thanks! We'll need you. Remember not to tell them about my undercover work. They only called because they knew I gave Holly support."

Robert chuckled and shook his head, then sobered. "Let's go." He clicked off the TV and hurried out to his pickup while Carolynn ran to her car in the garage.

A few minutes later they reached the Rawlings home.

Robert hurried right to Brittany and picked her up. "I'll take care of her while you're dealing with the other."

Tim nodded, unable to speak.

Silver clung to Carolynn, sobbing out her story. "I didn't want Gwen to see Brittany and maybe take her away from us, but I never wanted her dead!"

"Let's get to the church and see what we can see," Carolynn said calmly. She didn't feel calm. Murder was hard to face, especially when it involved people she knew and loved. Tim and Silver were special to her.

Carolynn drove Tim and Silver to the church and they all stepped from the car and peered inside Gwen's car. She was just as Silver had described. Carolynn turned to Tim. "Go inside and call Sheriff Farley Cobb." She gave Tim the sheriff's home number. "Tell him I'm with you and will wait here."

Tim started toward the office door of the church.

"Go with him, Silver," Carolynn said gently. She didn't want Silver to look at the dead woman any longer than was necessary. Besides, with both out of the way, she could check things more thoroughly.

Carolynn waited until Tim and Silver were inside the church, then she looked closer at the body. It looked like someone had struck the woman with a heavy club. Her purse was on the floor of the car. Carefully Carolynn lifted it out and checked inside. The woman was Gwen Nichols. She had over a hundred dollars in her wallet, so it hadn't been robbery. There was a letter to her from Tim Rawlings! "How strange," Carolynn muttered.

She hesitated only a fraction of a second, then opened

it and quickly read. She gasped in shock at one paragraph: "I don't want Silver ever to know about us or that Brittany is my baby. It would destroy her."

Trembling, Carolynn stuffed the letter back in the envelope, then pushed it into her purse. She couldn't let the police department or the newspaper get ahold of that bit of news. It would harm too many people.

She quickly looked through the rest of the contents in Gwen's purse, but there wasn't anything of interest. Who would kill Gwen and why?

Carolynn checked the back seat and the trunk of the car. There was nothing out of the ordinary.

She turned as Silver and Tim hurried out of the church. The street lights and parking lot lights flashed on all around, making the parking lot almost as bright as day.

"Sheriff Cobb said he'd be right here." Tim rubbed an unsteady hand across his jaw. "This is bad, Carolynn. We've never been involved in anything like this."

"I know." Carolynn patted Tim's arm and squeezed Silver's hand. Carolynn wanted to ask Tim about his relationship with Gwen, but bit her tongue. She'd talk to him privately at the first opportunity. "God's strength is yours. Don't forget that."

"I hope Robert thinks to put Brittany to bed," Silver said nervously as she looked at her watch. "She always goes to bed at ten. And she always has a 'sippy cup' of milk. Will he think to give her milk?"

"He probably will," Carolynn said. "He thinks of things like that because of our grandchildren. Little Caro is two, only a few months older than Brittany."

"I should be with her." Silver plucked at Tim's arm. "Don't you think I should be with her?"

Tim pulled Silver close to his side. He'd do anything to make it easier on her, but he couldn't. "The sheriff said to wait here. You found Gwen, so he'll want to talk to you."

From under her lashes Carolynn studied Silver. Was she capable of murder? If she learned about Tim and Gwen and the truth about Brittany, in her rage would she kill Gwen? Carolynn pushed the ugly thought aside. Silver could never kill anyone! Never! But then, she'd never dream that Tim would have an affair. Their marriage seemed so solid.

Just then Sheriff Farley Cobb drove up in an unmarked car, his own gray Chevy. He stopped near Gwen's car and hurried to it. He was about Carolynn's age with hazel eyes that saw everything and graying brown hair. He was short and ran toward being overweight. He wore jeans and a short-sleeved green plaid shirt. "Mrs. Burgess, what's this you have for me?"

"Sheriff." Carolynn smiled briefly. They were on a first-name basis only when no one was around. He knew her secret life and he kept it to himself. "This is Tim and Silver Rawlings. They called you. Silver found the body — found Gwen Nichols."

Sheriff Cobb studied the two, then turned to the dead body. "The others will be here shortly. Are things just the way you found them?"

Silver nodded.

"Do you two know the dead woman?"

Carolynn stood to one side and watched Farley's face

as he asked questions and the Rawlings answered them. She could tell Farley was suspicious of them by the look on his face and by the soft tone of his voice. The more suspicious he was the softer his voice got. By the last question his voice was just above a whisper. Carolynn bit her lower lip. She didn't like the turn of events one bit.

As the medical examiner drove in, followed by Deputy Littlejohn, Carolynn said, "Sheriff, let me take Tim and Silver home. They have a baby. Robert's watching her, but she needs her mom and dad. You know where to find them if you need them."

The sheriff studied Carolynn for a couple of minutes, then nodded.

She hurried them to her car before reporters arrived on the scene. They didn't need their pictures splashed over tomorrow's paper.

From the back seat of the car Silver wailed, "He thinks I did it! I could see it in his eyes. But I didn't do it. Honestly, Carolynn, I didn't. I found her dead."

"We believe you," Tim said, holding Silver close. "Calm yourself before you get home. You don't want to upset Brittany."

Carolynn drove them home and hurried them inside. She didn't want to take any chances that a reporter might've already learned their names.

★   ★   ★

Gil Oakes paced the tiny area of his apartment. He'd been waiting to hear from Dud Dumars about his birth mother. Maybe Mrs. Burgess hadn't gotten the information to Dud. Or maybe they didn't think he was important enough. He'd done his best to get Meg Dumars to feel sorry for him. He might have to 'run' across her in the grocery store again. It had taken him a couple of days to accidently run into her, but he'd managed it. He couldn't afford to hire the agency to find his birth mother, so he'd found another way to do it. He'd learned early on how to get his own way one way or another.

Had Carolynn Burgess seemed suspicious of him in the cafe or was he being overly sensitive? Maybe he should've told her he was sure his birth mother worked at Provincial House, but he couldn't learn who she was.

He poured himself a glass of milk, grabbed up the bag of cookies, and sat down to watch the eleven o'clock news.

*   *   *

The next afternoon Jeanna put on her best smile as the woman and little girl walked out of the fitting room toward her. Background music played softly as voices drifted from other areas of the store. The burr of the cash register and the ding-ding of the elevator added to the sounds. "Did the dresses fit?" Jeanna asked in her best saleswoman voice.

"Very nicely. We'll take both." The woman held them out to Jeanna and she rang them up and slipped them into a bag marked Maxi's.

"I want to wear one home," the girl said, tugging her grandma's hand.

"We have more shopping to do, but you can wear

one right after we get home." The woman ushered the girl away toward the escalator, talking with her as they walked.

Jeanna turned around, then stopped, a scream stuck in her throat. Nurse Wilder stood just inside the children's department, a scowl on her face. She looked different out of uniform. She was tall and thin with short brown hair with touches of gray and piercing blue eyes.

She stepped right up to Jeanna. "Your friend Kip Jennings said you'd be coming back soon to work at the Provincial House. I came to make sure you wouldn't."

Jeanna swallowed hard as shivers ran down her spine. "Kip's wrong. I don't intend to go back. I told you that."

"You told me a lot of things, most of them lies."

Jeanna looked helplessly around. What would she do if Nurse Wilder tried to hurt her? Was anyone nearby to help her? Just then she caught sight of Sarah and Meg walking toward the children's department. Relief made her weak.

Nurse Wilder saw them coming and she leaned closer to Jeanna. "Just remember what I said. You stay away from the Provincial House!" Abruptly she turned and strode away with her head high.

Jeanna leaned weakly against a counter of shirts and tried to stop trembling. Sarah must not guess that anything was wrong!

"Hi, Jeanna." Sarah smiled and motioned to Meg. "We came to buy Meg a new shirt."

"Great! I'm glad you stopped by to see me." Jeanna

was glad her voice hadn't cracked. She noticed Meg looked more pregnant than the last time she'd seen her.

Meg pushed her blonde hair out of her pouting face. "I don't want to shop. I don't feel good."

"Don't give me any trouble, Meg, or we'll go right home and forget the shirt," Sarah snapped.

"Oh, all right." Meg tugged her blue tee shirt over her shorts, showing her rounded stomach even more. She flipped back her blonde hair and walked to the back of the room to look at little girls' dresses.

Sarah sighed and shook her head. "I don't know why I bother with her sometimes. She is impossible. I don't know what to do to help her."

"Maybe you can't, Sarah. Maybe it'll take someone else who has experience with this kind of thing."

"Maybe." Sarah leaned against the counter with her back to Meg. "You are so lucky to be working here."

"It's a good job for now."

"And I'm stuck with a babysitting job!" Sarah pushed the strap of her purse higher on her shoulder. "Look! Here comes Adrial. How's she doing in jewelry?"

"She likes it and Mom says she's doing a good job."

"She and Mick seem to hit it off very well. Aren't you worried?"

Jeanna hesitated. "A little, but I'm going to have a talk with Mick and set it straight.

"Good luck." Sarah grinned, then turned to greet Adrial.

"Hi, Sarah. Jeanna." Adrial looked pretty dressed in a tan skirt and a gold knit shirt. "I'm on my break and I thought I'd come visit."

Meg walked up to them just then and scowled. "Let's get out of here before I get sick all over the place."

"Meg, this is Adrial," Sarah said, flushing with embarrassment. "Jeanna's cousin."

Meg stared at Adrial, then shrugged and turned away. "I don't want to buy a shirt today. I'll wait for you at the front door." She ran to the escalator.

"Don't mind her," Sarah said tiredly. "I think I'll take her home and forget about shopping."

"Is Meg going to keep her baby?" Adrial asked.

Sarah shrugged. "One day she is, the next she isn't. I'm taking her to Children's Services to talk about adoption."

Jeanna's mind drifted to Nurse Wilder as Sarah and Adrial talked. Had Kip really said that she was going back to work at the Provincial House? Well, she would certainly set him straight first chance she got!

"I better go," Sarah said. She waved a hurried goodbye and rushed after Meg.

Jeanna sighed as she watched until Sarah was out of sight. She turned to Adrial. "Is Mom taking us home?"

"Mick is."

Jeanna's mouth turned dry. "He didn't say anything to me."

Adrial looked down at her long fingers. "We went for a ride last night and set it up then. I hope you don't mind."

"Why should I?"

Adrial licked her lips. "Sometimes I think you're mad at me."

Jeanna forced a smile. "Don't be ridiculous. I'll meet

you later and we'll ride home with Mick." And then she'd take Mick aside and talk to him about Adrial.

Adrial lifted her hand in a small wave. "See you later, Jae. Don't work too hard."

"I'll try not to." Jeanna watched Adrial walk away, then turned back to work, forcing her mind on what she was doing so that she wouldn't think about Nurse Wilder.

Later Jeanna walked ahead of Adrial to the escalator and rode down to the main floor. Smells of perfume and fabric and people filled the air. Noise rose up around her and hurt her ears. It would be good to get out of here. She stepped out the heavy side door into the hot afternoon. Her skirt felt heavy and hot.

"There's Mick!" Adrial's voice rose in a lilt and her cheeks flushed a rosy pink.

Jeanna walked slowly toward the brown Chevy as Adrial's high heels clicked loudly ahead of her. She reached the car and slid into the front seat. Jeanna frowned, then walked around to the driver's side. Mick stood beside the open door and smiled at her.

"You don't mind riding in the back, do you, Jae?"

She hesitated, then shrugged, too tired to argue. She could relax in the back and kick off her shoes to rest her weary feet. She froze as she spotted Kip in the back seat.

"Hi," he said with a wink.

She hesitated a second longer, then slid in beside him, her hands locked over her purse.

He touched her hand and she jumped and he chuckled softly.

Adrial and Mick talked and laughed as Mick drove out of the crowded parking lot. Jeanna knew that Mick didn't notice when Kip slid close to her, but she knew, her entire body and heart knew, and she trembled.

"Did you have a nice day, Jae?"

She shot a look at him. "Nurse Wilder stopped in. She said you told her that I would be back to work at the home."

Kip shrugged. "I figured I could change your mind. I'm sure she wants you back as much as I do."

If only he knew! "I am not going back and I told Nurse Wilder that, too, so don't you dare tell her differently!"

"Don't get so upset, Jeanna."

She forced herself to relax. "I'm not upset. I just wanted to set it straight."

He shrugged.

She turned her head to look at him. A flame leaped in his eyes and she tried to draw away, but he slipped his arm around her shoulders and she couldn't move. She frowned at him, but his eyes were on her wide mouth and she trembled and her lips tingled as if he'd kissed her. She could smell his cleanness and a faint odor of chlorine from the swimming pool.

Frantically she looked out the window beside her to see how close to home they were and she panicked to see that they were out in the country just driving past a large dairy farm. "Where are we going?" Her voice was only a croak, but Kip heard the question.

"For a ride in the country," he answered close to her ear. "Mick and I decided you girls needed fresh air after

working all afternoon. We told your parents our plan
so they wouldn't worry. So, here we are."

How could she endure another minute this close to
Kip? She glanced at Mick, but he was busy talking with
Adrial and didn't hear Kip. Jeanna moved restlessly.

"Your grandma asked about you today," Kip said.

"She did?" Jeanna frowned. "What about?"

"The Provincial House."

Jeanna froze. Why would Grandma want to know
about that? "What'd she want to know?"

Kip shrugged. "She didn't say. She said she'd call you
or come see you tonight sometime."

Jeanna bit her lip, then suddenly realized Grandma
might be just the one to tell about what'd happened
at the Provincial House. Grandma didn't get upset easily
and she always seemed to have the answers. Yes, she'd
talk to Grandma!

Mick drove into a state recreation area and parked
near a grassy field beside several other cars. "Let's walk
for a while to get some fresh air."

"I can't walk in these shoes," Adrial said.

"I got shoes for both of you. They're in the trunk."
Mick walked to the back of the car and Adrial followed.

Jeanna started to push out of the car to go to Mick,
but Kip held her back. She lifted her brow questioningly.

"They're planning to go together without us."

"Not Mick!"

"Yes, Mick. With Adrial. Face it, Jeanna."

She didn't want to, but she stayed beside Kip and
watched Mick and Adrial walk away together.

"Now we can go." Kip helped her change her shoes and then he caught her hand and pulled her along with him. "Get your mind on me and forget about those two."

She stumbled over a branch and would've fallen, but he wrapped his long arm around her narrow waist and steadied her. "I'm all right now," she said in a strangled voice.

"No, you're not, Jeanna."

She stopped and looked up at him in alarm. A nearby stream gurgled and the hot sun tried to break through the shade of the large tree beside them.

"Jae, please tell me what happened to make you stop going to the Provincial House."

"I already told you!"

"No. No, you didn't." His dark hair hung a little over his wide forehead and his brown eyes searched hers for an answer. "You're afraid of something and I want to know what it is so I can help you."

"Your imagination is running wild."

"Do you trust me, Jeanna?"

She shrugged. "Maybe."

He squeezed her hand and she shivered.

"We came to walk, didn't we? Let's walk and stop talking."

He sighed and turned and walked with her, his arm around her waist. Birds sang in tall trees along a narrow path near the stream. Children shouted from a playground across the grassy park. A gentle breeze cooled Jeanna. Finally she looked up at Kip.

"Did you finish the oil painting you were working

on?"

"Not quite. It seems I have other things on my mind lately."

"What things?"

He stopped and held both her hands in his. "Mostly you, Jeanna Marie Shaneck."

She drew back, startled. "No. No!"

"Yes! The sooner you believe it, the sooner we can get on with it."

She didn't want to ask, but she whispered, "With what?"

"With us." He lifted her hand and held it against his broad chest.

"Don't do this, Kip. You aren't interested in me. We don't even like each other that much."

"Don't we?"

"You never noticed me until recently, and then only to tease me."

"You were just a little girl next door that always hung around Mick until all at once I looked and you were grown up and beautiful and wonderful."

She jerked free, shaking her head, her eyes flashing. "Don't talk to me that way! I know how you are with girls! You get them to love you and then you drop them!"

"I do not!"

"I know the girls that have loved you! They'd make friends with me just because we're neighbors and they'd fall for you and then I'd hear all the details about you and them."

"You can't believe everything you hear, Jeanna." He

stabbed his fingers through his dark hair. "Sure, I've gone out with a lot of girls, but I never treated them badly. I never broke any hearts."

Jeanna tossed back her hair. "That's where you're wrong, Kip. I have talked to plenty of girls with broken hearts. That's why I don't believe any of this silly talk you've been giving me. I don't want anything to do with you now, or ever!"

Pain darkened his eyes and he stared at her as if he couldn't believe what she was saying, then he pushed his hair back and his hand trembled.

She knew she'd hurt him. She had to turn away before she burst into tears. Now, maybe he'd leave her alone so that she could get back to a normal life.

She bit her bottom lip and hunched her shoulders as she slowly walked to Mick's car. Kip followed her and they sat side by side in the back seat without touching and without speaking. She sighed in relief when Mick and Adrial returned.

The only sounds to be heard as they drove back to town were the car radio and Jeanna's racing heart. When she saw her house she breathed, "Finally."

"Saved at last," Kip said sharply.

Adrial and Mick slid out and walked away. Jeanna started out, but Kip caught her hand and pulled her off balance so that she fell against his broad chest. He brushed his lips against her flushed cheek and the blood raced through her veins at an alarming rate.

"See you soon," he said softly.

"No!"

"Oh, yes!"

She stumbled from the car, her head spinning. She remembered Grandma would be calling and she hurried inside. When Grandma hadn't called by ten-thirty, Jeanna called her while Adrial was out of the bedroom. "I hear you wanted to talk to me, Grandma."

Carolynn's mind was full of the previous night's murder, but she pulled her thoughts together. "Yes. Yes, I do."

"What'd you want to know?" Now maybe she'd find help!

"Tell me about Nurse Wilder."

Jeanna almost dropped the phone. She sank to the floor beside her bed and gripped the receiver. "What about her?"

"Why is she so set against you?"

Jeanna's face turned as white as the stuffed bunny on her bed. "Who told you?"

"News gets around, Jeanna. Suppose you tell me all about it."

Tears welled up in Jeanna's eyes. How she'd wanted to tell someone! Now, finally, she could. But before she could talk Adrial burst into the room and flopped on her bed. Jeanna's heart plunged to her feet. "I'll have to talk to you later, Grandma. Goodnight."

"Tomorrow we'll talk, Jeanna. For sure."

"For sure."

"I love you, Jae."

"I love you, Grandma." Jeanna slowly hung up, her heart a little lighter. Soon she wouldn't be carrying the terrible secret all alone.

Chapter 4

Carolynn sat in the rocking chair in the corner of Jeanna's bedroom with Jeanna on the floor at her knees. She'd forced away all her thoughts of Silver and Tim and the terrible murder. So far Farley hadn't arrested Silver. Carolynn hadn't said a word about it to Jeanna and she obviously hadn't seen it on the news or read it in the paper. It was late morning. They'd been together for several minutes just passing the time of day. Carolynn smiled at Jeanna. "Now we can talk about the Provincial House."

Jeanna took a deep breath. She was more than ready. "It's a really terrible story, Grandma."

"Tell me anyway." Carolynn rested her hand on Jeanna's shoulder. "You'll feel better if you do."

"I know." Jeanna turned until she was facing her grandmother fully, then told what had happened.

A week after Easter she'd walked down the corridor of the Provincial House, dressed in the uniform that showed she was an aide. The strong odor stung her nose and she was thankful that she didn't live in such a place. Just as she walked past a small room before the turn in the hall, she heard a faint voice calling, "Help. Help me."

She poked her head in, then rushed to the bed where a small, white-haired woman was hanging half in and half out of bed. Jeanna caught her as she toppled from the bed. The room smelled stuffy and dusty.

Carefully Jeanna helped the woman back onto the bed. "Are you all right?"

The woman nodded wearily, but clung to Jeanna's hand. "Stay with me, please. I'm afraid to be alone. My, how pretty you are! How young! I once was young and pretty. I haven't seen you before."

"I'm Jeanna Shaneck and I come twice a week to help."

"How nice. I'm Grace Meeker. Please call me Grace, and be my friend. I get so lonely!"

"Don't you have a family, Grace?"

"Not around here, but I have a daughter in England. She's lived there the past seven years. She has red hair and freckles. My husband had red hair and freckles, too. He died close to ten years ago, or was it twelve? Time seems to get away from me, dear. But it's not like that for young people like you. Did you say your name's Jeanna?"

"Yes."

"It's a pretty name." Grace said it over several times and nodded. "Yes, a pretty name."

Jeanna talked several more minutes before she excused herself with a promise to visit often. During the next several days she spent a lot of time with Grace Meeker.

The day after school let out for summer vacation Jeanna went to work early to have more time with Grace. Jeanna smiled as she looked at the rosebud she'd bought special for Grace for her seventy-third birthday. Jeanna had learned that Grace loved roses and that she'd had a large rose garden at her home before she'd been forced to move to the Provincial House.

With a smile Jeanna pushed open Grace's door, then stopped with a frown. Nurse Wilder stood over the bed, an angry scowl on her face, a small paper pill cup in her hand.

"You must take this medication, Mrs. Meeker! Don't be so obnoxious or I'll be forced to call an orderly to force you to take it."

Grace cringed back. "I'm not supposed to take anything today! Dr. Browne said so!"

"Ridiculous!" Nurse Wilder lifted Grace roughly and tried to force the medication into her mouth. Grace tossed her head back and forth, her mouth closed tightly and whimpering noises pushing out her throat.

Jeanna jumped forward and caught Nurse Wilder's arm. "Don't do that! You're hurting her!"

The nurse dropped Grace and spun around to glare at Jeanna. "Get out of here right now and mind your own business. She is going to take her medication now and that's all there is to it!"

"But she said the doctor doesn't want her to."

"He doesn't!" Grace cried, shivering.

Nurse Wilder whipped around and glared at Grace. "Do you think I'll take your word for it? I know what you are supposed to take. I've been forced to work here the past three years and I've learned how to handle you difficult patients!"

Jeanna tried to push past Nurse Wilder to reach Grace to comfort her, but the nurse blocked the way. Jeanna didn't know if she should believe Grace or the nurse, but she was not going to allow Nurse Wilder to be so rough with Grace. "I want to talk to her and calm her down. Let me do that, at least."

Nurse Wilder's face darkened with anger. "Do you think this is the only patient I have? I don't have time for this."

Jeanna helplessly backed up and watched in horror as Nurse Wilder forced the medication down Grace's throat. Finally the nurse stepped away from the bed, a triumphant look on her thin face.

"That's that," she said smugly, straightening her white uniform. She squared her shoulders and marched out, closing the door behind her.

Jeanna sprang to the bed and Grace burst into tears.

"She was wrong, Jeanna! I shouldn't have taken that medicine! I shouldn't have."

Jeanna patted Grace's shaking shoulder. "There, there. Don't worry about it. Dr. Browne would've let her know what to give you."

"But maybe he forgot! He talked to me not more than an hour ago. He said he was cutting back on my medicine because it was having a bad effect on me. He did say that, Jeanna."

"Just don't think about it. You're all worked up and you should lie down and relax and sleep awhile. I'll come back later when you're rested."

"No, no! Don't leave me! Please!"

"I'll stay a few minutes, but you must lie down." Jeanna saw the woman's ashen face and heard her rapid heartbeat. "I just remembered something, Grace."

"What?" she asked weakly, tugging the sheet up to her chin.

"Happy birthday!"

Tears glistened in Grace's eyes. "Yes, it is my birthday, isn't it? I had forgotten."

"I brought you something." Jeanna reached for the rose that she'd set on the table beside the bed. "Look!"

"A rose. A beautiful red rose!" Grace held it to her and closed her eyes and sniffed the aroma. Finally she opened her eyes and smiled at Jeanna. "Thank you, Jeanna. You are a joy to me. I will rest now and I'll meet you in the sun room to listen to you read afterwhile."

Jeanna kissed the wrinkled cheek. "See you later. Rest now and enjoy your rose."

Later Jeanna read to the people in the sun room, then talked to them, glancing regularly at the door for Grace. She never came and Jeanna hurried to her room to speak with her before it was time to ride home with Kip.

Just outside Grace's room Dr. Browne blocked her way.

"You can't go in."

"I came to see Grace." Shivers of fear ran over her body.

The doctor rubbed his balding head with a pale hand. "Sorry, young lady. Grace died about five minutes ago. It's to be expected in a woman her age."

Jeanna fell back, her mouth open, her heart hammering painfully. "She can't be dead! I just talked to her two hours ago!"

Dr. Browne muttered something just as Nurse Wilder walked out of Grace's room. She gripped Jeanna's arm and led her down the corridor. Jeanna didn't have the strength to resist.

"I want you out of here now and I don't want you to come back!" Nurse Wilder's fingers bit into Jeanna's arm. "Do you know why that woman died?"

Weakly Jeanna shook her head.

"She was trying to get to you! She had no business being out of bed when she wasn't feeling well, but she was determined to talk to you. You are the reason she's dead!"

"No, no," Jeanna said hoarsely, her eyes wide in alarm. "That's not true!"

"You don't want to believe it because it's a terrible thing to be responsible for someone's death, but it's true." Nurse Wilder narrowed her eyes to two blue slits. "You have no business working around these people. You get them to care for you and then you kill them."

Jeanna gasped, her trembling hand at her throat.

"I want you to get out of here and never, never return. If you do, then I'll tell everyone just what you did. You could go to prison for it. I shouldn't be helping you, but I don't want the scandal that it would bring to this place, so I'm going to keep quiet — only if you promise never to come here again."

Numbly Jeanna nodded. Grace had died because of her. No one must ever know.

"I'll tell Mrs. Dillen that you're quitting. You won't have to see her at all."

Jeanna had found her purse, then had stumbled into the parking lot to Kip's car. She'd told him as calmly as possible that she wouldn't be working there again. He'd shrugged and accepted it then. But now he couldn't understand why she wouldn't go back, now that he'd suddenly taken an interest in her. She'd said she'd never go back and she'd kept her word.

Now she stared up at her grandmother in the rocking chair. "I'm sorry for what I did to Grace. I am so sorry!"

Tears filled her eyes and slowly ran down her cheeks to splash on her trembling hands locked together in her lap.

Carolynn gathered Jeanna close and held her just as she had when Jeanna was a baby. "There, there, sweety. I'll get to the bottom of this. I don't believe you're to blame for Grace's death. I remember when it happened." Carolynn almost told Jeanna about looking into Grace Meeker's death when it had happened, but she stopped herself in time. She and Jay Sommers had been sure something shady was going on at the Provincial House, but they'd been wrong. But after hearing Jeanna's story, she'd look into it again. Maybe she and Jay had overlooked something.

After a long time Jeanna wiped her eyes and blew her nose. "I'm glad I told you, Grandma."

"Me too. I knew something was bothering you, but I thought it was boy trouble."

Jeanna rolled her eyes. "It sure is hard to grow up."

"God is with you, Jae. Remember that always."

Jeanna nodded. "Sometimes I get too busy to remember."

"That's easy to do. But don't let it happen. Take time to ready your Bible and pray. Without God's help none of us can make it."

Jeanna laid her head on Grandma's knees again. "I

love you, Grandma."

Carolynn stroked Jeanna's hair. "Heavenly Father, thank you for helping Jeanna every day of her life. Fill her with your peace and your love. May her steps be ordered by you each day. Thank you, Father. In Jesus' name, Amen."

"Amen," Jeanna whispered. As long as she could remember her grandma had prayed with her and for her. "Grandma, someday I want to help others as much as you do."

Carolynn smiled and the laugh lines spread from the corners of her eyes to her dyed, light-brown hair. "You don't have to wait until 'someday.' You can do it right now. You have people around you who need help. Just think about the ones near you, and see how you can help them."

Jeanna thought of Adrial, then of Sarah and Meg. They especially needed her help. Right then she vowed to do what she could for Meg.

A few minutes later Carolynn drove away for her meeting with Jay and Silver.

Jeanna sank in the rocking chair and closed her eyes.

The bedroom door opened and Adrial hurried in. "Here's your mail, Jeanna." Adrial held out the large envelope.

"Thanks!" Jeanna seized the envelope and read the return address. Her heart sank. It was from the magazine where she'd sent her story. She could not open it in front of anyone, not even Adrial.

Adrial opened her drawer, lifted out red shorts and a floral knit shirt, and slipped them on. "I'm going to

Sarah's again today, Jae. She has some music for me to look at and I'm going to help her with a new hair style." Adrial dabbed perfume behind her ears and on her long slender neck. "I like Sarah a lot. She sure needs help with Meg. I don't understand why their mom doesn't do something."

The large envelope grew heavier and Jeanna stared down at it, her ears closed to Adrial. A sick feeling rose from deep inside, and she didn't hear Adrial walk out. The silence lengthened and finally she opened the envelope and pulled out the typed pages of her story. A letter fluttered to the floor and she gingerly picked it up and read it. "Sorry, but this is not for us. We would like to be able to comment on it, but our work load is too heavy." It was signed "The Editors."

Jeanna slumped back and tears filled her eyes and ran down her ashen cheeks. How could they turn down her beautiful, wonderful story? She had to show it to Mick so he could share her grief.

With a sob she ran downstairs and outdoors into the hot summer morning. Blacky pushed against her legs, almost upsetting her. A car honked and sounds of rushing traffic from Madison Street filled the air.

She found Mick in the swimming pool and she stood on the edge and called, "Mick. Mick!"

He turned, then swam to her and pushed out of the pool, spraying water around. "What's wrong, Jae? Is it Adrial?"

"No, no. It's — It's —"

"Where is Adrial? Are you sure she's all right?"

"She went to see Sarah." Jeanna gripped Mick's arms.

"Will you listen to me?"

He moved restlessly. "If it's not Adrial, then what is it?"

Jeanna bit her lip and pulled away from him, wrapping her arms around herself. "I just got a rejection. The magazine turned down my story."

"That's too bad, Jae." Mick rubbed his hair with his blue towel. "Do you know when Adrial will get back? Maybe I should pick her up."

"Mick, please, listen to me! Help me."

"What can I do, Jae? I am sorry, but I can't make them take it, can I?"

"I just need to talk to you, Mick. We haven't seen much of each other and now I need you."

He tugged one of her curls. "I'm sorry, Jeanna. Now, tell me your problem and I'll see if I can help."

Tears stung her eyes. "I already told you."

He spread his hands wide. "Maybe the story wasn't good enough. Maybe you need to write it again, or toss it out and start all over."

"Oh, Mick! What has happened to us?"

He moved restlessly. "Nothing. We're friends, as always."

"Nothing more?" she whispered hoarsely.

"Well, of course, a whole lot more, but it's hard to put into words. We've never needed words, have we?"

"I guess not."

He draped the towel around his broad shoulders. "I wish I could make you feel better, but I don't know how."

She swallowed hard and nodded. "That's all right,

Mick. I guess no one can understand, or help." She walked slowly back to her yard with Blacky on her heels. She sank down under a maple, pulled her knees to her chin, and buried her fingers in Blacky's thick hair. She closed her eyes and sniffed back the tears. A cricket sang somewhere near the picnic table on the patio. A dog barked in the distance and a door slammed. Music drifted across the yard from the house in back of her.

Blacky lifted his head and barked one short bark. Jeanna's eyes flew open to find Kip standing over her, a concerned look on his face.

"Go away," she whispered. She'd stayed away from him since their drive to the country.

"I saw you sitting here, looking as if you'd lost your best friend and I came to help you." He wore jeans and a short-sleeved, pull-over shirt.

"I'm all right, Kip. I don't need your help." She pushed herself up and took a step toward her house.

"Don't go," he said softly and she turned slowly and saw the look in his brown eyes and she couldn't move. "Please, stay."

She nodded, then sank to the grass with him beside her. They leaned against the maple, shoulder to shoulder.

"Now, tell me why you're so unhappy, honey."

With a quivering sigh she locked her icy fingers together. "My story was rejected."

"Oh, babe! I am so sorry!" He turned and gathered her close.

She pushed her face into his neck and burst into tears. Finally the tears stopped and he pushed a tissue into her hands. She smiled weakly as she wiped her eyes. "My makeup is smeared, isn't it?"

"You look beautiful."

"I don't know why I was so upset over a little story."

"You worked hard on it and it's only natural to be upset. Find another place to send it and you'll feel better. You've read about writers who had their work rejected several times, only to have it sell later. Don't give up, Jae. Never give up!"

She touched his arm, then leaned forward, and kissed his cheek. "Thank you." She pulled back with her fingers on her lips. "Sorry about that."

"Don't be sorry. I liked it." He tipped her face up and she closed her eyes for a moment, suddenly weak. He lowered his head and barely touched his lips to hers. Her fingers curled around his arms. He kissed her again, but this time it was different and her hands slid around his neck. Her senses spun and a fire leaped inside her.

"I knew it would be like this for us," he whispered with his mouth against her ear.

She stiffened and pushed against him and he let her go. "Don't, Kip." Her voice was shaky and she flushed.

"Don't pull away from me, Jeanna."

"Don't play with me, Kip! You had no right to kiss me."

"What a baby you are! Why won't you face the truth?"

Her hand trembled as she pushed his hands off her arms. "I know the truth about you, Kip. This is a game to you, nothing serious at all."

"If that's what you think of me, then I can't change

your mind, can I? You might as well go back to playing games with Mick. With him you don't have to involve your heart."

She fled to the house, her heart racing. With trembling hands she locked her door, then flung herself across her bed and buried her face in her pillow.

Kip had kissed her!

She had kissed him!

She moaned with shame and curled into a tight ball. She'd kissed him and he'd kissed her and she'd liked it! How could she feel that way when she didn't love him?

Mick had never kissed her the way Kip had. She had never responded to Mick the way she had to Kip. What could it mean?

Someone knocked on the door and she froze. How could she face anyone now? "Go away!"

"It's Mom, Jeanna. I need to talk to you."

She pushed herself up, sniffed and wiped her eyes. She'd thought her mother was at work. Maybe she'd come home for lunch. She sometimes did that. "Can't it wait, Mom?"

"It's important, Jae."

She looked at her reflection in the dresser mirror to see that her eyes sparkled and her lips were redder. Could her mom tell that she'd been kissed? She flushed and turned quickly away to unlock the door and swing it open.

Christa Shaneck walked in and stood in front of her, her face thoughtful. Her brown hair was neatly combed and her flowered blouse was tucked into her yellow skirt.

"What is it, Mom?"

Christa pushed her hands into her skirt pockets and hunched her shoulders. "Jae, Mrs. Griffin reported that several items are missing from your department."

"Oh, Mom!" Jeanna's hand fluttered at her throat.

"More shoplifting, Jae."

"I never noticed anyone, Mom. I didn't see anyone remotely suspicious at all!"

"I've asked the house detectives to walk through the children's department periodically after this, but you keep your eyes and ears open, too."

"I will." Jeanna shook her head and clicked her tongue. "I can't imagine anyone walking into your store and walking out with stolen items."

Christa sighed heavily. "It certainly cuts into the profits."

"I'm sorry."

"These past few weeks have been worse. Are you sure you haven't noticed anyone suspicious?"

"I haven't! I wish I could catch the culprit."

Christa tapped Jeanna's shoulder. "Don't do anything to put yourself in danger, spitfire." Christa laughed and Jeanna did, too. "You are more important to me than a few items of clothing." She hugged Jeanna, then held her away and studied her thoughtfully.

Jeanna saw the questions in her mom's eyes and she flushed and ducked her head.

"Jae, I know that something's been going on lately. Can't you tell me what it is?"

Jeanna rubbed her hand down her mom's arm. "I can't

talk about it, Momma. Please, don't take it personally. This is something I have to handle myself."

"Is it Kip?"

Jeanna froze. "Kip?"

"Never mind. I thought he was showing a little interest in you."

"Don't worry about me, Mom. I'll be fine." Maybe she should tell her about Nurse Wilder. Abruptly she pushed the idea away. Grandma was the only one she'd tell.

"Jae, when are you going to the Provincial House again?"

She flinched and caught her breath. Had her mom read her mind? "I don't think I'll ever go back. Why do you ask?" It was hard to talk around the painful lump in her throat.

"I know you enjoyed the work, and the people you met must miss you." Christa fingered the top button of her blouse. "Did you know that woman who died so mysteriously awhile back?"

Jeanna's heart stopped and she stood very still, her eyes wide in her pale face. "Yes, I knew her. Why?"

"I was just wondering. Your dad and I thought that might be what's been bothering you. We know how close you were to some of those people and we thought maybe her death had upset you."

Jeanna's stomach tightened. "It did. But I'm all right now."

"I wonder what did happen."

Jeanna shrugged, but couldn't speak.

Finally Christa walked out, closing the door.

Trembling, Jeanna sagged against her desk.

★   ★   ★

At Children's Services Adrial stood beside Sarah and Meg. "It's really for the best, Meg," Adrial said softly. She'd wanted to tell Jeanna they were taking Meg to Children's Services today, but hadn't. It was hard to tell Jeanna anything.

Meg looked down at her stomach with a pout. "I should've got an abortion."

Sarah gasped. "Don't even say that! You can't murder your baby!"

Meg glared at Sarah. "Don't start that again! I said I'd come here, didn't I?"

Adrial had helped convince Sarah to bring Meg to Children's Services. "And you were wise to do it," Adrial said. She looked around for Clara Breech, the woman they'd spoken to on the phone. Only a man was there, sitting at the computer.

The man looked up and smiled. "Can I help you girls?"

"We want to see Clara Breech," Adrial said. "We have an appointment."

The man glanced at the pregnant girl and his heart sank. He obviously hated to see teens pregnant and needing the help of Children's Services. "I'll get Clara for you." He hurried away with tears in his eyes. Here was another girl giving up her baby. Clara was the one they talked to when that's what they planned to do. Clara always made the arrangements.

A few minutes later the girls were seated with Clara.

The man listened as the girls introduced themselves and Clara explained the procedure of putting a baby up for adoption. He knew the spiel by heart. He also knew Meg would put the baby up for adoption. It wasn't right! Didn't she know that?

Suddenly he froze in place as a brilliant idea popped into his head. Why hadn't he thought of it before this? He could kill Meg while she was still pregnant. It would solve the baby's problem as well as punish Meg. It was a wonderful plan. He looked at Meg and smiled. She was going to get just what she deserved, only this time even the baby would be saved from years of agony living with an adoptive mother.

A few minutes later the girls left. Clara dropped the information beside the man for him to enter into the computer. When her back was turned he jotted Meg's name and address on a scrap of paper, then stuffed it in his pocket. He'd take care of Meg, maybe then he'd be free to get on with his life. He might marry Dena and move away, maybe to Colorado. He'd heard it was nice there.

★   ★   ★

Her eyes wide with terror, Silver stared at Deputy Littlejohn as he held up the tire iron. It was in a plastic bag with a red tag on it. She'd just put Brittany down for a nap when the deputy had called her downstairs to the front room. He was tall and thin with high cheekbones and raven black hair.

"I found this under a mat in the back seat of your car."

"What?"

"It doesn't fit your car, Mrs. Rawlings. Do you know where it came from?"

Silver shook her head as shivers raced up and down her spine. "I've never seen it before in my life! My tire iron doesn't look like that at all."

"I know. I found yours in the trunk with the jack."

"Why would anyone put it there? I don't understand why it's such a big deal."

Deputy Littlejohn cleared his throat and looked upset. "It's probably the murder weapon. It's the right shape to make the mark the woman had on her head. It has a little blood on it even though it's been carefully wiped off." He hesitated, his dark eyes alert. "It was as if someone wiped it off, yet carefully left a smear of blood."

She rubbed her hands nervously down her jeans. "Would somebody deliberately put it there so I'd be blamed for the murder?" she asked hoarsely.

Deputy Littlejohn cleared his throat again. "Is there anyone you want to call? You shouldn't be alone at a time like this."

Silver nodded as she looked at the phone on the table beside the couch. "My husband. He had to go to church for a meeting, but he'll come home if I call. He said he'd be here by two."

"It's almost two now."

She pushed her long, brown hair behind her ears. "Then he'll be home." She fingered the necklace at her throat. "He never breaks his word."

The door opened and Tim called, "I'm home!"

"In here, Tim!" Silver wanted to run to meet him,

but she felt glued to the carpet.

Tim hurried in, then stopped short when he saw the tire iron in a plastic bag in Deputy Littlejohn's hand. "What's that?"

Silver ran to him and clung to him. Hysterically she said, "He said it's probably the murder weapon! It was in *my* car! It has *blood* on it!"

Tim's blood froze in his veins. He didn't want to suspect Silver, but she'd been very determined about Gwen not seeing Brittany. He turned to the deputy for an explanation.

"It was under the mat in the back seat of her car." Deputy Littlejohn looked toward the door. "I'm taking it in to have the blood checked. The sheriff won't want you leaving town."

Silver whimpered and pushed her face into Tim's neck. She couldn't lose her baby, her husband, her home and her freedom over something she didn't do!

As the deputy walked out Tim led Silver to the couch and sat with her. "Is Brittany asleep upstairs?"

Silver nodded. "I thought about sending her to Holly's for the day, but with Holly at work and only the babysitter there, I couldn't. Brittany needs us as much as we need her."

Tim agreed.

Just then the sheriff walked in, his hat in his hand. He stopped near the entertainment unit and cleared his throat. "Tim, I was talking with your neighbor and he said you left here last night on your bike. About eight-thirty, he said."

Silver stared at Tim in shock. "I didn't know that,"

she whispered.

Tim flushed. "I was supposed to meet Gwen Nichols at the church like I told you. But I couldn't find my car keys. I loaded Brittany in the baby carrier on the bike and started for the church."

Silver gasped. Why hadn't Tim told her?

"And did you make it to the church?" Sheriff Cobb asked in a very quiet voice.

Tim shook his head. "Brittany started fussing, then spit up all over herself, so I came back. I changed her and was going to go out again, but Silver came home with the terrible news."

Sheriff Cobb settled his hat in place and pulled out his notebook. "Why didn't you mention this before?"

Tim shrugged. "I didn't think to. Why?"

Silver saw the suspicious look on the sheriff's face. She wanted to say something to protect Tim.

"You had the opportunity to kill the woman."

"But I didn't get to the church!" Tim wanted to jump up, but his legs had turned to water.

"Since you planned to go there, why didn't you drive?" Sheriff Cobb's voice was almost too low to hear.

"It was my fault," Silver said weakly. "I took his car key so he couldn't meet Gwen. I'd do *anything* to keep him from taking the baby to Gwen!"

The sheriff lifted his gray brow. "Anything?"

Silver clamped her hand to her mouth and shook her head.

"She wouldn't *kill,* sheriff! And neither would I. Ask Carolynn Burgess about us. She knows we wouldn't kill anyone."

"Mrs. Burgess said she's only known you the year you've been here in Middle Lake."

"But she knows we couldn't kill anyone!" Silver cried.

Tim narrowed his eyes. "If Silver did kill Gwen, why would she hide the tire iron in her car? Why wouldn't she get rid of it?"

"Maybe she planned to later."

"I didn't! I never even knew it was in my car!"

Sheriff Cobb pushed his hat to the back of his head. "The next time I talk to you, I suggest you have an attorney present."

Silver burst into tears and pushed her face against Tim's arm.

Tim sat helplessly beside Silver, a prayer locked in his icy heart. He was getting just what he deserved for what he'd done. Maybe Gwen had told Silver the truth and she'd struck her, accidently killing her. But if Gwen had said anything, wouldn't Silver confront him? Tim absently patted Silver's arm. She could've blocked the truth out because of the horror of it. Absolutely no one else had a motive to kill Gwen Nichols.

Sheriff Cobb studied the young couple as they huddled together on the couch. He wished Carolynn was here with them to comfort them. He'd call her from his car and see if she could come right away.

★   ★   ★

Carolynn sat in Nurse Wilder's office, waiting to talk to her when she finished her phone conversation. The office was small, but pleasantly decorated in shades of blues with a splash of green here and there. A bouquet of roses in a glass vase sat on a table near the window. Even the phone Nurse Wilder was using was blue. Her wooden desk was of medium size with only the phone on it. Her high-back desk chair was made of blue leather and looked comfortable enough for napping. Carolynn crossed her legs and leaned back in the leather chair. It was pretty comfortable too, but it didn't recline. It was totally for business.

Finally Nurse Wilder hung up and lifted her brows questioningly. "Now, what can I do for you?"

Carolynn smiled and leaned forward. "This is really silly, but when you lived in Flint wasn't your name Melanie Reeve?"

Bess Wilder blanched. "Who wants to know?"

"No one you'd know. I know it's really an invasion of your privacy, but I'd really like to know."

"I don't see that it matters to anyone, but yes, it once was my name. After I left Flint I got married. He liked my middle name, so I decided to use it. I haven't been known as Melanie Reeve for over twenty years."

"There's a young man looking for you. Gil Oakes is his name."

Bess Wilder shook her head impatiently. "I never heard of him. What does he want?"

"I'll let him tell you. Would you meet with him to talk?"

"I really don't have time for foolishness. What's he selling?"

Carolynn chuckled. "Nothing. He only wants to talk. He could meet you here if it's easier for you."

"Why didn't he come instead of you?"

"You can ask him. I have no idea." Carolynn stood, her purse in her hand. Bess Wilder didn't seem the type to open her arms to a son she'd given away at birth. "Would tomorrow afternoon at three work for you?"

"I suppose."

Carolynn started for the door, then turned back. "I almost forgot. Did Grace Meeker's family claim her personal belongings?"

Bess Wilder's face turned ashen. Slowly she pushed herself up. "I really have no idea. I'm not in charge of such things."

"I was sorry to learn about her death. It seemed very — sudden. Didn't it?"

"She was old, Mrs. Burgess. That's life." Bess strode to her door and opened it. "I really don't have time for chitchat. If you'll excuse me." She held the door wide, looking expectantly at Carolynn.

Carolynn switched her purse from one hand to the other. "I heard a rumor that Grace Meeker died because she was given the wrong medication."

Bess trembled, then steeled herself to stand tall and steady. "I never listen to rumors!"

"I think I'll ask Dr. Browne about it."

"You are quite a busybody, aren't you, Mrs. Burgess? Dr. Browne doesn't have time for gossip. Please, leave now. And don't bother the doctor!"

Carolynn walked slowly to the reception area where Sue sat at the desk.

Sue laughed softly. "I heard her clear out here. What'd you say to make her angry?"

Carolynn grinned and shrugged, then leaned close

to Sue. "She doesn't know I'm Jeanna's grandma. Please don't mention it, okay?"

"I won't. Any reason?"

"I don't want to make trouble for Jeanna because of my curiosity."

"Jeanna said she wasn't coming back, but Kip Jennings said she was." Sue glanced toward the women sitting in the lounge watching TV. "I hope she does come back. She's good with the patients. Mabel Pranger especially."

"Did you hear the gossip about Grace Meeker?"

Sue bit her lip. "I did, but I gave my word to keep quiet about it. Nurse Wilder called a special meeting for that very reason. Sorry."

Carolynn shrugged. "That's all right. I shouldn't be so curious anyway."

"I don't think her death has anything to do with Jeanna leaving. They were friends, though."

"Do you know who she named in her will? Her family?"

Sue looked quickly around. "I suppose I can tell you that much. She left her possessions to the Provincial House."

Carolynn bit back a cry of surprise. "Does that happen often?"

Sue lifted a shoulder and let it fall. "If a patient is unhappy with her family, he or she will often leave her money to the Provincial House."

"Is it privately owned?"

"I really don't know."

Carolynn jotted a mental note to check into it. "I

must be going, Sue. It's been nice talking to you."

"Tell Jeanna hello for me."

"I will." Carolynn hurried to her car. She'd stop by to tell Dud to set up a meeting between Gil Oakes and Nurse Wilder.

Carolynn drove out of the parking lot and into traffic. "I think I'll be here tomorrow at three just to see how that meeting goes."

Chapter 5

Carolynn sat in Sheriff Cobb's office, her hands locked over her purse. He was on his second cup of morning coffee. It smelled as if it was strong enough to walk away by itself. He usually wasn't in on a Saturday, but he had a few things to wrap up. She had to hurry back home to go to breakfast with Robert. She'd told him she had to talk to the sheriff in person, but wouldn't be gone long. "Farley, you have to realize those two are innocent!"

"I told Mrs. Rawlings to have an attorney present when I talk to her again. You see that she does, Carolynn. The woman's in deep trouble."

"Give me a few days, Farley. Please. I'll investigate the murder." Carolynn pushed aside thoughts of Gil Oakes and his problems. He could wait awhile. "I'll see who had both motive and opportunity."

"Mrs. Rawlings had motive."

"I know." Carolynn moved restlessly. Silver had more of a motive than Farley could even imagine. But then maybe she didn't know about Tim and Gwen Nichols.

"I'll drag my feet a bit on this one, but I can't do it for long." Farley poured himself another cup. "You sure you don't want one?"

"No thanks." Carolynn waited until he sat down again. "I'll appreciate all the time you can give me. Thanks, Farley."

He sipped his coffee and smacked his lips. "I wouldn't do this for anyone else."

"I know."

"You make sure she doesn't run."

"She won't." Carolynn talked a bit longer, said goodbye and drove to Dud's office. He was alone.

"I got news you don't want to hear," Dud said as he motioned for her to sit down.

"Bess Wilder really isn't Gil's mother?"

Dud chuckled, then sobered. "That young man never called me, so we didn't set up a meeting with Nurse Wilder."

"That's strange."

"My news has nothing to do with him. It's worse."

She watched him as he leaned back on his desk, his hands in his pockets. She hoped it wouldn't take Dud long to get the story out. She was hungry and Robert would be too. "Then tell me and let me work it out."

Dud jangled his change and keys. "Gwen Nichols's family hired Lavery to find her killer."

Carolynn shot from her chair. "No!"

"I told you it was bad."

"Did you tell her not to take it?"

"I couldn't without making her suspicious."

Carolynn sank back down to the folding chair. She thought of the letter from Tim to Gwen she had concealed in her purse. What would Lavery do if she learned about the affair? She'd never keep it to herself no matter how many people it hurt. Carolynn looked helplessly at Dud. She'd have to solve the case fast before Lavery learned about Tim.

*　　*　　*

Sunday afternoon the man parked across from Meg's house. Maybe he'd get lucky and be able to kill her yet today. She should've known practicing safe sex was a lie. Abstinence was the only answer. Well, she wouldn't have to think about it after today. She'd be in a cold coffin deep in the ground and her baby would be right there with her for all eternity.

He drummed his fingers on the steering wheel and hummed a tune under his breath. Waiting was hard, but it was part of the job.

After two hours he frowned impatiently. Where was she? Her sister had left with her skinny boyfriend a long time ago. Was this going to be the only day she stayed in? Maybe he could ring the doorbell and kill her when she answered it. He played with the idea for a while, then shrugged. "I'll go get a strawberry shake and come back later. I just might be lucky."

*　　*　　*

Carolynn sat on a bench in Tim's back yard and watched Silver carry Brittany into the house for a nap. Carolynn crossed her legs. She sometimes liked a Sunday afternoon nap, but today she had more important things to handle. "Could we talk, Tim?"

He sat down beside Carolynn and nervously rubbed his hands down his jeans. "You don't think Silver's guilty, do you?"

"No." Carolynn hated to say what she knew she

must. She tried to choose her words carefully, but finally blurted out, "I know about you and Gwen Nichols."

Tim gasped and the color drained from his face.

"I know Brittany is your natural child." Carolynn told him about the letter she'd taken from Gwen's purse.

"I'm so ashamed, Carolynn! I thought I left my past behind me when we moved here, but it seems I can't really do that."

"I assume Silver doesn't know."

"Not unless Gwen told her."

Carolynn sat very still at the implication Tim had made. "Wouldn't Silver say something to you?"

"Not if she blocked the whole thing out of her mind." Tim stabbed his fingers through his hair. "A year and a half after we were married, Silver had a miscarriage. She blocked it out of her mind and continued to think she was pregnant. It took prayer and therapy before she could admit the truth."

"Let me know if she says anything." Carolynn hesitated, then said, "I learned Gwen's parents hired a private investigator to find her killer."

Tim groaned.

"Do they know about you?"

"I don't think so. But Gwen might've told them."

"Maybe you should tell Silver the truth before she hears it from someone else."

Tim helplessly shook his head. "I can't, Carolynn! I can't do that to her."

"You had an affair. You did that to her."

"I know," Tim whispered. "I was at a low point in

my life. I know it's no excuse. I couldn't pray or read my Bible. I met Gwen and it — just happened."

Carolynn frowned.

"I know. It didn't *just* happen. I listened to Satan's lies and I gave in to temptation. I've asked God to forgive me and I know He has." Tim's voice broke. "But I continue to pay, Carolynn."

"I'm sorry, Tim. I truly am. But you should tell Silver. If she hears it from someone else, it'll be even harder on her." Carolynn laid her hand on Tim's arm. "Who would hide the tire iron in Silver's car? Someone wants to blame her for the murder. But, Tim, why would anyone choose her of all the people in Middle Lake? Why? It must be because of your connection to Gwen."

Tim groaned. "I hadn't thought about that."

"Suppose you tell me about Gwen. I might be able to see if anyone has a motive to kill her."

"You, Carolynn?"

She frantically searched for the right thing to say. "At this point I'm thinking clearer than you, Tim. You can't talk about this to anyone else. Am I right?"

Tim nodded. "No one else knows." He took a deep breath. "She lives — lived — near Lansing in an apartment by herself. She has a brother as well as her parents. I don't know if she dated much. She wasn't seeing anyone when we — met."

"Did you ever meet her parents or her brother?"

"Her brother Andy. I was afraid he'd find out about us."

"And did he?"

Tim shrugged.

"Would he kill his own sister?"

"No! I don't know." Tim rubbed an unsteady hand over his face. "It's all so terrible, Carolynn!"

"I know, Tim, but it happened and we have to deal with it." She pulled out her notebook and pen. "Give me Andy's address."

"I don't know it. He lives in Lansing. At least he did. He could've moved." Tim helplessly shook his head. "I don't know why you'd suspect him."

"It had to be somebody close to Gwen — somebody who knew about the two of you. Why else would he or she hide the tire iron in Silver's car? It always comes back to that."

"Maybe it was only a coincidence. Did you ever think of that?"

"Yes. It could've been. Gwen could've seen something she wasn't supposed to see and got herself killed. Or somebody could've tried to rob her or rape her, she struggled, and was killed. But there wasn't a sign of struggle. Nor of rape or robbery." Carolynn was quiet a long time. "How long does it take you to ride your bike to the church and back?"

"Five, ten minutes each way. Why?"

"Sheriff Cobb will get to thinking about that, Tim. He might think you could ride to the church on a bike quicker than Silver could drive there, kill Gwen and ride home before Silver got back."

Tim sagged and shook his head. "This is the worst nightmare I've ever had."

"You and Silver know how to pray, Tim." Carolynn

patted his arm again. "You'd better both pray fervently because this nightmare is only beginning."

★   ★   ★

Jeanna jerked her jeans and green tee shirt over her flowered swimsuit. Somehow she had to forget her terrible secret, let Grandma help and get on with her life. She had to go with her friends to keep busy this long Sunday afternoon and forget what had happened at the Provincial House.

Her hands trembled as she hung her church clothes in the closet. As she turned, Adrial walked in, humming happily. She stopped when she saw Jeanna and cleared her throat nervously.

"Did Mick get another person to go with us today, Addie? Five would be an awkward number."

Adrial tucked her yellow tee shirt into her tight jeans, then tied her walking shoes. Her strawberry blonde hair was pulled back and up and braided in a French braid that showed off her high cheekbones and widely set eyes. "Mick said he'd find someone. I talked to him a few minutes ago and he said he'd handle it."

Jeanna studied Adrial thoughtfully. "Is anything wrong?"

Adrial flushed and lifted her chin. "Why do you ask?"

Jeanna shrugged. "Well, is there?"

"Sarah's your best friend, Jeanna."

"So?"

"So why aren't you helping her with Meg?"

Jeanna flushed. She'd been so caught up with her own problems that she'd ignored everyone around her. But it certainly wasn't Adrial's place to mention it. "It's really not any of your business."

"I've been making it my business! I went to Children's Services with Meg and Sarah. Meg's going to put the baby up for adoption."

"That's good." Jeanna looked down, feeling really rotten for not being there for Sarah. Finally Jeanna glanced at Adrial. "I'm glad you went with Sarah."

Adrial shrugged. "I couldn't let her go alone. She wanted you there. I wish you'd deal with whatever's bothering you."

"I'm trying to!" Jeanna snatched up her pack. "Let's get out of here." She held the bedroom door wide and waited for Adrial to walk through. Her perfume drifted along with them downstairs and outdoors to the Jennings' driveway, where Jimmy and Sarah were waiting in Jimmy's parent's station wagon.

"Ready to go?" Sarah asked with a happy laugh.

"I am!" Adrial pushed the bag of food into the cooler in the back of the wagon.

Jeanna pulled Sarah aside. "How's Meg?"

Sarah made a face. "She's home alone today. I know I should've stayed with her, but I just couldn't stand to!"

"Of course not! You're not her keeper, Sarah."

"I'm her sister and I want to help her."

"I know."

Just then Jimmy called and Sarah ran to join him.

Jeanna glanced at Kip's silver Toyota and quickly away. Was he inside right now watching them load up to leave? With a frown she forced away thoughts of Kip and tried to talk to Jimmy. In his baggy shorts and tank top Jimmy looked taller and thinner. His Adam's apple bobbed as he talked.

Mick stood at the side of the wagon and beckoned to Adrial. Jeanna frowned. When would Mick get around to talking with Adrial about his feelings for her? Jeanna chewed her bottom lip thoughtfully. Maybe she should push Adrial aside and cling to Mick all day long.

"I'm ready." It was Kip's deep voice, and Jeanna's heart zoomed to her feet as she whirled around to face him. He smiled at her, then caught her arm and pushed her into the very back seat. "We'll take the back and leave the middle seat for Mick and Adrial."

"No." Jeanna flushed. She'd intended to say it firmly, but it came out in a mere whisper. She cringed against the seat, but her pulse leaped as Kip sat beside her, his shoulder pressed against hers.

"Relax, honey," he said close to her ear.

Just the feel of him made her dizzy. "Let me go," she whispered through a parched throat.

He laughed softly and his brown eyes twinkled. "Not a chance. Let's enjoy today and forget about our yesterdays."

The idea appealed to her, but how could she manage it?

With a chuckle he held up his left hand and then his right hand. "Choose, Jae." He waited and she didn't speak. "So, you like them both equally. That's great. Today's going to be a wonderful day!"

She shook her head and laughed. "You are hopeless, aren't you?"

"Not on your life! I am hopeful, always hopeful."

She had to find a safe area of conversation and she searched her racing mind. "Why don't we talk about your art? That should keep us occupied for the hour drive to Bear Lake, shouldn't it?"

He rubbed his forehead against her curls, then drew back. "Art, it is. What exactly shall we discuss?"

"Dad told me that the bank bought one of your oils. He said it was beautiful."

"I like it and of course I'm glad they hung it at the bank." He reached for her hand and she let him take it. "You know, I sometimes wonder if I dare take money for the things I create. It doesn't seen right, somehow."

"Why should you feel that way, Kip? You put time and energy and talent into your pictures. You should get paid for it."

He sighed and turned his head to look at her. "Do you ever daydream what it'll be like when you're rich and famous?"

She nodded.

"I do, too. I think about the masterpiece I want to paint so that others can see beauty that I see. You use words to say something and I use my art. We're sharing our feelings and thoughts with others in a way that's all our own."

"That's beautiful, Kip. I feel that same way, but I've never put it into words. I like it when I write just the correct word to make the reader laugh or cry. The painting that you have hanging in the office of the high school shows that you want to do the same thing."

"I wish I could give it to you, Jae, but it belongs to

the school. I'll paint a picture for you, one that will speak to you alone."

She squeezed his hand. "Thank you."

"My pleasure."

She sat quietly beside him while Jimmy drove down the highway. Soft music filled the car and blended together with voices. The air conditioner blew cool air around them.

"Did you send your manuscript out again, Jae?"

She nodded with a sigh. "The day after I got the rejection. I want it to sell so badly."

"I can understand that. And it'll happen as long as you hang in there."

A semi roared past them. Sarah laughed at something Jimmy said; Mick and Adrial talked together in low, excited voices.

"Did you read about the murder in the church parking lot?" Kip asked.

"I heard my folks talking about it."

"There's gossip that Silver Rawlings is guilty."

"No! I can't believe that!"

"Me either."

Jeanna stared down at a green gum wrapper on the floor. She couldn't handle hearing about a murder that a friend might've committed.

Kip tapped the back of her hand with his finger. "By the way, Mabel Pranger asked about you again. I told her that you wouldn't be back to work and she begged me to take you to visit her. What'd you say?"

Jeanna's stomach tightened painfully and she kept her head down. "I don't want to visit her or anyone else at the Provincial House. I told you that. Please don't ask me again."

He raked his fingers through his thick brown hair. Music from the cassette player drifted around them, cutting off any other sounds. "I can't understand you, Jae! What happened to change you? I know something is bothering you and I want to help."

She cradled herself with trembling arms. What if she took him seriously and suddenly told him everything, then threw herself into his arms? Oh, she didn't dare! This was Kip Jennings, the boy who had pushed her away all his life because she was a kid. He wouldn't want to know what had happened to her, what she'd done. Once he lost interest in her, he wouldn't give her a second thought. She peeked up at him and found him watching her closely.

"Stop giving out those inviting vibes, Jeanna."

"Me? Vibes?" What was he talking about?

He tapped the tip of her nose. "My, but you sound innocent. You know the messages you send to me every time we're within calling distance of each other. And then when we're this close, the message is so loud and strong that I can barely keep my hands off you."

She pressed her trembling hands to her flushed cheeks. "I don't do that, Kip! I don't!"

"Stop teasing me. Let's have fun today, and help Adrial to enjoy herself." Kip glanced at Mick and Adrial and bobbed his dark brows. "I think she'll have a happy memory of today. I didn't know my little brother had it in him."

Jeanna bristled. "Had what in him? And he's not

little!"

Kip frowned and caught her hand and she stared at him in surprise. "Jae, don't pretend you still are in love with Mick. You aren't and you never were."

"You're wrong, Kip! I love him and he loves me!" Her voice was low and hoarse and she wondered if she was trying to convince Kip or herself. "Mick wants Adrial to have a good time. He told me that. He would never forget our love."

Kip pressed her imprisoned hand to his heart. "Mick's heart never raced like this because you were near him. And your pulse didn't leap over him the way it does with me."

Her face flamed and her insides felt like Jell-O that had been left out in the hot sun. "Don't do this, Kip. Please."

He released her hand abruptly. "I am tired of waiting for you."

He sounded tired and depressed and her heart went out to him, but she sat still without speaking and watched out the window as Jimmy drove into Bear Lake access. She pulled her large, round sunglasses off the top of her head and slipped them into place. Feeling safe behind them she turned to Kip. "We'll have fun today, Kip. I won't give you a hard time and you won't tease me."

He rubbed his hand down his jeans and finally nodded.

"You aren't mad, are you?"

"Should I be?"

"Oh, Kip, I don't want us to fight. I want to be

friends. Can't we be?"

He smiled and nodded and she smiled in relief.

Several minutes later Jeanna picked up her bag and the case of 7-UP and waited for Mick to join her. He smiled and spoke, but walked past her to Adrial.

"I hate walking through the sand." Adrial frowned at the long stretch of beach ahead of them.

"I'll carry you," said Mick.

"No." They laughed together, then ran along the sand, stopped and she spread out a bright blanket. He set up a huge beach umbrella with bright red polka dots against a white background. Waves washed up on the sand, leaving wet, packed sand. Children shouted and played several feet away.

Jimmy set the cooler down under the umbrella, then pulled out a bag of ruffled potato chips from a sack that Sarah carried. "I'm hungry. Anybody want to eat now?"

"Jeanna and I are going swimming first," said Kip, and she found herself nodding in agreement.

She raced beside Kip to the water and plunged in. It felt as soft as velvet against her skin as she swam toward the buoy with Kip beside her, matching her speed. She knew that he could have left her behind and she smiled thankfully at him. At the buoy she said, "I'm swimming in now. Want to come?"

"Not right now, but I'll join you later."

Lazily she swam to shore, then walked alone to the blanket. The beach wasn't as crowded as usual and she was thankful as she sat down and wrapped her yellow towel around her shoulders. With her knees up to her chin she watched the multitude of colors around her. She smiled as Mick strode toward her and dropped to the blanket beside her. Water dripped from his hair.

"Oh, Mick, it's a beautiful day, isn't it?"

He nodded as he rubbed his light-brown hair with an orange towel. He turned toward her, his face serious. "I came in because I saw you alone."

She smiled and touched his arm. "Thanks. We haven't had much time together, have we? I've missed you."

"You have?" Absently he rubbed the towel over his muscled leg, then draped it around his broad shoulders. "Jeanna, I do have something to say, something important."

"What is it? You know you can tell me anything."

He swallowed hard. "I'm in love with Adrial."

Jeanna's eyes widened and her stomach cramped. "What?"

"You can't be surprised, Jae. She and I have spent all of our free time together since she came."

"Oh, Mick!" Tears filled Jeanna's eyes.

"I thought you'd be glad for me."

"Why?"

"You've fallen in love and I thought you'd be happy that I have too."

Her mouth dropped open and she couldn't speak.

"I'm not blind, Jae. I've seen you and Kip together."

"But you know Kip. He doesn't fall in love. And I'm already in love with you." She clutched the towel to her.

"You are not, and never have been. We're friends. I realized the difference when I fell in love with Addie."

A tear trickled down Jeanna's pale cheek. "I don't

want things to change between us."

"Don't cry." He sounded as if he would.

"I'm not crying." She rubbed away the tears seeping from under her lashes.

"I don't want to hurt you. I thought you understood how it is with Adrial and me. What you and I have is totally different from what Adrial and I have. If you're honest with yourself, you'll be able to see that we never were in love."

Jeanna lifted her chin and narrowed her eyes. "It's Adrial's fault!"

"Don't blame her. Be honest with yourself, Jae. It's all right to love Kip."

"Don't," she whispered in a strangled voice.

Just then Adrial ran up and caught Mick's hand. "Ready for a walk along the beach?"

"Ready." He jumped up and they ran off together.

Jeanna pressed her forehead against her knees and groaned. Mick and Adrial really were in love. Where did that leave her? She did not dare consider loving Kip!

He dropped beside her and she looked up with a scowl.

"What did I do now?" He grabbed his towel and rubbed his hair.

"It's not you. It's Adrial. She thinks that she's queen of the universe."

As Kip leaned forward, she could smell his wet skin. "You have considered Mick your private property for years now. I guess it's only right for you to be a little jealous."

"Me jealous?"

"Yes, you, but you'll get over it as soon as you admit that Mick's only a special friend and nothing more." Kip's breath whispered against her cheek. "Admit how you feel about me."

"Go bury yourself in the sand!"

He laughed and pulled out a sandwich from the cooler. "I think you're hungry. Want one?" He held it out and finally she took it and bit into it. "That'll keep away the flaring temper. I've noticed that when you're hungry, you're not at your best."

She laughed.

"That's better. We agreed to enjoy today, and we're going to."

She nodded. "You're right." Tomorrow she'd think about how she felt about Mick and Adrial.

Chapter 6

Monday morning Carolynn started up the steps of the police department to see the sheriff.

"Carolynn Burgess! Paying off a parking ticket?"

Carolynn froze at the sound of Lavery's smooth voice. Slowly Carolynn turned to face Lavery. She looked impeccable as usual in a light-weight, light green suit. Her black hair hung to her slender shoulders. Her blue eyes were full of suspicion. "Morning, Lavery." Carolynn noticed the man beside her. She stuck out her hand. "Morning. I'm Carolynn Burgess."

The man gripped her hand for a second without smiling. "Andy Nichols."

A jolt went through Carolynn, but she didn't let it show. "Any relation to the murdered woman?"

"We don't have time for chitchat," Lavery snapped.

"Her brother," Andy said.

"Do you live here in town?"

Andy nodded.

"We're too busy to stand and talk." Lavery tried to urge Andy on.

"How long have you lived here?"

"Several months."

"I trust you're enjoying it."

Andy shrugged. "One place is as good as the next."

"I was sorry to hear about your sister's death."

"Come on, Andy!" Lavery tugged his arm, but still he wouldn't move.

Carolynn forced back a grin.

Andy looked off across the street, then back at Carolynn. "I didn't approve of my sister's lifestyle. I told her more than once it wasn't right to give her own flesh and blood away. A baby isn't an automobile that you can trade off."

Lavery shot another angry look at Carolynn. "We're in a hurry."

"I'm not stopping you." Carolynn smiled at Andy. "I really am sorry about your loss. It's always hard to lose a loved one."

"He's not going to give you any pertinent information, Carolynn, so stop fishing for it!"

"Lavery, don't judge everyone by your standards." Carolynn lifted her hand and walked back toward her parked car.

"Aren't you going the wrong way, Carolynn?" Lavery called. "Did I upset you so much you forgot your errand?"

Carolynn bit her lip, then finally turned and managed to smile. "I guess I did forget where I was going. But it can wait. I have to get to the store and buy milk and bread. I have grandchildren coming later for lunch." Carolynn walked to her car and drove away. Caro, Bobby and Heidi were coming for lunch and she did have to buy bread and milk. She'd talk to Farley when Lavery wasn't at the police station.

"What did Lavery want at the station?" The words hung in the car over the hum of the air conditioner. Carolynn stopped at a red light and drummed the steering wheel. Andy Nichols was kind of strange. But maybe he was still in shock over his sister's murder. Was it possible Andy knew about Gwen and Tim? Would Andy kill Gwen and try to frame Silver or Tim?

The light changed and Carolynn drove on. Silently she prayed for the answers she needed to solve the case. While she was praying, she prayed again for Jeanna.

Later at home Carolynn sat at the kitchen table with Robert. Only a few weeks ago she'd struggled with telling him about her secret life. Now that he knew, they often talked together about her cases. "I've been thinking about Jeanna so much it's hard to concentrate on Tim and Silver and their problems."

"What'd you learn about the Provincial House?"

"Nothing! I tried to find out at the courthouse, but they were too busy and I had to leave."

"How about if I do it for you?"

Carolynn stared at Robert in shock. He'd never offered to help with anything she'd been interested in. "Would you? That'd be great!"

He shrugged, pleased with himself. Truth to tell, it felt good to get involved in a little intrigue — especially if it helped Jeanna.

"I expect you'll find that Nurse Bess Wilder owns the place. I could be wrong, of course, but I'm usually not."

"I'll go right away. We've got to make Jeanna realize just because Grace Meeker was trying to get to her, she wasn't to blame for her death. It was wrong for Nurse Wilder to even suggest such a thing to her!"

Carolynn smiled, then dashed around the table and hugged Robert. "I like it when you fight to right a wrong."

He chuckled and his eyes twinkled. "You do, huh? I guess I'll have to do it more often."

⋆   ⋆   ⋆

Jeanna walked listlessly back to the children's department after her morning break. Several people called to her and waved. Once she thought she saw Kip and her stomach tightened alarmingly. He probably wouldn't want to see her again after Sunday's picnic when she wouldn't give him an opportunity to talk seriously with her. She had to be only a passing interest and she dare not take him seriously.

She pushed her purse under the counter near the cash register, then looked up as Mrs. Griffin walked toward her. She wore a sand-colored dress that swirled around her long legs and her long, brown hair curled prettily around her well made-up face and down her slender shoulders. She frowned as she stopped in front of Jeanna.

"Three items are missing from Saturday, Jeanna. Are you sure you haven't seen anyone shoplifting?"

"I'm sorry, but I didn't and I've been watching closely. I know most of the people who come in."

Mrs. Griffin picked up a pair of socks and fingered them nervously. "You must remember that everyone is suspicious. The shoplifter could be someone you know."

"No!" Jeanna shook her head. "That's too terrible to consider!"

"But it is possible, so watch everyone. We're keeping

an eye on the department, so you aren't alone."

"Thank you." Jeanna leaned weakly against the counter as she watched Mrs. Griffin walk away in a cloud of rose perfume. Music played softly and someone laughed. Just then she saw Adrial walking toward her and she turned away, her suddenly icy hands doubled into fists at her sides.

Adrial cleared her throat. "Jeanna, I'm on break and I came to buy a gift for a friend back home."

"Fine. Help yourself. I have to price these pajamas."

"You're not still mad, are you?"

Jeanna shot a sharp look at her and she nervously bit her bottom lip. "This is not the place to discuss private things."

"Yes. Yes, I suppose you're right. It's just that I am having a hard time concentrating on my work and I thought — thought maybe we could get this settled. About Mick, I mean." Adrial's voice died away and tears sparkled in her eyes.

"I thought you came to buy something." Anger sharpened Jeanna's words.

Adrial picked up a tiny raccoon. "How much is this?"

"The tag is on it!"

"Oh, yes, so it is." Adrial sounded very uncertain and Jeanna faced her with a set look on her face. "Jae, please, don't do this to me." Adrial dropped the raccoon into her purse. "I love you and I never wanted to hurt you. I — I didn't know there was something special between you and Mick until it was too late."

Jeanna's stomach tightened and she gripped a pair of white pajamas. "I don't want to talk about it."

"You love Kip, not Mick, so you leave Mick alone and let us be happy!"

Jeanna fell back a step, her eyes wide. "I love Mick," she whispered hoarsely. Adrial couldn't understand that what she felt for Kip was just physical attraction that had nothing to do with love. It wouldn't last. It couldn't. But what she and Mick had together had already lasted for years and would continue to do so. "I won't give him up, Adrial. You've taken him over while you're here, but once you're gone, he'll be mine again. And there's nothing you can do about it."

Adrial stumbled away, her head down, and Jeanna stared coldly after her. Suddenly a tall man gripped Adrial's arm and marched her back into the children's department.

"What's wrong?" Adrial cried, trying to pull away.

"Call your mother, Jeanna," the man said, keeping a firm hold on a startled, struggling Adrial. "I want her to witness the shoplifting."

"What?" Adrial cried, her blue eyes wide and her face pale.

Jeanna frowned. "What're you talking about?"

"Look in her purse." The man motioned to the purse and Jeanna looked inside and saw the small raccoon.

"I forgot to pay for it," Adrial said in a small voice. "I didn't steal it. Tell him, Jeanna."

Jeanna hesitated, then shrugged. "I'll call my mother. I told her that I wouldn't protect anyone I know." She couldn't look at Adrial's stricken face as she dialed extension 402. Adrial wouldn't shoplift, but this man didn't know. Maybe her mother would fire Adrial and she'd have to go home. Jeanna flushed painfully. How could she be so mean? "Mom, can you come here right now?"

"Oh, Jeanna!" Adrial burst into tears. "You know I didn't steal the raccoon."

"You did, miss," the man said sternly. "Mrs. Shaneck will deal with this."

Christa hurried toward them, her bright dress flapping around her knees. "What is it, Ralph? Adrial?" Christa turned to Jeanna, her brows cocked. "What's going on here?"

Jeanna flushed guiltily. "Ask him."

Christa turned to Ralph.

Ralph told about catching Adrial with the stolen item in her purse. "I know the girl is your niece, but you said to stop the shoplifter no matter who."

"I know." Christa nodded. "I'll take care of this, Ralph." She waited until Ralph was out of hearing. "All right, girls, what's going on?"

Adrial wiped away her tears with a tissue from her purse. "I did mean to pay for it. We were talking and I forgot."

Christa frowned at Jeanna. "Well?"

"How was I to know she was going to pay for it?"

"Jeanna!" Adrial cried.

"I don't know what's going on here," Christa said impatiently. "But we can't settle it now. Adrial, get back to your department. Jeanna, get back to work. Both of you meet me in my study at home after dinner so we can talk." She scowled at them and then strode away.

Adrial gulped and fled.

Jeanna leaned weakly against the counter, her face flushed with guilt. Finally she forced herself back to work and finished her shift.

Later Joyce Benson walked in to take over and Jeanna said a quick goodbye and grabbed her purse. She had to get away from everyone before she burst into a million pieces.

At the escalator she stopped with a gasp. "Kip! What are you doing here?" He wore navy dress slacks and a white shirt open at the throat. He looked out of place in the children's wear department.

"Hi," he said softly as he took her arm.

Her mouth felt cotton-dry. "Why are you here?"

"I'm taking you home." He stepped on the escalator with her and she almost lost her balance. "Careful, honey. I wouldn't want to lose you now."

She looked back and up at him and her heart leaped to her mouth at the warm look in his eyes. The smell of his cologne enveloped her.

"Don't look at me like that or I'll kiss you right here in front of everyone."

Her legs almost gave way and she clutched the railing and looked down. What would he do when he learned what she'd done to Adrial?

The hot afternoon sun burned down on her as she walked across the parking lot to his car. She slid in and kicked off her shoes, then leaned back with a tired sigh. "I thought Dad was going to get me."

"I offered and he accepted. He said he was going fishing with your grandpa and was glad for my offer."

Kip tugged her curl. "I think you need a cold chocolate shake."

"That does sound wonderful."

"Tell me about your day." He stopped the car at the end of the parking lot and waited for three cars to pass before he pulled onto the busy street.

She talked about the customers, but she didn't tell him about Adrial and the raccoon. "What did you do today?"

"Painted until about an hour ago and then I had an overwhelming desire to see you."

She moved in agitation. "Stop that!"

He glanced at her, then turned back to his driving. "I mean it. I usually mean what I say."

She found a cassette, clicked it on and music filled the car. She caught Kip's quick look, but ignored it. She dare not let her feelings for him get out of control or she'd be very, very sorry. He would lose interest and not be around to watch her cry her eyes out over him. He'd be off dating other girls.

Later at the Dairy Queen he handed her a shake and she sipped it thankfully, savoring the cold chocolate ice cream. He sipped his and the silence lengthened. A car honked and someone shouted.

Finally he drove away from the Dairy Queen and onto a side street. He slowed for a small boy on a bike, then drove on.

"Where are we going, Kip? I thought you were taking me right home."

He didn't speak and her nerves jumped.

"Kip, where are you taking me?"

At a stop sign he turned to face her. "To see Mabel Pranger. I said that I would."

"No! I told you I'd never go to the Provincial House!" She jerked on the door handle to get away, but he caught her arm and held her and she turned like a spitting kitten.

"Stop it, Jeanna! What's wrong with you?"

"Don't make me go, Kip. Don't!"

"You can't hide away all your life. Face what's bothering you and get it behind you so you can get on with your life."

"There is nothing to face," she said grimly.

"Oh, Jae, what am I going to do with you?"

She turned on him, her eyes flashing. "Leave me alone! That's all I want from you!"

He shook his head as he gripped the steering wheel until his knuckles turned white. "Something is wrong and I mean to find out what it is."

"Take me home."

"Don't you trust me!"

"Kip, take me home now!"

He sighed and slowly drove away from the stop sign. "I am losing you, honey, and I don't know what to do about it. I have to be with you or my day isn't complete. I want to talk to you and have you listen to what's going on with my life. I want to hold you close and feel your heart beating against mine, but you won't let me. I know your feelings for me are as strong as mine are for you."

Tears filled her eyes. "Don't, Kip. Please, don't."

He glanced at her, then glanced again. "You're

crying!" He increased his speed, then pulled into the city park and stopped. He pushed open his door, then in seconds had hers open. "We have to talk, Jeanna. I must get past the barrier that you've put up between us."

She stumbled with him to a grassy spot secluded by bushes. She saw the determined set of his jaw and she trembled. She couldn't tell him about Nurse Wilder or Grace Meeker! He must never know that she'd caused the kind woman's death.

Kip stopped with her and lifted her chin so that he could look deep into her eyes. "I see a sadness, honey. What is it? Can't you share it with me?"

She cleared her throat. "It's Adrial. You should know that."

"No, it's not Adrial, nor Mick. Now, what is hurting you?"

She pulled away, her back stiff. "Take me home."

He pulled her close and she pushed hard against him to get away. She felt his heart thudding against her palm and a fire raced through her, leaving her weak. "Let me go," she whispered.

"No."

Her eyes locked with his and the desire for his kiss and his touch washed over her. With a sigh she lifted her mouth to his and slipped her arms around his waist.

He pulled away and she groaned. "I'd better take you home, honey." He smiled gently. "You see the way it is with us."

"Don't say that," she whispered helplessly.

"Is it so painful to admit it, Jae?"

She nodded and he stroked her cheek and she wanted to move into his arms again.

"We have something precious between us, honey. Don't push it away or deny it. I'm always here for you when you're ready to talk to me and share with me what's hurting you so deeply."

She ran to the car, trying to stop her rush of feelings.

He followed, sliding in under the steering wheel and filling the car with his presence.

"Kip, I don't think we should see each other again." The words hurt her and she couldn't go on.

"I won't consider that, Jeanna. We are going to be together as much as we can and you're going to learn to believe your feelings for me. I know you could if you didn't have something else on your mind. You're not giving me undivided attention, and that's what I need."

"Did it ever occur to you that I just don't care about you?"

He grinned. "The thought crossed my mind, but I wouldn't let it stay. It would hurt too much."

Her heart leaped. "Would it?"

He nodded.

She turned away to look out the window. His ego was probably what he meant. No girl had ever turned him down that she knew about.

An ambulance whizzed past with a loud wail. A cloud passed over the sun and thunder rumbled in the distance.

"Jeanna, are you sure you don't want to visit Mabel Pranger?"

Jeanna locked her hands in her lap. "I'm sure." How wonderful it would be to see Mrs. Pranger and talk to her and listen to the stories she told of her past. "Just take me home, Kip."

He studied her for a minute. "Something happened at the Provincial House and I'm going to find out what it was."

Panic seized her and she gripped his arm, her nails biting into his skin. He'd hate her if he knew and he'd be in danger from Nurse Wilder. "Don't, Kip! It's nothing! Leave it alone!"

"I thought for a while it might be because you were upset about Grace Meeker's death, but I know it's more than that."

"If you don't take me home, I'll get out and walk. I mean it!"

"Don't be ridiculous!"

"Then take me home." She gripped her purse and stared across the park at the trees and grass and children playing.

With a sigh he pulled out of the park and turned toward home. "Jae, could we at least have dinner together tonight?"

She remembered the meeting she was to have with Mom and Adrial and she saw this as a way out of it. "Yes. Yes, I guess we could."

"Don't sound so overjoyed."

"Sorry."

He didn't speak for a while. "One of these days I might wake up and see how crazy I've been for trying to open your eyes."

"Yes, you probably will."

He gripped the steering wheel. "You are next to impossible, Jeanna Shaneck. But then I think about how wonderful you are I have to keep on trying."

She studied him from under her dark lashes. He seemed to mean what he was saying. Could it be that he really did care for her? Her nerve ends tingled. Was it possible?

He pulled into his driveway and turned off the engine. The cool air stopped and hot air from outdoors seeped in. "See you tonight."

She stiffened. What was she doing? It took being with him only a short time and she was ready to fall into his arms and believe everything he said! It couldn't happen! "I'll call you." She couldn't tell him that she was going to call to beg off, or he'd find a way to make her change her mind.

"We'll go out together, Jae. Just the two of us."

She slipped from the car and ran across to her yard, her heart racing wildly. Since she was away from him, she'd get over this need for him.

She stopped just inside the back door and took a deep breath. How would it feel to go ahead and just fall in love with Kip Jennings?

Oh, what was she thinking? Thoughts of his kiss pushed through her mind and she gingerly touched her tingling lips.

★   ★   ★

Later when he could get away by himself the man drove to Meg's house. He didn't know if she'd be home,

but he had to start somewhere. It wasn't long before
her baby was due and he had to kill her before she gave
birth. It was important to keep the baby from suffering
long years of living with people who weren't his blood.
Why wouldn't anyone tell Meg that? It might keep her
from giving her baby away.

He watched a gang of boys skate past, their
skateboards humming against the sidewalk. Warm
wind blew through his open car window. Should he
walk right up to the door and ring the bell? She or her
sister Sarah could be home. If Sarah answered, he'd say
he was selling encyclopedias. But if Meg answered, he'd
kill her on the spot. "If nobody's watching," he said
grimly. His stomach knotted. It wasn't always easy to
kill even though the person deserved it.

He slipped out of his car and stood beside it. A robin
landed on a nearby branch of a large maple. He smiled.
He liked robins. When he was little he'd tried to catch
one and had accidently shot it with his BB gun. Mother
had locked him in his bedroom for a whole day for it
even though he'd told her it was an accident. He still
liked robins, though.

He squared his shoulders, hiked up his pants and
slowly crossed the street. He stood on the sidewalk
outside the house. It took courage to go right up to
the door. He thought of the poor innocent baby and
his courage surged inside him. He could do anything
to save that little baby!

Before he could move, the door burst open and Meg
ran out with Sarah right behind her.

"I want ice cream right now!" Meg cried, looking

over her shoulder at Sarah.

He could've easily stuck out his foot and tripped her. But that might've killed the baby, not her, so he moved out of the way.

Sarah ran after Meg. "Will you slow down? You'll hurt yourself if you run all the way to the Dairy Queen!"

Meg slowed to a walk and Sarah caught up with her. "I could kill them both," he muttered impatiently. But he wouldn't. Sarah didn't deserve to die. Slowly he walked back to his car and drove to the Dairy Queen. Maybe he'd find a chance to kill her there.

★   ★   ★

Tim paced the living room while Silver fed Brittany in the kitchen. "I can't tell her," he whispered raggedly. It could mean the end of their marriage. Why hadn't he thought of that before he'd let himself get interested in Gwen?

Impatiently he picked up the phone book. He'd marked Jack Paine's name in case they really did have to call an attorney. Tim flipped open the pages. He'd told Pastor Alton Craig what the sheriff had said. Al had suggested Jack Paine, he said he was a Christian and a fine man. "I hate calling an attorney," Tim muttered. "It makes everything seem too real."

His stomach was a ball of ice as he grabbed up the phone and punched the numbers before he lost his courage.

"Jack Paine, Attorney-at-Law. Davina Littlejohn speaking."

Tim's mouth turned bone-dry. He'd forgotten Deputy Littlejohn's wife was Jack Paine's secretary. Tim cleared his throat. "This is Tim Rawlings. I need to speak to Mr. Paine as soon as possible."

"He's not in right now. Would you like to leave a message?"

"Have him call me." Tim rattled off his phone number, then quickly hung up. If Jack Paine didn't call, he'd forget the whole thing. The sheriff would surely find the killer soon and he and Silver would be in the clear.

Tim strode to the window and looked out. A warm breeze fluttered the leaves of the oaks and maples. A red car drove past and turned in at the Petersons a few houses down. Could life really go on in a normal way after what had happened?

Carrying Brittany on her hip, Silver walked in and stopped at the baby's walker. "What're you looking at, Tim?"

He turned slowly. "Nothing."

Silver stood Brittany at a chair and she immediately toddled to Tim with her arms out, chattering in her baby talk. Her round face looked freshly scrubbed and her light-brown hair was brushed back.

Laughing, Tim squatted down. "Are you trying to tell me what Momma fed you? Did you drink all your milk?" He kissed her dimpled cheeks, then stood to face Silver. "We have to talk."

She saw the pain in his eyes and she sank weakly to the couch. "Maybe we should wait until Brittany's asleep."

Tim shook his head. "I've waited too long already. Something keeps coming up." He sat beside Silver and took her hand. It was icy to his touch and he rubbed it gently. How could he tell her and break her heart?

Brittany walked to the window and pressed her palms against the glass. She chattered as she looked out.

Silver saw the handprints along the big window, but just shrugged. She'd rather see handprints then have a sterile house without a baby.

Tim released Silver's hand, picked up a throw pillow, and absently traced the design of the flower on it. How could he begin? He'd prayed about it, but the agony of telling her the truth had kept him from hearing an answer.

"If it's so hard to say, then don't say it," Silver whispered as she nervously pushed back her long hair. Her blouse and shorts suddenly felt too hot, yet her feet were icy-cold in her sandals.

Tim thrust the pillow away. "I have to tell you."

Silver stared at him in alarm. "Did *you* kill Gwen Nichols?"

"No!" Tim shook his head in horror. "How could you even think that?"

She shrugged. "It's just that you're having a really hard time telling me what you want to tell me. I figured it was something really bad."

Tim's stomach knotted painfully. "Carolynn said Gwen's family hired a private detective to solve the case. Lavery is her name. She'll be snooping around and prying into our business."

"Why is that upsetting you? We have nothing to

hide."

But he did! He couldn't tell her. He just couldn't! "I just wanted you to know in case she starts questioning you."

"She's not the police. We don't really even need to talk to her, do we?"

Tim grabbed at the tiny straw. "You're right! We don't need to talk to her. Nor anyone else. Only the police."

Silver frowned slightly as she nodded.

"So, don't let anyone in if they aren't with the police."

"I won't."

Tim sagged back in relief. "Good. I feel a whole lot better." Silver would never learn about him and Gwen. It was going to be all right after all.

*　　*　　*

Dud Dumars tapped his yellow pencil on his desk as he studied Carolynn Burgess. "What's going on?"

"I don't know." She paced the space from his back door to his desk and back again. "I had the meeting all set up for Gil Oakes to meet his birth mother, but he didn't even call you to find out who his mother is and what time to meet her."

"I've called him several times, but no answer. He doesn't have an answering machine. Maybe you should run over to his home and talk to him."

"I already tried that, Dud. He wasn't there and his landlady said he usually was at that time."

"Did you check where he works?"

Carolynn nodded. "Sure did. He missed the last two

days. Called in sick, she said."

"Yet he wasn't at home." Dud abruptly stood and dropped the yellow pencil on his desk. "Why is it we get these weird cases? I should've told my wife to tell the guy to get lost."

Carolynn laughed. "Sure, Dud. I could see you doing that."

He chuckled. "Me, too. The guy goes to all that trouble to get our help, then won't take it."

"Maybe he'll call you tomorrow. Or stop in and see you."

"Maybe."

Carolynn leaned on the back of the folding chair and looked intently at Dud. "Do we know this man who says he's Gil Oakes is really Gil Oakes?"

Dud flung his arms wide. "I didn't check. Did you?"

Carolynn shook her head. "But I think I will now. I could check the Flint schools to see if a Gil Oakes attended there, then if so, look at the yearbooks. He's still young enough for me to be able to pick his photo out."

Dud sank back on his desk. "Next time my wife runs into someone at the grocery store that wants help, I'll tell her to forget it. We don't run a charity here, you know."

Chapter 7

Gil Oakes walked listlessly through the park. Things weren't going right for some reason. He kicked a clump of dirt and sent it spraying out in front of him. He'd thought it would be so simple to confront his past and deal with it. Why hadn't he called Dumars' Agency to find out who his birth mother was, so he could meet with her? Was he afraid? He wasn't a teenager any longer! He should be able to come face to face with his past. But what if she rejected him? That would be a cruel blow. He couldn't handle being rejected yet again by the woman who'd given birth to him.

He slumped down on the bench, his elbows on his knees. Too bad Carolynn Burgess wasn't his mother. He could love her. She really cared about her family and the people around her. Maybe he should find a reason to get to know her better. She might even invite him for Sunday dinner. How would it feel to sit around the dinner table and talk and laugh with a family who cared about each other? Maybe she'd make fried chicken with real mashed potatoes and a chocolate layer cake for dessert. His mouth watered just thinking about home cooking.

Gil groaned from deep inside. Something was going on with him. But what? Maybe it had something to do with Carolynn Burgess saying she'd pray for him. She'd been serious! Had anyone ever prayed for him? He shook his head. Nobody had. Maybe he should go see Carolynn Burgess. She might help him find the courage to face his birth mother. Or maybe she'd talk him out of it — leave well enough alone.

⋆　　⋆　　⋆

Silver ran her finger around the rim of her teacup. Something was wrong with Tim — something more than the murder. What could it be? Was he afraid people would learn Gwen was Brittany's birth mother? If so, why should it matter? Maybe he didn't want the stigma of the murder hanging over Brittany's head.

"Mom, I wish I could call you," Silver muttered. The corners of her wide mouth turned down, she shook her head. Her mother didn't believe in adoption. "If God wanted you to have children, you'd be able to give birth to them," Mom had said many times. "Don't thwart God's plan by adopting."

Silver sighed from deep inside. Was it wrong to adopt? Impatiently she shook her head. "It's not!" Children without parents desperately needed homes. *She* desperately needed children. It was God's will for them to adopt Brittany — and even a baby boy, when they could.

The doorbell rang and Silver almost jumped out of her skin. Maybe it was someone saying they'd found the murderer.

Silver flung the door wide and warm air rushed in along with the roar of a lawn mower. A woman dressed in a bold red and white dress stood there. "Yes?"

"Silver Rawlings?"

"Yes."

"I'm Lavery."

Silver's eyes widened and she started to close the door. "My husband says not to talk to you."

"Why? Do you have something to hide?"

"Of course not!"

"Then it won't hurt to talk to me." Lavery stepped inside. Her red and white heels sank into the thick carpet. Her red and white earrings danced on her shoulders. "I came to talk to you about Gwen Nichols. How well did you know her?"

Silver looked uncertainly from Lavery to the open door. "I don't want to answer any questions."

"You want this case solved." Lavery looked right into Silver's eyes. "Don't you?"

"Of course!"

"Then why not help me? The police can't do the work alone. I'm known for my quick results." Lavery flipped back her long, dark hair, sending her long earrings dancing again. "Shall we sit down to talk?"

Silver reluctantly closed the door. It took a minute for the air conditioner to cool the warm air she'd let in. Tim had said not to talk to Lavery, but what could it hurt? Having the case solved was indeed the most important thing. Silver walked to the flowered chair and sat even as she motioned for Lavery to be seated.

Lavery set her red and white purse beside her. "I understand the murder weapon was found in your car."

Silver gasped. "I hadn't heard that the sheriff was certain of that."

"He is." Lavery crossed her mile-long legs, looking more like a high-fashion model than an investigator.

"He must know I'm not guilty."

Lavery shrugged. Actually she expected the sheriff to arrest Silver Rawlings before the day was over. "How well did you know Gwen Nichols?"

"I didn't know her at all!"

"Why did she want to see you?"

Silver's mouth dried until it was hard to speak. "Who says she did?"

"Her brother Andy. Do you know him?"

Helplessly Silver shook her head. "I don't know anything about her! Nor her brother."

Lavery watched Silver closely. "You must know she gave birth to the baby you adopted."

Silver gripped the arms of the chair. "Who told you that?"

"Andy did. He said she planned to see you and talk to you."

Silver's head spun. Was that true? If so, why hadn't Tim told her? He'd said Gwen wanted to meet with him only to see Brittany. Had Tim lied? The thought left Silver weak.

"When did you first see Gwen?"

"I don't think I want to say anything more to you," Silver said in a voice that shook.

Lavery lifted her perfectly shaped dark brows. "Why is that?"

"I don't know." Tears welled up in Silver's eyes and she stood uncertainly. "I'm so afraid I might say something that'll make me sound guilty. And I'm not!"

Smiling, Lavery stood with lithe grace. "Did *I* say something that made you feel as if *I* thought you were guilty?"

"No." Silver wrung her hands. "Oh, I don't know! Could you please leave? Tim said I shouldn't talk to you. Well, not just you, but not to anyone but the police."

"That's very strange. Does *he* think you're guilty?"

Helplessly Silver shook her head. What if she was guilty? What if she'd killed Gwen, then blanked out like she had when she'd had the dreadful miscarriage?

Just then the door opened and Tim walked in with the attorney Jack Paine. He was in his early forties, lean, with light-brown hair and bright summer-blue eyes. Tim stopped short and scowled at Lavery, then at Silver. "I told you not to let her in," Tim said gruffly.

With a strangled sob, Silver ran to him and clung to him.

Smiling and with her hand out, Lavery stepped forward. "Jack, how nice to see you. Are you representing Silver Rawlings?"

Jack shook hands with Lavery and chuckled. "You're as gorgeous as ever, Christine."

Bristling, she jerked her hand away and scowled. "Lavery. And you know it."

"You'll always be Christine to me." Jack frowned, "What're you doing here? Having tea with Silver?"

His mind racing, Tim listened to Jack and Lavery talk. Tim wanted to shake Silver and demand to know why she'd let Lavery in. Just what had Lavery told Silver? Did she even know anything to tell her?

Jack turned to Tim. "Would you like me to see Christine out?"

Tim nodded, still unable to speak.

"I have a few more questions," Lavery snapped, backing away from Jack.

Smiling, he shook his head. "Afraid not, Christine. It's time to say *adios*." He gently took her arm and escorted her out. He watched until she reached her car, then he closed the door. "She's gone."

Abruptly Tim held Silver from him and frowned at her. "Why on earth did you let her in? We agreed not to!"

Silver brushed at her tears. "She kind of pushed her way in."

"She's like that," Jack said crisply. "I'll have a talk with her and try to keep her from coming here again."

"Thank you," Tim said in relief. He turned back to Silver. "What did she ask and what did you tell her?"

Shaking her head, Silver sank numbly to the couch. "I don't remember."

Tim groaned. "You must remember! Think, Silver!"

Jack clamped a hand on Tim's shoulder. "It's not important, Tim. Let's sit down and talk calmly, shall we?"

His whole insides churning, Tim dropped down in the flowered chair. "I can't understand why the sheriff can't find the killer so we can get on with our lives!"

"He will." Jack sat near Silver on the couch. Smiling, he gripped her hand briefly, then let it go. "Don't worry about what you did or did not tell Christine. You're innocent, so there's nothing you could've said to cause any harm." Jack looked across at Tim. "Is there anything I should know that could be used against the two of you?"

Tim forced back a guilty flush. He couldn't tell an outright lie, so he answered Jack with, "What could there be? Neither one of us killed Gwen Nichols."

Silver cleared her throat. "Lavery said Gwen wanted to see me. Gwen's brother told Lavery that."

Tim's nerves tightened to the breaking point. Gwen had wanted to see Silver, but he'd absolutely refused to let her. He'd never told Silver that bit of information. What else did Andy know? Was it possible he knew the truth about Brittany?

★   ★   ★

Carolynn sat beside Robert on the couch. She looked down at their clasped hands and smiled. Years ago they'd always held hands, then they'd stopped. They'd stopped communicating, stopped a lot of things. Finally she'd realized a big reason for them drawing apart was the secret she'd kept from him for years — that she was an undercover investigator for Dumars Investigative Services. Now that he knew, they were finally getting close again. He didn't spend nearly as much time in the basement building birdhouses and working with other woodcrafts. She talked about her work with him and he responded with thoughts and ideas of his own. He always had a different view of situations than she did and his insights helped her to see things clearer.

"I found out who owned the Provincial House," Robert said proudly.

"Nurse Bess Wilder?"

"Nope."

Carolynn pulled sharply away and stared at Robert. "Who then?"

Robert laughed. "First admit you're not always right."

She jabbed his arm. "Tell me!"

He shook his head.

With a laugh she said, "All right! I'm not always right." She waited a few seconds. "But I am most of the time."

Robert kissed her, then looked very smug. "Guess."

"A corporation here in Middle Lake."

"Nope."

"Tell me! Come on, Robert, who?"

"Dr. Raymond Browne."

"You don't say!" Carolynn narrowed her eyes. "Do you suppose there's hanky-panky going on with the patients?"

"Murder for profit, you mean?"

She nodded.

"I hate to think that." Robert reached for Carolynn's hand again. He hated to think bad about anyone. "It could be Grace Meeker's death was an accident just like you discovered when you investigated it before."

"I doubt it, Robert, after what Jeanna told me. What if Nurse Wilder had a different motive for killing Grace Meeker. Not everyone kills because of greed."

"Give me the list," Robert said with a laugh.

Carolynn took a deep breath, then let it out. "Envy, lust, hatred, malice, guilt, greed, financial need, revenge, irresistible impulse, retribution, setting right a wrong. And probably many more."

Robert shook his head in wonder. "How on earth

do you know that?"

"I've been at my job a long time."

"I'm amazed."

Just then Stan walked in, carrying a glass of milk and a handful of chocolate chip cookies. He was their youngest son and still lived at home in order to save money. He wrote the successful Skip Reagan Mystery Series for boys and was also a substitute English teacher at the Middle Lake Middle School. He saw his parents holding hands and he grinned. "Am I interrupting anything?"

"Not at all," Carolynn said.

"Sit down and share a cookie with me." Robert held out his hand.

Laughing, Stan gave Robert two cookies and Carolynn one. "Want to share my milk too?"

"No thanks," Carolynn said.

"I might," Robert said around a bite of cookie.

Stan sank to the rocking chair that his mother usually sat in. "Any news about Silver and Tim?"

Carolynn shook her head. "Not that I've heard."

"I can't believe someone was actually murdered in the parking lot of our church!" Stan frowned. "And to think the police are questioning Silver and Tim about it! It's preposterous."

Robert nodded. "It's a hard time for them."

Carolynn wanted to change the subject before she or Robert said something that would make Stan suspicious of her involvement. He didn't know about her secret life and she wanted it kept that way. "How's Holly? And the kids?"

"We haven't seen much of them," Robert said.

Stan flushed. "We had a little disagreement."

"I'm sure you'll get it settled." Carolynn wanted to say a whole lot more. Ever since Holly's husband had died Carolynn had wanted Stan and Holly to get together and eventually get married. They seemed so right for each other. She knew Stan was a little frightened about marrying a woman with two children, but she'd thought he was overcoming his fear with God's help. Stan had loved Holly in high school, but she'd married Ben Loudan and broken Stan's heart.

"That's why I wanted to talk to you both." Stan took a deep breath and slowly let it out. "I asked Holly to marry me and we set the date."

"Wonderful!" Carolynn cried.

"Congratulations." Robert reached over and patted Stan's back.

Stan groaned. "Now, she says she can't think of marriage until this whole thing is settled with Tim and Silver."

"Holly and Silver are very close," Carolynn said.

Stan frowned. "I don't think it's fair to put aside our plans though."

Robert leaned forward. "Son, Holly probably wants to be married when she can think of only the two of you. It'll be better that way."

Carolynn stared in surprise at Robert. She'd never dreamed he'd side with Holly. "You're right, Robert." She turned to Stan. "Be patient a little longer, son. I don't think it'll take long to solve the case."

"You sound very sure of yourself, Mother. Do you

have inside information?"

Carolynn flushed and didn't know what to say.

Robert laughed. "You know your mother. She has very strong opinions."

Carolynn thankfully squeezed Robert's hand. "Stan, love Holly and give her all the support she needs right now. Both of you continue to pray for Silver and Tim." Carolynn jumped up. "Could you both excuse me? I have a phone call to make." She hurried away to call Sheriff Farley Cobb to see if there were any new developments.

⋆   ⋆   ⋆

Sobbing, Meg rushed out her door with Sarah right behind her. Even though she was dressed in shorts and a loose top, Meg felt hot and uncomfortable. She looked over her shoulder. "Don't follow me, Sarah! I just want to be alone!"

Sarah hesitated on the sidewalk outside their house. Dare she leave Meg alone? It didn't seem wise with her being so close to her due date. What if Meg was off by herself and went into labor? She wouldn't know what to do. Sarah nervously rubbed her hands down her pink shorts. She really wouldn't know what to do either, but she'd be able to stay calmer than Meg.

Just then Sarah looked across the street. A man sat there in his car. She'd never seen him before. Wait! She had seen him earlier today when Meg had insisted they go for ice cream. What was he doing here again? He didn't live in the neighborhood. Was he visiting someone? She shrugged. Why worry about him? She had to think about Meg.

The man in the car watched Sarah run down the street toward the park after Meg. Maybe he could catch Meg alone today and kill her. He pulled away from the curb and slowly drove after the girls. He passed them, drove to the park, and parked in the shade of a giant oak. He rolled his car window down and waited. He hummed softly to himself. Things had to go right for him — they usually did.

Gasping for breath, Meg reached the park and sank down on the nearest green bench. She rubbed sweat off her face. She felt old and ugly and awkward. She should've listened to Sarah and not let Logan touch her. Sarah had said she'd never have sex until she was married. Jeanna had said the same thing. Meg groaned. She'd tried to stay a virgin, but most of the girls in her class weren't, and they'd teased her because she was. Logan had been so persuasive that she'd finally given in. How she wished she hadn't! It never occurred to her that she'd get pregnant. She knew five of her friends had already had abortions, but she couldn't bring herself to kill her baby even though she'd told Sarah she was planning to. She glanced around for Sarah and saw her at the wishing well. "Probably wishing I wasn't her sister," Meg muttered. She looked toward the parking area and her heart stopped. She saw the same man she'd seen a few other times. He was looking right at her! A whisper of fear tickled the small of her back. Was he following her? If so, why? Groaning, she pushed herself up. "Sarah, let's go!"

Sarah heard the panic in Meg's voice and ran to her.

"What's wrong?"

"Nothing!" Meg looked toward the car again. The man was still looking at her. She hesitated, then whispered, "Sarah, don't look now, but there's a man watching us."

Trying to appear nonchalant, Sarah glanced around. Her bones turned to icicles. It was the same man! "Meg, let's cut across the park and go to Jeanna's house. It's closer than ours."

Meg nodded. "He scares me, Sarah."

"It's probably nothing, but we don't dare take chances." Sarah wanted to run to Jeanna's, but she knew Meg couldn't keep up with her.

Several minutes later they rang the doorbell at Jeanna's. Sarah looked around for the man, but he wasn't in sight. They'd probably lost him by cutting across the park. She breathed easier.

"I don't think anyone's home," Meg said frantically as she rang the doorbell again.

Blacky ran to them, wriggling and sniffing their ankles.

Suddenly the door burst open and Jeanna stood there, her eyes and nose red. "Sarah! Meg! I thought it was someone else." She'd thought it was Kip, but she didn't want them to know.

Sarah looked closely at Jeanna. "Is something wrong?"

"I had a bad day. Come in."

"We need a ride home," Meg said, looking around nervously. "There was this weird guy following us."

Jeanna gasped. "Really?"

Sarah shook her head. "We don't know for sure, Jeanna." She told about seeing the man twice today. "We couldn't take a chance."

"I don't have a car or I'd drive you home." Jeanna glanced across to the Jennings' driveway and the silver Toyota. No way could she ask Kip to take them home, but Sarah could. "Kip's home. I'm sure he'll give you a ride."

Before she'd finished speaking Meg was running awkwardly next door.

Sarah touched Jeanna's hand. "Are you sure you're all right?"

Jeanna shrugged.

Sarah bit her lower lip. "Jeanna, we're best friends. Aren't we?"

"Yes," Jeanna whispered.

"You can tell me anything! You know that."

Jeanna started to say something, but Meg shouted for Sarah. "I guess you'd better go."

"We'll talk later. We will, Jeanna!" Sighing, Sarah ran to Meg and Kip.

＊　　＊　　＊

Jeanna paced her bedroom with the door locked so that Adrial couldn't walk in. Somewhere outdoors a dog barked and Blacky answered with three sharp yaps. With a groan Jeanna turned away from the long mirror on her closet so she wouldn't have to see the guilty look on her face. How could she tell Mom that Adrial was guilty of shoplifting? How could she do a lot of things she'd done lately? It had all started with Grace Meeker's death.

Tears stung Jeanna's eyes and she blinked them away. If only she could share her grief with Kip, maybe the nightmare would end. She stopped pacing and stood in the middle of the room with her icy hands clenched. Oh, she dare not tell Kip! What was she thinking? Kip was the last person she'd tell. He might confront Nurse Wilder, then he'd be in danger too. Jeanna trembled. Danger? Why danger? Jeanna bit her lip as a picture flashed across her mind of Nurse Wilder forcing medication down Grace's throat. Had Nurse Wilder *killed* Grace Meeker either by accident or on purpose?

Jeanna pressed her hand over her mouth. Was that really why she was afraid? Was that really why she couldn't tell Kip, of all people? What if she weakened and told him tonight? At first she'd planned to call him and tell him she wouldn't go, but then she'd changed her mind and told herself that if he called her, she'd go with him.

"Oh, Kip! I don't dare!" She tugged her shirt over her red shorts and stared at the door, willing it to open so that she could dash through to Kip.

Someone knocked and she froze, her eyes wide in alarm. Had she conjured up Kip outside her door? About an hour ago he'd taken Sarah and Meg home. Maybe he was coming to tell her she should be a better friend to Sarah.

"Kip's on the phone for you, Jae," Dad said through the locked door. "He says it's important."

She sucked in her breath and pressed her hands to her racing heart. "Tell him I'll call him later, Dad. I can't come to the phone now."

"I'll tell him, but I don't think he'll like it."

Jeanna dropped to the edge of Adrial's bed and burst into wild tears. She turned and flung herself down with her face pressed into Adrial's soft pillow. Racking sobs tore at her throat. Tears soaked Adrial's pillow. Finally the tears stopped and Jeanna pushed herself up. Her nose and eyes were red and her throat sore. She must keep control of her emotions or her secret might come out when she least expected it to. She sniffed, then noticed the wet pillow case. With a trembling sigh she picked up the pillow. Under it lay a pile of clothes marked with price tags from Maxi's. Gingerly she picked the things up and her heart plunged to her feet. "The stolen children's clothes! Adrial? She really did steal them!"

Someone knocked and Jeanna whirled around. "Who is it?"

"Jeanna, it's me. Adrial. Let me in."

The color drained from Jeanna's face. She stared in horror at the bundle of children's clothing in her hand, then ran to the door, unlocked it, and pulled Adrial inside. "Look, Adrial!" Jeanna shook the clothes in Adrial's face. "I found them under your pillow!"

"Oh, no," Adrial whispered as she sank to the edge of her bed.

Jeanna flung the clothes down beside Adrial. "I should've known it was you after the raccoon deal!"

"No! It wasn't me. It wasn't!"

"Then who was it? Talk fast or I'll call Mom right now. After the raccoon deal I know she'll be ready to send you packing."

"I can't explain. Don't ask me to!" Adrial lifted a haggard face to Jeanna. "I was going to take them back in the morning and sneak them into place."

"Sure, I bet."

"I was!"

"Tell me another one, Adrial." Jeanna whirled around so she wouldn't even have to look at her cousin.

Adrial sighed heavily. "Oh, I forgot. Kip is downstairs and he wants to see you right now. He said if you don't come down, he'll come up."

Jeanna shuddered. "I can't see him." She hated to ask a favor of Adrial, but she had to. "Go tell him I'll talk to him tomorrow. And please don't let him come up here!"

Adrial sighed heavily. "I'll tell him, but he might not listen to me. He looks really upset."

"I don't care! Just tell him what I said!" Jeanna closed her eyes and pressed her hands to her head.

"Go talk to him, Jae," Adrial said softly. "Don't put it off. You know you want to see him."

"Mind your own business!"

"It is my business!" Adrial's eyes flashed as she stood in front of Jeanna. "If you got things settled with Kip, you wouldn't be mad at me or at Mick. Then you'd see other things clearly — like the shoplifting."

"Things are settled and I see everything perfectly clear! You're just trying to get out of being sent home in disgrace because of your shoplifting!"

Adrial shook her finger at Jeanna. "You know I didn't take those things. I can't tell you how I got them, but

you know I didn't do it. You are just trying so hard
to hang on to Mick and push Kip away that everything
is distorted. You know in your heart you love Kip."

Jeanna covered her ears with trembling hands and
backed away. "I will not listen to you, Adrial!"

Adrial caught at her arm and tugged. "You'd better
listen to somebody. There's something really wrong
with you and you need help. I came here because I
knew you'd teach me how to be strong in the Lord.
But you haven't even done that!"

The words struck Jeanna in the heart. She knew it
was true.

The doorknob rattled and Kip pounded on the door.
"I want to see you now, Jeanna!"

Jeanna fell back a step, her mouth dry, her pulse
racing.

Adrial thrust the pile of clothes back under the
pillow, then leaped to the door and flung it open. Kip
sprang in. Adrial ran out, leaving Jeanna to face Kip
alone.

Kip stood there, towering over Jeanna, his arms
folded across his broad chest and his feet apart. "Talk
to me, Jeanna."

She shook her head.

"I mean it!"

"Don't," she whimpered. "Don't do this, Kip."

"I haven't done anything. I waited. And waited. Then
I called you and waited some more. I was excited about
going to dinner with you. I thought finally we could
be together and talk and reach an understanding about
our feelings."

"There's nothing to say."

"Tell me to my face to stay or to leave. Tell me to my face to get out of your life."

She stepped toward him, then drew back. She dare not get too close or she'd be lost and never be able to escape him, never be able to hold back her terrible secret. "Get out of my life, Kip," she said quietly, calmly.

His face turned white and he dropped his arms to his sides.

"I've told you that I don't want anything to do with you." The words cut razor-sharp through her tight throat.

"You've told me, but your actions said differently."

"You judged them wrong."

"Don't do this, Jae. Please. I've never begged anyone for anything before, but I'm begging you. Don't do this to me. To us. I can't survive if you do."

Pain squeezed her heart. "Leave me alone, Kip."

He shook his head.

She saw the tears in his eyes and she couldn't believe he would cry over her decision.

"Don't break my heart," he said hoarsely.

"Goodbye, Kip." She stood before him, her face drawn and white. If he stayed any longer, her legs would give way and she'd fall to the floor at his feet.

"Don't do this."

"Goodbye, Kip."

He shuddered, then whirled and strode away out of her life forever. His footsteps echoed on the stairs and she crept to her bed and curled into a ball in the middle of it and hugged her pillow to her.

Several minutes later her bed moved and the springs creaked and she smelled Dad's after-shave and felt his work-roughened hand on her head.

"Don't cry, Jae."

She sniffed. "I won't."

"Do you want to talk?"

"No."

"I saw Kip's face. You hurt him, honey." Ian stroked her hair, then rubbed away her tears with his thumbs. "He's a fine boy and I hate to see him hurting."

"He'll get over it, Dad." But would she? He would soon forget her and turn to someone else, but she'd never, never be able to forget him.

Ian sighed and stood up, his hands resting lightly on his hips. "I wish you'd let me help you the way you did when you were younger. I'm still your dad and I love you very much."

She rolled over and sat up and managed a teary smile. "Thanks, Dad. I love you, too."

"And do you love Kip?"

The truth hit her and almost knocked her off her feet. She loved Kip! Her feelings were not just physical attraction for him. Finally she nodded and whispered, "Yes, Dad. I do love him."

"Does he love you?"

She shook her head, her eyes dry. "No."

"Are you sure, Jae?" Ian rattled the change in his jeans. "He was in a great deal of pain when he ran out."

"Dad, to him I am only the little girl next door that

he finally realized grew up. Once the initial interest lags, he'll be off to find someone more suitable."

"I think you're wrong, Jae, but you'll have to learn that yourself the way you've had to in the past with everything." He squeezed her shoulder. "Think about it carefully, Jae. Pray about it."

She nodded, then watched him walk out of the bedroom. She couldn't think about Kip loving her, or she might convince herself it was true and run to him, only to be rejected.

Adrial burst in, her face ashen. "Did you tell Uncle Ian about the clothes you found under my pillow?"

Jeanna pulled her mind off Kip to answer Adrial. "No." She sighed heavily. "No, I didn't tell Dad. I think it'll be better all the way around if I take the things back myself the first thing in the morning." Suddenly it didn't matter if Adrial stayed or went home. And she was free to have Mick.

Adrial reached thankfully for Jeanna's hand then drew back. "Thank you," she said stiffly.

"I'm not doing it for you, but for Mom and Dad. They love you."

Adrial backed away, then sank to the edge of her bed. "I'm thankful you're not going to tell."

Jeanna slowly pulled off her clothes and slipped on her short yellow nightie. She peeked at Adrial from under long lashes. She looked very unhappy. "You'd better get to bed. You have to work tomorrow."

Adrial pushed her long hair back from her pale face. "Jeanna, I have reached a decision."

"Oh?"

"I'll break up with Mick and leave and you can get back together with him."

Jeanna gasped.

"I love you, Jae, and I don't want to lose you over anyone, not even Mick." Giant tears filled Adrial's eyes and slowly ran down her cheeks as she fingered the gold chain around her slender neck.

"Oh, Adrial!" Jeanna caught Adrial's icy hands. "Don't do that! I'm not worth it!"

"I love you, Jae."

"Oh, Addie! I love you, too." Jeanna wrapped her arms around Adrial and they clung together, sobbing softly. Finally Jeanna pulled away. "Addie, I don't love Mick, and even if I did, I know that he loves you and you love him. I won't let you break your heart or his because of me. He does love you."

"I know."

Jeanna stepped away from Adrial. "I'm very tired, Addie. We'll talk more in the morning."

Adrial nodded, sniffing back tears.

The next morning Jeanna looked in the mirror at the dark circles under her eyes, then turned to find the same with Adrial. "I see you didn't sleep much either."

"I couldn't."

"Addie, did you steal those clothes?"

"No, but I can't tell you who did."

"Maybe you should tell Mom you can't continue to work for her."

Adrial lifted her head in alarm. "Don't you believe me?"

"I've tried to." Jeanna found a Maxi's bag and pushed

the clothes into it. "I'll talk to you when I get home."

"Oh, Jae!"

Jeanna hurried to the kitchen to find Dad drinking a cup of steaming coffee at the kitchen table. "Where's Mom?"

"She left for work about ten minutes ago. Why?"

"I wanted a ride." Jeanna set the bag on a chair with her purse, then poured herself a glass of orange juice. The smell of coffee and toast filled the kitchen. "Could I borrow your car, Dad?"

"Not today, Jae. I have to check the men at the construction site, then I'm going fishing again with Grandpa." Ian studied her thoughtfully. "I thought you didn't work until this afternoon."

Jeanna swallowed the juice and set the glass beside the sink. "I want to go in early. Maybe I can catch a ride with Mick." She quickly said goodbye and stepped out into the bright sunlight. Blacky ran to her with a happy bark. She patted his head. "Lie down, Blacky. I don't have time to play this morning." Blacky padded to his doghouse, turned around, then stretched out in the shade with his head on his paws.

Jeanna ran across the grass to find Mick, then stopped at the sight of Kip walking toward his car. Butterflies fluttered in her stomach and she gripped the bag tightly. He stopped dead when he saw her and the color drained from his face.

"Are you waiting for me?" he asked stiffly.

She longed to say that she was, but she shook her head. "I was hoping to catch a ride with Mick."

"He's still in bed. I'll take you. I should have my head

examined, but come on."

How could she ride with him? If he was nice to her at all, she'd fall into his arms and tell him of her love, and then maybe even spill the story about Grace Meeker. "I don't really want to ride with you, but I must get to the store."

"Have it your way."

Reluctantly she slid into the passenger seat and buckled her seat belt. The car moved when he sat down. He smelled of soap and after-shave lotion and it blended with her cologne. Shivers of awareness ran over her.

"You aren't supposed to work until two-thirty," he said.

"I have to get in early today."

The tension in the car increased as he drove toward the store. She peeked at him, but he stared straight ahead, seemingly occupied with the morning traffic. One hand gripped the steering wheel and the other rested on the gearshift on the floor between the bucket seats. If she moved her hand a bit to the left she'd touch him. She shivered and pulled tighter into herself.

"Can't you relax?" he asked gruffly as he pulled around a yellow Mustang. "You're coiled tighter than a spring. If you go off, you'll ruin yourself and the interior of my car!"

The plastic bag slipped from her hand and she caught it before it fell to the floor.

"What are you gripping so protectively?" He shot her a look and her eyes locked with his with a force that took her breath away. He turned back to his driving. "You look very guilty, Jeanna. Do you have a bomb in that bag?"

"I can't talk about it," she said barely above a whisper.

"Then you do have something in the bag that is upsetting you. I thought it was me that was doing it to you. Will you please tell me what's wrong so I can help?"

Tears filled her eyes at the gentle sound of his voice. "I think Adrial shoplifted some things from Maxi's."

"Not Adrial!"

"Why not?"

Kip drove in silence, then pulled into Maxi's parking lot that was almost empty. He stopped beside a black Cadillac, then turned off the ignition and turned to Jeanna. "Adrial wouldn't shoplift and I think you know that."

"How do you know?"

"I know Adrial."

Jealousy shot through Jeanna. "She took the clothes that I have right in this bag! I found them under her pillow."

He tugged his tie loose and cleared his throat. "I've talked with Adrial often when she came over to see Mick. She wouldn't steal any more than you would."

"Then how do you explain these clothes?" Angrily Jeanna shook the bag under his nose. "I say she did and I say I'm going to tell Mom."

Kip caught Jeanna's wrist and then released it abruptly as if it had burned him. "There has to be another explanation. If you weren't so jealous you'd know it, too."

"She looks like an angel and acts like one and you

fell for it just like Mick did!" Jeanna slid out of the car.

"Do you need a ride home?"

She glared at him. "If I do, I'll call a cab!"

Kip roared out of the parking lot and she watched him go while every fiber of her being wanted to run after him. Slowly she walked to the door marked "employees only" with tears stinging her eyes.

Chapter 8

"Jeanna!"

She kept her hand on the doorknob to the door marked 'employees only' and looked over her shoulder to find Sarah running across Maxi's parking lot toward her. Sarah's fine, blonde hair flopped lifelessly on her narrow shoulders. Her blue shorts and white tee shirt looked wrinkled and soiled.

"What is it, Sarah?" Fear pricked Jeanna's skin.

"Adrial called me. She told me what you're going to do." Sarah nudged the bag and tears filled her eyes. "I have to talk to you."

"Did Adrial tell you about this?" Jeanna frowned. "I know that you and Adrial have become good friends, but I didn't know she'd tell you about this."

Sarah blinked away her tears. "Adrial didn't steal them, Jae."

"How do you know?"

"It was — it was Meg."

Jeanna gasped. "Meg?"

Sarah nodded. "I found out a few days ago and I've been going crazy. I asked her why and she just shrugged. Ever since she got pregnant she's been doing things she never did before."

"Oh, Sarah, I'm sorry."

"Me, too. Yesterday when Addie came over I was in tears and when she asked me what was wrong, I broke down and told her I'd found out that Meg was shoplifting. Addie said she'd take the things back and that no one would have to know. But you found out."

"And blamed Adrial." Jeanna flushed.

"I will make sure Meg doesn't do it again, Jae. I promise you."

"How can you do that, Sarah? You can't watch her twenty-four hours a day."

"I won't let her out of my sight."

Jeanna shot a look at her watch and gasped. "Oh, no! Look at the time! The store's already opened. I hope I can get these back in place before anyone sees me. I should have been in there before this."

"I'll wait for you."

"No. No, you go home and I'll call you later."

Sarah gripped Jeanna's hand. "Jae, thank you! You're a good friend. I just wish I could help you."

Jeanna moved restlessly. "Do I need help?"

"With Kip. With whatever's been bothering you since the beginning of summer vacation. With the great sadness that I feel inside you."

"I don't need help," Jeanna said stiffly, clenching the bag tighter.

"I happen to know that Kip loves you, but you won't believe it."

"Don't, Sarah. Don't."

"It's true. And I know that whatever's bothering you could be taken care of if you'd face what it is and deal with it. You won't even let God help you. And that's not like you at all." Sarah nervously twisted a strand of lifeless, blonde hair around her finger. "If what I said makes you mad, then I'm sorry, but I had to say something. I don't like to see you this way."

"Don't say any more, Sarah. Please." Jeanna fumbled with the doorknob and finally pushed open the door and stepped inside. The air-conditioned coolness made her shiver. Smells of perfumes and fabrics filled the air. How could Sarah believe that Kip loved her? How could Sarah know that something was bothering her? Had it been that evident?

On the main floor Jeanna hurried past several customers to the escalator. She spotted Ralph and her heart raced in alarm. If the security man saw her with the merchandise, she'd be sunk.

In the children's department Lois smiled and said hello, then stopped folding jeans. "Did you forget that I'm working this morning, Jeanna?"

Jeanna forced a laugh that sounded fake even to her ears. "I had to take care of something."

"It's been a little slow in here so far, but it'll pick up. Enjoy your free time and I'll see you later today." Lois turned back to her work and Jeanna walked slowly toward the blouse section, nervously glancing around.

A tall woman with a large purse blocked the aisle and Jeanna turned to walk down another. The woman walked to Lois and talked with her while Jeanna fumbled with the bag, trying to pull out the clothes without being seen. Suddenly the bag fell from her hands, spilling the clothes to the carpet. With a gasp, she dropped to the floor, gathering the things together.

"What have we here?"

Jeanna looked up at the tall woman who suddenly seemed twenty feet tall. "I — I dropped something."

The woman swooped down and picked up a handful of clothing and they draped over her hand. "Call Mrs. Shaneck, Lois. We have our shoplifter."

Jeanna wanted to sink through the floor. "I'm not!"

"You've made a mistake," Lois said in a small voice, staring at Jeanna as if she didn't know what to believe.

"Call Mrs. Shaneck!" barked the tall woman.

Jeanna leaned against the counter filled with underwear and tried to think of something to say. Her mind remained blank and she couldn't speak until her mother stood in front of her.

"What's going on, Jeanna?" Christa's voice was crisp.

"It's a mistake, Mom." Jeanna rubbed her clammy hands down her jeans. "I can explain."

Christa turned to the ladies. "Mrs. Keepers, Lois, I'll handle this. Go back to work." Christa gripped Jeanna's arm and strode toward her office, her face gray.

"I'm sorry, Mom," Jeanna said in a small voice.

"Save it until we get to my office!"

Finally Jeanna stood facing her mom in her office, knowing she expected to hear every detail. Jeanna swallowed hard. "I — I can't tell you who took the things. I promised I wouldn't."

"You'll have to break that promise."

"I can't," Jeanna whispered, gripping her hands together. "I can't."

"It seems like you can't tell me anything lately, Jeanna." Christa leaned back against her oak desk. Bright rays of the sun shone through the windows behind her. "You can't tell me what's ruining your life. You can't tell me who took these clothes." Christa stood straight and faced Jeanna squarely. The smell of her perfume filled the air. "Just what can you tell me? I am your mother and I want to help you. But you won't give me a chance. You won't even help yourself." Her eyes flashing, Christa gripped Jeanna's arms. "You get your life back in order or you won't have a life left that's worth living! You are beginning to look like a walking skeleton with those dark circles under your eyes. You jump at every little noise. Just how long is this going to continue?"

"Please don't, Mom." Tears flooding her eyes, Jeanna hung her head.

"I love you, Jae! Jesus loves you too. Can't you understand that? He wants to help you. *I* want to help you. I know others that want to too and you won't let them. Kip talked to me. Do you know that?"

Jeanna's head shot up and she stared at her mom with wide eyes.

"Kip asked me if you were sick. He said he knows something is wrong but he said you won't confide in him, or let him help you. You can't go on like this, Jeanna. You have to settle your life so that you can live, really live again."

Tears ran down Jeanna's ashen cheeks and she nodded slightly. "I'll think about what you said."

"I'll take you home and I don't want you to come to work today. I'll get Lila to come in." Christa's fingers bit into Jeanna's arm as she led her to the elevator to take them to the ground floor.

Outdoors Jeanna blinked against the blazing sun as her mom walked her to the car. "I can find my own way home, Mom," Jeanna said weakly.

"I'm taking you!" Christa pulled her car key out of her purse, then looked as a car pulled into the lot. "Wait. There's Kip. I'll ask him to drive you home."

Jeanna bit back a gasp. Sarah's words rang inside her head, 'I know Kip loves you, Jae.' Did he? Was it possible? She shook her head and cringed against her mom's car.

Kip stopped beside them and looked questioningly at Christa.

"Kip, could you please see that Jeanna gets home?"

"Yes, but I do have a couple of errands to run first."

"That's all right." Christa walked Jeanna around the car and opened the passenger door.

Jeanna hesitated, then slid in, clutching her purse. She stared straight ahead, her heart racing as Kip drove from the parking lot.

"I came back for you," he said gruffly.

She turned with a gasp. "You did?"

"I should have my head examined! I knew something was wrong. I had to make sure you were all right."

Her pulse quickened. "I am all right."

"So I see."

Tears filled her eyes and she turned but not before he saw them.

He groaned, "Oh, honey."

She wanted to creep into his arms and stay close to his heart no matter if he rejected her or not.

"Please, Jae, tell me what's wrong."

She saw that he really wanted to know and before she could stop herself she blurted out about Adrial and

Sarah and Meg and spilling the bag of clothing and Mrs. Keepers' accusing voice.

Kip parked in Thompson's parking lot and turned to face her. Cars whizzed past on the street. In the distance a siren wailed. "Jae, tell your mom the truth. She has a right to know and Meg has a right to get help. Sarah shouldn't have to deal with Meg's pregnancy and her shoplifting. It's too much responsibility on her."

"But I promised her!"

"Talk to her again and tell her that you were wrong to promise. I'll take you to Sarah's if you want."

"No!"

Pain crossed his face and he quickly masked it. "I won't argue. I know it doesn't do any good." He opened his door. "I have business in the furniture store and I'll be right out to drive you home."

"Are they buying one of your oils?"

"Yes. Mr. Thompson said he sold the other one yesterday and that I should get another one to him."

"You must be very proud."

Kip shrugged. "I guess I am. It's just that other things have been on my mind." He gave her a knowing look and she quickly turned away to open her door.

"Is it all right if I go in with you?"

"It's up to you," he said stiffly.

She walked around to the trunk with him and waited while he lifted out the wrapped, framed painting. She knew she'd hurt him again and pain squeezed her heart. How could she ease his pain? "Kip, before long you'll be so famous that everyone will want a painting of yours."

He glanced at her, then away as he walked to the front door. The bell tinkled as he pushed the door open. Stiffly he motioned for her to enter. With color flushing her cheeks she walked in just as a wiry, short man hurried to greet them.

"Mr. Thompson, this is Jeanna Shaneck."

The man smiled and Jeanna managed to also. "So, did you want to see how Kip's pictures would look hanging with my furniture?"

Jeanna nodded as Mr. Thompson unwrapped the canvas and held up the still life.

"It's beautiful, Kip," Jeanna said breathlessly as she stared at the oil painting of an old butter churn with eggs, fruit and a wooden apple crate.

"It certainly is," Mr. Thompson said. "I'll hang it in our dining room display. It'll be perfect. I'm sure this will sell as fast as the other."

"I'll try to have another one ready soon." Kip took the check that Mr. Thompson held out to him and slipped it into his pocket. He was silent as he walked Jeanna to the car.

She stood beside his car with the sun shining brightly overhead and cars driving past on the street. A boy on a bicycle whistled cheerily as he pedaled past. "I liked the picture a lot, Kip."

He nodded without speaking and finally she slipped into her seat. She wanted him to talk to her, assure her with his pleasant banter that he hadn't given up on her, but he never spoke until he'd driven several blocks.

"I'll take you back to Maxi's so you can talk to your mom."

"Thank you." Jeanna moistened her dry lips with the tip of her tongue. Could she talk to Mom and tell her about Sarah and Meg? "I suppose you're right. I suppose I should tell her the truth and then talk to Sarah."

"I'll be with you to help you."

She was silent, unable to speak without bursting into tears. Maybe he really did love her. Her heart leaped at the thought. She peeked at him sideways and saw a muscle jump in his jaw.

"I just remembered that I have something else planned," his voice was gruff and she stared openly at him.

"Are you angry at me, Kip?"

"Me? Angry? Why should I be?"

She moved restlessly as he stopped at a red light. "I don't know. You tell me."

"Forget it, Jeanna." He stopped in the parking lot and drummed his fingers on the steering wheel. "I'll wait here for you."

She opened the door with a jerk. "Never mind. I'll find my own way home." Her legs trembled and she clutched the door to keep from falling. "Thank you for the ride and the help."

His eyes narrowed. "Help? Since when have you let me help? You have a secret locked up inside you that's eating you alive and you won't let me help with that. I've given up trying. You don't want my help and you don't want me. It's just too bad that we live next door to each other and will run into each other. But then that won't bother you at all, will it? Your heart won't be broken." He reached across and slammed the passenger door shut and roared away.

"Oh, Kip," she whispered, blinking back tears. "What have I done to you?" She crept to the side door of Maxi's and stood in the shade with her shoulders drooping. "What have I done to myself?" Why hadn't she faced Nurse Wilder and Dr. Browne and settled her guilt over Grace Meeker's death? Was she going to be a coward all of her life and let it hang over her head so that she could never lead a normal life?

"Heavenly Father." Her voice broke and she couldn't go on. "I'm sorry, Father, for pulling away from you when I should've run to you for help. I need your help now more than I've ever needed it. Show me what to do." She prayed softly while she stood all alone at the employees' entrance. Finally she lifted her chin and squared her shoulders. Today with God's help she'd settle everything! She'd tell Mom about Sarah and Meg, then she'd talk to Sarah. After that she'd drive to the Provincial House and face Nurse Wilder.

Jeanna reached for the doorknob. Butterflies fluttered in her stomach and shivers of fear ran up and down her spine. She ignored them as she walked inside the store and rode the elevator to the office.

A few minutes later she stood in front of the large oak desk, facing her mother. "I have to tell you the truth, Mom. It's not right to keep it a secret." Jeanna swallowed hard. "It was Meg Butterworth, Sarah's sister, who took the clothes."

Christa made a tent with her fingers and looked over the top of them as Jeanna talked.

"I promised Sarah I wouldn't tell, but I had to, Mom."

And now I have to tell Sarah what I did. She might not forgive me."

"You can handle it, Jae." Christa looked at a calendar on her desk. "I'll check my schedule and see when I can talk to Mrs. Butterworth and Meg. I want to see them today and get this settled. I'll see what I can do to get help for Meg."

"Thank you!"

"I wish you'd told me sooner."

"Me too."

"Has Meg decided what she's going to do with the baby?"

Jeanna nodded. "Put it up for adoption with Children's Services."

"I pray she's doing the right thing."

"Me, too. Mom, may I use your car? I have to talk to Sarah and then make a trip to the Provincial House." Jeanna almost choked. "I'll be back by three at the latest." Was she really going to settle it today? Maybe by tomorrow she'd be in jail. She forced back a shiver.

Hesitantly Christa held the car keys out to Jeanna. "Provincial House, huh?"

Jeanna nodded.

"Are you sure you don't want to talk about it?"

Jeanna shook her head, then walked around the desk and kissed her mom's cheek, "Thanks."

"For what?"

"Loving me and being patient with me."

"You'll come out on top, Jae."

"With God's help, Mom." Jeanna's voice broke and she quickly said goodbye and ran to the elevator. The ride down seemed to take only seconds as the enormity of what she was going to do hit her.

★   ★   ★

Carolynn Burgess slowly hung up the phone and walked to her kitchen table. She'd been wrong. Again. She'd been so sure Gil Oakes wouldn't be who he said he was. "But he really is Gil Oakes." She'd overnighted a snapshot of him to the school in Flint from which she'd learned he'd graduated. The call was to tell her he was indeed who he said he was. He'd graduated seven years ago. "So, what's with him?" Carolynn muttered as she fingered her glass of iced tea. Maybe he was too frightened to face his birth mother. "Sometimes you make everything too complicated, Carolynn." She chuckled. "Talking to yourself again? Better watch that."

Just then someone knocked on the back door. Carolynn hurried through the laundry room where the washer was just finishing the spin cycle and opened the door. Sheriff Farley Cobb stood there, his hat in his hand. "What a surprise, Farley!"

He grinned. "Now that Robert knows your secret life I can come see you without making him suspicious."

Carolynn led him to the kitchen. "Iced tea?"

"Sure could use a tall glass with plenty of ice." Farley sat at the round oak table and dropped his hat on the chair beside him. "Things aren't good, Carolynn."

Her hand trembled as she handed him a glass of iced tea. The ice cubes clinked. Slowly she sat facing him.

"Tell me, Farley."

"I'm going to arrest Silver Rawlings for the murder of Gwen Nichols."

"But she's innocent!"

"So you say, Carolynn. She had motive, opportunity and the murder weapon was found in her car."

"She's not strong enough to swing a blow hard enough to kill someone."

Farley took a long swig of the tea, set the glass down and wiped his mouth with the back of his hand. "She's been pumping iron the past several months."

"I didn't know that," Carolynn said weakly. "But I do know she's innocent. She wouldn't be able to keep such a dastardly secret."

"She could've blocked it out of her mind." Farley rubbed a hand along his jaw. "I checked into her past and I know what she did when she miscarried a baby."

Carolynn's mind whirled with ways to stop Farley from arresting Silver. "Why'd you come see me?"

"To let you know my plans."

"Can't you give me more time? I'm checking into Gwen's brother Andy. He had motive."

"But not opportunity. I checked his alibi."

Carolynn fingered the napkin beside her glass. "I know. I checked it too. But maybe he was lying and maybe somebody's covering for him."

"I figured you'd say that. I'll give you time to check it out."

"Thanks, Farley. I appreciate it."

"While you're checking, check out Tim Rawlings. Would he kill the woman, then pin it on his wife?"

"Farley! That's a terrible thought."

"If it crossed my mind, it crossed yours too."

Carolynn flushed. "You're right, but I couldn't bring myself to say it aloud."

"Maybe they did it together. Andy said his sister wanted her baby back. Maybe they were afraid she'd try, and succeed."

Carolynn thought of Tim's affair with Gwen and wondered if Farley was right. Maybe Gwen was planning to tell Silver the truth and take both Tim and Brittany. "Farley, how much time can you give me?"

Farley wrinkled his forehead in thought. "I could lose the paperwork for, say, another twenty-four hours."

"Thanks." Carolynn's pulse quickened. Could she find the killer by then? She'd run into dead-ends so far. She talked a few more minutes with Farley, then saw him out. Slowly she walked back to the table, her hands clasped at her heart. "Heavenly Father, thank you for wisdom in this case. Help me to see with a clear eye and lead me to the killer."

★   ★   ★

In the car Jeanna gripped the steering wheel and waited for the air conditioner to cool the interior. Dare she face Nurse Wilder? Maybe she should call Kip to go with her.

"No! I have to do this alone! I can't back out now!"

Slowly she drove from the parking lot and turned toward Sarah's house. Maybe after today she wouldn't have Sarah for a friend. Maybe after today she wouldn't have anyone for a friend.

Fear rose inside Jeanna. She remembered the Scripture that said God hadn't given her the spirit of fear, but of love and power and a sound mind. "Thank you, heavenly Father! Fear does not belong to me! I am full of love and power and I have a sound mind!" Finally she was in control of her own life! She'd face Sarah and her other problems and she'd win! She gripped the steering wheel until her knuckles ached and she shivered.

At Sarah's she parked at the curb and slipped out of the car as she looked at the weathered white house. Before she could walk to the door Sarah burst out and ran toward her. Sarah had washed her hair and it hung in a pretty tail down her back.

"What happened, Jae? I thought you were going to call." Sarah gripped Jeanna's arms. "What happened?"

Jeanna swallowed hard as she pulled away from Sarah. "Don't get mad at me, but I had to tell Mom the truth."

"No!" Sarah pressed her hand to her mouth.

"I had to, Sarah. Meg needs help and if you kept this a secret, she wouldn't get help."

Sarah glared at Jeanna. "So, suddenly you want to help everyone around you, but you won't let anyone help you. Where do you get off being the great helper of the year? How will I face Meg? Or Mom? And your mom? How could you tell her, Jeanna?"

Tears flooded Jeanna's eyes and she numbly shook her head. "Mom's coming here later to see Meg and your mother."

"Oh, no!"

"I'm sorry."

"No, you're not! You want everyone to be as miserable as you are. Get out of here and leave me alone!"

Jeanna chewed her bottom lip. "I'm going to the Provincial House now, but I'll call you later when you're calmer."

"Don't bother!" Sarah flipped around, then stopped short.

"What's wrong?" Jeanna asked sharply.

"See that car? That's the man that's been following us."

Jeanna looked just as the man pulled away from the curb and drove away. "I didn't get a good look at him."

"I wonder what he wants."

"Why don't you call the police and tell them somebody's been watching you and following you."

Sarah scowled at Jeanna. "Oh, sure and have them mad at a false report? We don't need that." Sarah ran to the house, slamming the door behind her.

A dog sniffed at Jeanna's feet and she absently rubbed its head. Three boys ran past, calling to each other. Slowly Jeanna walked to her mom's car and drove away.

Jeanna trembled. Could she really go to the Provincial House? Fear pricked her skin, but she kept driving. It was time to face her problem. Her heart sank. Would she ever be the same again? Maybe she'd spend the rest of her life in prison.

She slowed the car as she looked down the street at the Provincial House. Soon she'd know her fate. Why hadn't she allowed Kip to come with her?

Did he really love her? Was it possible? If he loved her, really loved her, she could face anything and win.

She parked in the Provincial House parking lot and stared at the large brick building. Perspiration dotted her forehead and shivers ran up and down her spine. Could she really do this, or should she run for her life? Whimpering, she backed out of the parking place and drove quickly away.

★   ★   ★

Silver sat under the shade of the umbrella on her deck while she watched Brittany play with a shovel and pail in the sandbox. Silver absently sipped her Pepsi. She'd wanted to stay locked inside the house with Brittany, but she'd decided it was better for the baby if she kept the same routine.

The gate creaked and Silver jumped. She watched as a man about her age walked into the back yard. Silver leaped to her feet and faced the intruder. "You're trespassing! Please leave before I call the police!"

The man took a step toward Silver. "I'm Andy Nichols, Gwen's brother. I have to talk to you."

Silver shivered as she dropped weakly back in the deck chair. "I don't want to listen."

"You'll want to hear what I have to say." Andy pulled out a chair and sat down. The shade of the umbrella covered him. "Did Gwen get to talk to you before she died?"

Silver helplessly shook her head. "What could she say to me? I certainly wouldn't give my daughter up!"

Andy watched Brittany spill sand out of the bucket, then he turned back to Silver. "Didn't you ever wonder who the natural father was?"

"It wasn't on the birth certificate, they said at Children's Services."

"Tim is Brittany's natural father."

Silver blanched. "How can you say that? It's a lie!"

"Tim and Gwen had an affair that lasted almost three months. He broke it off because of you. But Gwen was already pregnant."

Blood roared in Silver's ears and she thought she'd topple over in a dead faint.

"They worked it out with Children's Services that he'd adopt Brittany. Gwen agreed because she knew she couldn't raise a baby alone. But she was sorry from the first day. She's been trying ever since to get the baby back."

Helplessly Silver shook her head. "Why are you telling these lies?" she whispered hoarsely.

"I'm telling the truth." Andy pulled a letter from his pocket and laid it on the table in front of Silver. "It's from Gwen."

"I won't read it. I can't!" A bitter taste filled Silver's mouth and she thought she'd vomit.

"I'll leave it with you. I made a copy of it, so it won't do any good to tear it up." Andy stood behind his chair and gripped the back of it. "I've decided to take back what belongs to my sister. I'm going to take Brittany."

"No!" Silver jumped up, knocking her chair over with a bang. "You can't have her!"

"I'm going to court to take her away from you."
Andy turned and strode across the yard and out the
gate.

Sobbing, Silver raced to Brittany and scooped her
up in her arms. She ran inside and grabbed the phone.
Holly Loudan would know what to do. She punched
the quick dial on the phone that belonged to Holly,
then remembered she'd be at work. Silver hung up, then
called Holly at work. It took an eternity before she got
her. Between sobs she said, "I need you to come here
right now, Holly. Please! It's urgent."

"Calm down, Silver. It'll take me about ten minutes
to get there, but I'm coming. Hold on. I'll be right there.
And I'll be praying for you."

Silver dropped the receiver in place, then dashed
upstairs. She threw Brittany's clothes into a giant diaper
bag, then grabbed the whole pack of disposable diapers.
Brittany wiggled and burst into tears. Silver held her
close and quieted her, then ran to her room and packed
a bag. She put Brittany in the crib and carried both bags
downstairs and set them outside the front door, then
raced back up for the baby. She hurried out just as
Holly drove in.

Her mint-green skirt flipping about her legs, Holly
ran to Silver. "What's wrong? What're you doing?"

"Please take me to your house. I'll answer your
questions later." Silver ran to the car and slipped inside
with Brittany on her lap.

Holly carried the bags and put them in the back seat.
Her heart raced as she quickly drove to her house. What
on earth had happened to upset Silver this much? Holly

bit back all her questions until Brittany was playing with Paige and Noah, and the babysitter was watching all three. Holly led Silver to her bedroom and closed the door for privacy. "Okay, Silver. What's wrong?"

Shuddering, Silver pulled the letter Andy had given her from her pocket and handed it to Holly.

She quickly read it, her heart sinking lower and lower. She looked up at Silver. "Is it true?"

"I don't know! It must be!"

Holly dropped the letter to the bed and pulled Silver close. "Heavenly Father, in Jesus' name comfort Silver. Bring peace to her heart. Help her to see with a clear mind." She prayed awhile longer, then stepped back from Silver. "I'm so sorry about all this. I'll do anything to help you."

"Let me stay here! And don't tell Tim where I am!"

Holly brushed back her short, dark hair. "I don't know, Silver. It's important for you two to talk this out."

Silver shook her head hard. "Not yet, Holly. I just can't do it yet!"

"You're welcome to stay as long as you need to. I won't tell Tim." Holly thought about Carolynn Burgess. She'd need to know what had happened and that Silver was here instead of home. Carolynn would keep it a secret.

Much later when Silver was busy with Brittany, Holly called Carolynn and told her what had transpired.

Carolynn clicked her tongue and shook her head. "Holly, it's even worse than you think. Sheriff Cobb has given me only one more day to find the killer. If

I don't, he's going to arrest Silver."

"Oh, no! What're you going to do?"

Carolynn sighed. "Check everything again. Maybe someone saw something the day of the murder and isn't talking." She paused. "Keep praying, Holly."

"I will. Thanks for your help, Carolynn. I wish I could tell Silver what you're doing for her."

"Please don't."

"I won't."

"Thanks."

"Carolynn, will you give Stan a message for me? Tell him it's off for tonight. I can't take a chance on him learning Silver is here. I don't think he'd see it the way we do."

"I'll tell him." Carolynn was quiet awhile. "Holly, it might be a good idea to tell Stan, then help him understand why you're doing it. He might be able to help."

"I'll think about it." Holly talked a bit longer, then slowly hung up. Could she keep Silver and Brittany hidden from Tim and the police?

Holly walked to the front-room picture window and looked out on the driveway and the street. A police car cruised past and she jumped back, her hand at her throat. Was this how she'd have to live until the killer was found?

Chapter 9

Carolynn sat in the church parking lot and looked around. She knew neither Silver nor Tim had killed Gwen. "So, who did?" Carolynn said under her breath. No one in the area had admitted to seeing anyone or anything. She slipped from her car. Warm wind blew against her pink slacks and blouse. She walked slowly away from her car and her pink shoes sounded loud on the pavement. The smell of diesel exhaust drifted back from a passing truck. A few days ago at this very time Gwen Nichols had been killed in the exact spot where Carolynn now stood. She slowly turned, scanning the area. The homes on either side of the vast parking lot were hidden by large oaks and maples. Directly across the street was a vacant house for sale by Bell Realty. The homes on either side were occupied, but the families were gone on vacation for another two weeks. "All dead-ends," Carolynn said impatiently. She walked to the sidewalk and looked up and down the street. Had someone driven past and seen something? Once again she turned to the house directly across the street. She pulled out her notebook and made sure she'd jotted down the phone number and name of the realty company. It was there in her neat handwriting and so was the agent's home number. She'd tried to talk to the agent who was in charge of showing the house, but she'd been out of town. "I'll try again right now," Carolynn said firmly. Maybe someone had looked at the house that day. She was grasping at straws, but she didn't dare not grasp.

Sighing, Carolynn walked slowly toward her car. Just then a car pulled into the parking lot and stopped near her. She peered closer and saw it was Tim Rawlings. Her heart zoomed to her feet. She hadn't wanted to see him yet.

His face pale and haggard, Tim ran to Carolynn. "I don't know where Silver is! She has the baby with her. She didn't leave a note or anything."

Carolynn patted Tim's arm. "Calm down, Tim. Tell me what happened."

He flung his hands wide. "I don't know! I got home just after four from the church and the house was empty. Her car is still in the garage, but she and Brittany are gone! Would Silver run away?" Tim breathed as if he'd been running the marathon. "Could she be guilty? Is that why she ran?"

"Tim, now's the time to pray, not faint. Don't start believing lies about Silver. We both know she's not guilty."

"Do we?"

"Tim! It's your own guilt talking."

His face flamed bright-red. "I know. How could I do such a terrible thing to my wife? To myself?"

"I've learned Gwen's brother knows the truth about Brittany. About you and Gwen."

Tim hung his head. "I was afraid of that. I have to find him and talk to him. Do you know where he lives?"

"You won't do anything rash, will you, Tim?"

"No. I just want to talk. I want to convince him to

keep what he knows to himself."

"Wait, Tim. Maybe the more you beg, the more determined he'll be to spread the story. He's very upset about Gwen's death. He's not rational right now. It would be wise to stay away from him."

"I don't think I can."

Carolynn gripped Tim's hand with both of hers and looked earnestly into his eyes. "Tim, this is the time to go to war in the spirit world. Satan is out to destroy you and your family. It's up to you to stop him. You do that by praying, by standing firm on God's promises."

"I feel too weak, Carolynn."

"You don't go by feelings, Tim. You live by faith in the Word of God. You think about that! You hear me?"

Tim slowly nodded.

"Get Al to pray with you. Or Robert. Call him. He'll be glad to go to your house to pray with you." Carolynn was glad to know it was true. Robert knew how to pray and he was glad to pray with others. She squeezed Tim's hand again, then released it. "Go home right now, Tim, and call someone to pray with you. The pastor or Robert. Or someone else you can trust."

Tears filled Tim's eyes and he nodded. Slowly he walked to his car and drove away.

Carolynn breathed a great sigh of relief that she'd not told him where to find Silver. "She should've stayed home and faced him and resolved the problem. Running away never solved anything." She grinned wryly. She of all people should know that. She'd never physically run away from Robert, but emotionally she had. But no longer! And she'd do her best to talk Silver out of running.

A few minutes later Carolynn stood at an outside phone booth waiting for Peggy Dunbar of Bell Realty to answer the phone. Finally she did in a high, sing-song voice. Carolynn explained who she was and what she needed to know.

"I don't think I showed the house that day, but let me get my book. I have to write down everything or I don't remember."

Carolynn tapped her toe and waited. The street lights flashed on all around. She knew Robert would be wondering about her. Finally Peggy Dunbar came back on the phone.

"I'm sorry it took so long, but my dog had somehow gotten my book and dragged it under the table. He's a fine animal, but mischievous, if you know what I mean."

"Did you show the house that day?"

"You know what? I did! At nine in the morning."

Carolynn's heart sank. "Are you sure it wasn't nine at night?"

"Let me think about that." Peggy was silent awhile. "You know what? It was! Yes. I remember because I was thankful it wasn't on a Sunday or Wednesday night. Because of the mob of people at Christian Center on those nights. Ties up traffic, you know."

Carolynn's pulse quickened. "What time did you finish showing the house?"

"I remember coming out after the couple had left and

seeing two cars in the church parking lot. I've showed the house when the parking lot was full and I couldn't get away. Well anyway, just as I was ready to leave one car drove out."

Carolynn gripped the receiver. "Man or woman driver?"

"Man. You know what? I don't know for positive, but I'm almost 85% sure it was a man."

"Thank you. Could you tell me what the car looked like?"

"I can't. I'm not good with cars. I think it was blue and it had two doors. But it could've been gray. But it had two doors. That I'm sure about because we have a two-door car and I want a four-door one so badly I can taste it." Peggy laughed. "Taste it. Does that mean taste the door?" She laughed again.

Carolynn managed a small chuckle. "Thank you for your help."

"I read about the murder in that church parking lot. Do you suppose it was the killer I saw leaving?" Peggy gasped. "You know what? If it was and if he'd seen me, I'd be dead now too. Wouldn't I be? I just never gave that car a thought until right this minute."

"I appreciate your help." Carolynn ended the conversation as quickly as she could. Her pulse racing, she slipped into her car. Silver's car was a four door! So was Tim's. Peggy Dunbar probably had seen the killer drive away. A man in a two-door car. Now to find just such a man connected with Gwen Nichols. "I wonder what kind of car Andy Nichols drives."

Carolynn started to turn the key in her car, then

stopped. Farley should know what Peggy Dunbar had said.

At the pay phone on the corner, Carolynn dropped in a coin and punched Farley's phone number. He answered on the second ring in an impatient voice. "Having a bad evening, Farley?"

"I was ready to get in the shower, Carolynn. What've you got that's so all-fired important?"

She told him as quickly as she could. "An eye-witness, Farley. Does that give you enough to hold off arresting Silver Rawlings?"

Farley sighed. "Enough to lose the paperwork a couple of days more. I sure don't want to arrest an innocent woman, and you know that, Carolynn, but I got pressure on me to get this case solved."

"I know. I appreciate you holding off. So does Silver. And her baby."

"Yah, sure. Can I take my shower now?"

"Who's stopping you?" Laughing, Carolynn hung up and hurried to her car.

*   *   *

Meg slowly walked out the front door of her house and awkwardly sank to the steps. Would she ever be normal again? The doctor had said her baby was due, but maybe she'd carry it forever.

Sarah opened the door and peered out. "Oh, here you are, Meg."

She frowned over her shoulder. "Don't be such a shadow!"

Sarah closed the door and sat beside Meg. "I can't

help it, Meg. I've been jittery ever since we saw that man twice in one day."

"It probably wasn't anything." Meg glanced up and down the poorly lighted street. The car or man weren't in sight. She jabbed Sarah. "I'm all right out here. Leave me alone, will you?"

Just then a car pulled right into the driveway. Meg shrieked and Sarah jumped up, ready to protect Meg.

Jeanna slid out of the car. "Hi, girls."

"Jeanna!" Relief washed over Sarah and she ran to Jeanna.

Meg wiped sweat from her face and slowly relaxed.

"Dad let me use his car, so I thought I'd drop in. Is that all right?"

"Sure." Sarah had gotten over her anger at Jeanna. "How're you feeling, Meg?"

"As light as a feather," Meg answered sharply.

Sarah caught Jeanna's arm. "Let's go inside, shall we?"

"Sure. All right. Talk to you later, Meg."

"I want to be left alone!"

"Meg! Jeanna's only being nice."

"It's all right," Jeanna said softly. They walked inside, leaving Meg alone on the step.

Meg moved restlessly. A moth fluttered at the window, trying to get inside to the light. Fireflies flickered across the lawn at the neighbor's house. She thought about the talk she'd had with Christa Shaneck, Jeanna's mom.

"I thought your mother would be here, Meg."

"She couldn't wait around." Meg knew she'd gone off drinking, but she didn't tell Mrs. Shaneck that.

Christa sat down on the shabby sofa and studied Meg where she sat in the only other chair in the room. "I know you shoplifted at my store, Meg."

She hung her head. "I'm sorry. I won't do it again."

"How do I know that, Meg?"

She shrugged.

"I've been trying to decide what to do — talk to the police and have them send you to juvenile court, or deal with it myself."

Meg's eyes widened. She'd thought for sure she'd be sent to jail — even have her baby there.

"I prayed about what to do on the way over here. And I'll continue to pray for you."

Meg flushed. It had been awhile since she'd prayed. She used to go to church all the time with Sarah, but she hadn't the last year.

"I've decided to let you work off your debt."

"But I can't do anything!"

"Not right now, but after the baby's born you can do odd jobs for me at home as well as in the store. I'll keep track of your hours, then when your debt is paid, you'll be free to stop working."

Meg had struggled against tears. "Why're you being so nice?"

"I care about you, Meg. God loves you and He wants me to give you another chance," Christa had said softly. "Will you take it?"

"Yes," Meg had said. Even now her eyes filled with tears at how kind Mrs. Shaneck had been. Meg rubbed her nose and sniffed. Why couldn't she have a mom like Mrs. Shaneck? Meg brushed tears from her eyes.

Why even wish?

Down the street the man slipped from his car, a knife in his hand. He'd been watching and waiting for just such an opportunity. It had finally come. He could easily sneak up on the girl and stab her. A knife was such a wonderfully quiet weapon. He'd have to watch not to stab her in the stomach and kill the baby. He'd stab her right in the heart or even in the neck so she'd bleed to death quickly.

He smiled. The light was dim so even if anyone saw him stab the girl on the steps they couldn't identify him. He touched the brown wig and the shaggy mustache he'd found in a thrift shop. Even if anyone saw him, they wouldn't really *see* him. He was hidden behind a mustache and under a wig. It was kind of fun to disguise himself. He'd never done it before. The whole idea caused him to chuckle softly.

Meg heard what sounded like a soft footstep. She glanced in the direction of the sound and saw the gray shape of a man. She screamed at the top of her lungs and struggled to stand.

The man panicked at the scream and almost dropped the knife. He had to take a chance. Soon it would be too late to carry out his perfect plan — killing her while the baby was safely inside her. He thrust out the knife, but she turned and the knife barely grazed her shoulder. She screamed again and lashed out at him. In panic he spun around and raced away.

The door burst open and Sarah and Jeanna dashed out. "Meg, what happened?" Sarah cried.

"Are you all right?" Jeanna asked in alarm.

Trembling, Meg pointed down the sidewalk, but already the man was out of sight. Soon a car barreled away from the curb and out of sight. "He tried to — to stab me!" She touched her bleeding arm.

"You're hurt!" Sarah cried.

"Get inside so we can see how badly." Jeanna helped Meg into the house.

Blood streamed down Meg's arm and dripped to the floor.

"We have to call the police." Sarah started for the phone.

"Wait!" Jeanna rushed Meg into the dollhouse-size bathroom to stop the flow of blood and clean her up.

Meg's head spun and she was thankful someone was taking charge. She sat on the stool and watched Jeanna turn on the faucet.

Frowning, Sarah ran to the bathroom doorway. "Why wait?"

Jeanna squeezed out the washcloth and held it against Meg's arm. "My grandma knows the sheriff. We'll call her and she'll call the sheriff."

Sarah took the washcloth from Jeanna. "I'll take care of her. You call your grandma."

Jeanna grabbed a towel and dried her hands as she hurried to the phone. Grandma might already be in bed, but she'd be glad to help anyway.

Carolynn answered her kitchen phone on the first ring. She'd just arrived home.

"Grandma, it's Jeanna. I'm at Sarah Butterworth's house. Her sister Meg was just stabbed."

"I'll be right there."

"I thought since you know the sheriff, you'd call him."

"I'll wait until I get there. Give me the address." Carolynn scribbled it down, then hung up. She turned just as Robert walked in. He was wearing his light-blue bathrobe. She told him what had happened. "I don't know what time I'll be back."

"I can go with you."

"There's no need. But thanks." Carolynn kissed him, then hurried to her car.

Several minutes later Carolynn stood with the girls and listened to the frightening account. She checked Meg's wound and saw it was not more than a scratch — not deep enough to require stitches.

"It wasn't the same man we saw following us," Meg said, shivering. "This man had kind of long hair and a big mustache."

After Carolynn quieted the girls she called the sheriff and told him what had happened. He said he'd be right over. "No sirens or flashing lights, please, Farley. The girls don't need a lot of curious neighbors hanging around."

A few minutes later Sheriff Cobb walked in looking and smelling as if he'd just had a shower. He took statements from the girls, then said, "I'll ask a patrol car to cruise the area regularly. If you spot the man you said was following you or the man who stabbed you, call immediately. A police officer will be here in minutes."

"Thank you," Sarah said with tears sparkling in her

eyes.

Meg couldn't speak around the lump in her throat. She'd almost been murdered tonight. She'd thought often that she wanted to die, but being so close to death, she realized she wanted to live. She didn't want just to live, but she wanted to make her life count! She'd talk to Jeanna and Sarah later when she was able to and ask them to help her — even pray with her.

Carolynn told the girls goodnight, then walked out with Farley. They stopped at her car. "What do you make of it, Farley?"

"Random killing?"

"I don't think so. It's strange, isn't it? Why would someone try to kill a pregnant child?"

"The boyfriend?"

"It's worth checking into. Logan Dimarco is his name. Or maybe the boyfriend hired someone." Carolynn shuddered. "What a terrible thought!"

"We got to think of 'em all, Carolynn — terrible or not."

"I know. But we don't have to like it. I especially hate it that my granddaughter has to be associated with a crime."

"Meg is somebody's granddaughter. They all are. Or grandson."

Carolynn swallowed the lump in her throat. "I know, Farley."

★   ★   ★

Andy Nichols looked out his apartment window at the morning sunlight. Flowers were in bloom, and birds were singing, but he felt like the dead of winter. He'd made a major mistake by telling Silver Rawlings about his plan to take Brittany. Now, she'd run off somewhere and he might not be able to find her. He'd tried to talk to Tim, but he'd slammed the door in his face.

Andy scowled. He'd go to the church and demand that Tim see him. If he refused, he'd tell the pastor just what kind of man Tim Rawlings really was. But maybe Tim wouldn't go to work today since Silver was missing. He might spend the day trying to find her.

"Maybe she ran off to her mom's," Andy said gruffly. He'd have to check that out.

★　　★　　★

Impatiently Tim rang Holly's doorbell. Where else would Silver go? Last night he'd called Holly, but she wouldn't give him any information. Maybe she would face to face.

The door opened and Holly stepped out, her purse in her hand. "I'm on my way to work, Tim."

"I want to see Silver."

Holly's cheeks flushed and sparks shot from her eyes. "Tim, you'd better pray for a miracle. It'll take that for Silver to speak to you ever again."

Tim groaned. "I know. But I can't pray, Holly. I'm frozen inside."

"Get yourself unfrozen. You're a minister. You of all people know how to fight against the works of the enemy." Holly slipped in her car and backed out of the driveway.

Tim looked back at the front door, then slowly walked to his car. Holly was right. He had to get help from God. Carolynn Burgess had said to get Al or Robert to pray with him, but he hadn't done so. He had to do something. Maybe he could drop in on Robert Burgess right now.

Tim backed out of the drive, hesitated, then drove home. He couldn't face anyone right now, not even kind-hearted Robert Burgess.

★   ★   ★

Gil Oakes stopped outside Dumars' Investigative Services. He finished the last of the hamburger and strawberry shake he'd picked up for lunch at McDonald's. Today he'd have the courage to ask Dud Dumars about his birth mother. Just because he knew who she was didn't mean he'd have to talk to her until he was good and ready. Carolynn Burgess would prepare him for seeing his birth mother.

Finally Gil Oakes walked into the front office. A tall, heavy-set woman was watering a plant. Her blonde hair was pulled back from her face and pinned in place at the nape of her neck. She wore a bright, orange-flowered dress with a wide black belt, but no jewelry, not even a watch. She turned to Gil with flashing hazel eyes.

"I'm Mable Green. May I help you?"

He hesitated. She was much younger than he'd first thought, probably close to his age. It left him tongue-tied.

"Do you have an appointment, sir?"

Sir! Gil managed to smile. "I'm Gil Oakes to see Dud Dumars. On business."

Mable looked at her book, then flipped back a page. "Your appointment was a couple of days ago."

"I know. I couldn't make it. It'll only take a minutes. Is he in?"

Ordinarily Mable would've brushed the man off, but Dud had said he might be in. "I'll see if he's available." Mable rang Dud's office. "Gil Oakes to see you."

"Send him right in," Dud said in surprise.

Mable hung up, then walked Gil to Dud's door and opened it. "If you need to see him again, Mr. Oakes, please make an appointment."

Mr. Oakes! He liked the woman. He might even see if she'd have dinner with him sometime. He pushed thoughts of her away as he walked toward Dud.

Dud shook hands with Gil and motioned for him to sit on the uncomfortable folding chair. Gil was better-looking than Dud had expected with neatly combed brown hair and nice brown eyes. His tan pants and green plaid shirt were clean and well-pressed. His brown casual shoes weren't new, but they didn't look shabby. Maybe he'd been wrong about Gil Oakes.

"I'm sorry I didn't make it before this." Gil cleared his throat and tried to find a comfortable way to sit on the folding chair. "I was too frightened to come. But I'm ready now to learn the name of my birth mother."

Dud sat on his chair and rested his elbows on his cluttered desk. He'd been looking over case reports from his investigators. Paperwork always did him in. "Maybe she doesn't want you to know who she is."

Gil sagged in the chair. "Did she say that?"

Against his will, Dud felt sorry for Gil. "I didn't tell her about you — said you'd explain yourself. You could just drop in on her. But she's a busy woman and you might not have a chance to see her without an appointment."

"What's her name?" Gil asked with a catch in his voice.

Dud hesitated, then shrugged. Why not tell the kid? He deserved to know. "Nurse Bess Wilder. Works at Provincial House."

The name rang through Gil's head and curled around his heart. Nurse Bess Wilder! "It was Melanie Reeve."

"Got married. Started using her middle name instead of her first. It wasn't a matter of trying to hide from anyone. Not that I learned anyhow."

Slowly Gil stood and held his hand out to Dud. "Thank you! You don't know how thankful I am. If I can ever afford to pay you, I will."

Dud waved his hand. "I told my wife I'd do this for you, and so I did it."

Gil brushed a hand across his eyes. "Thank you." He walked to the door, turned and thanked Dud again, then walked out.

Dud leaned back and smiled. "I hope it works out like he wants." He picked up the phone to call his wife to let her know he'd helped Gil Oakes just as he'd promised.

★   ★   ★

Carolynn pulled Jeanna aside while the rest of the family walked noisily to the dining room for a family dinner. "How's Meg, Jeanna?"

"Just fine. I talked to Sarah before we came over here and she said Meg has totally changed her attitude. She even asked Sarah to read the Bible to her."

"That's good. I'm surprised the shock of the attack didn't send her into labor."

"Sarah thought it had, but the pains quit after only three or four." Jeanna hugged Carolynn. "Thanks for helping her. And me. You're the best grandma in the world! I love you!"

Carolynn kissed Jeanna's warm cheek. "I love you, sweety. I can see you settled your problems. You're not tense like you were."

Jeanna smiled, then sighed. "I settled some of them, but I don't have the courage to do all I should." So far she hadn't been able to go to the Provincial House and she'd stayed away from Kip.

"You have courage because God is with you. When you realize that, you'll be able to deal with the other things."

"Thanks, Grandma."

Carolynn caught Jeanna's hand and walked to the dining room with her. Smells of roast beef, cooked carrots and mashed potatoes made Carolynn's mouth water. Wesley's wife, Kate, had spent the afternoon making the dinner. A glass bowl full of a brightly colored tossed salad sat near Carolynn's plate.

She sat at the foot of the table with Robert at the head. Eleena and Kail were still on vacation with their children and Holly had stayed home with her two children, so the table wasn't as crowded as usual. Stan looked lonely and sad without Holly. Kate and Wesley's three little ones were the only grandchildren present.

Robert smiled around at his family. "Shall we pray?" He bowed his head and asked the blessing on the food.

Soon the table rang with talking and laughter and the clatter of silverwear on plates.

Carolynn bit into the roast beef and savored the taste of it. She hadn't realized how hungry she was. Why, she'd actually forgotten to eat lunch!

In a lull the doorbell rang. Carolynn jumped up to answer it. She hurried to the front door and opened it. Gil Oakes stood there looking shy and frightened. "Gil, this is a surprise."

"I hope I'm not in the way." He smelled the food and his mouth watered. "I'm sorry. I got you away from dinner."

"Come in and join us. The family would be pleased to meet you."

Gil hesitated. This was exactly what he'd wanted, but now he didn't know if he could do it. "I'd better not."

Carolynn caught his arm and tugged. "Come right on in! My daughter-in-law cooked dinner and it's delicious. How long has it been since you've had a home-cooked meal?"

Never, he wanted to say, but he only shrugged.

Carolynn led Gil to the dining room. Everyone stopped talking to stare at him. "I want you to meet a new friend of mine. Gil Oakes. This is my family. I'll start with my husband, Robert, and go around the table. Don't be embarrassed if you don't remember all the names. There's a bunch of us." Carolynn laughed, then named off the members of her family, ending with two-year-old Caro in the highchair. "Jeanna, run to the kitchen and get Gil a plate, will you?"

Ian pushed a chair between himself and Robert and motioned Gil to it.

"We're drinking iced tea," Kate said. "But we also have water, diet Pepsi and we could make a cup of instant coffee if you want it."

Feeling overwhelmed by the kindness of the family, Gil sat down. "Iced tea would be fine. Or water if it's easier."

"Iced tea it is." Wesley filled a glass and set it near Gil's plate.

Carolynn watched proudly as her family made Gil feel right at home. At times she took her wonderful family for granted and forgot others weren't so blessed.

Later Stan served dessert — chocolate layer cake with vanilla ice cream on the side.

Gil bit into the cake and rolled the chocolate around on his tongue. It was better than in his dreams. If he'd stayed with his birth mother, would he have had happy times like this?

Smiling at Gil's pleasure in sharing family time with them, Carolynn silently prayed he'd find the happiness he was looking for. More than anything she wanted him to know Jesus as his Savior. She'd talk to him about that before he left today. Or maybe Robert would.

She smiled down the long table at Robert and he smiled back.

CHAPTER 10

Praying under her breath, Jeanna pulled into the parking lot, then cringed against the car seat and stared at the Provincial House. Could she find the courage today to walk inside? Just then a short, plump woman walked around the large building and Jeanna slid down in her seat. She wasn't ready to have anyone see her yet. The woman walked closer and Jeanna gasped. "That's Mabel Pranger! What is she doing outdoors alone?"

Jeanna frowned and sat up straight and watched as the elderly woman stumbled around a car. She was dressed in a baggy, cotton-print dress with fuzzy pink slippers on her tiny feet. She looked around furtively, then walked across the parking lot toward a clump of trees. She stumbled, caught herself, and walked on.

"She's running away!" Jeanna clamped her hand to her mouth and stared wide-eyed at Mabel Pranger. With a shiver, Jeanna slipped from the car and ran lightly across the grass at an angle with Mabel. She intercepted her at the edge of the woods. "Mabel." Jeanna caught her arm.

With a shriek, Mabel jerked in alarm and lifted scared, brown eyes. Deep wrinkles lined her face and neck and arms. "Oh, Jeanna! It's you!" Mabel burst into tears and clung to Jeanna. "Help me. Please, help me!"

Jeanna stood helplessly with her arms around Mabel while she waited for the tears to stop. Mabel smelled like dirty clothes and a hint of garlic. "Why are you running away, Mabel? You know you can't manage on your own."

Mabel wiped her tears away with her knuckles and lifted her wrinkled face to Jeanna. "Nurse Wilder is trying to kill me."

Fear stung Jeanna's skin, but she didn't let it show. "Now, Mabel, that isn't true."

"But it is!"

"Let's go back inside and get you back to bed. I'll stay with you until you're feeling better."

"I won't feel better until Nurse Wilder is caught and punished for what she did."

Jeanna shivered just thinking about Nurse Wilder. A grasshopper landed on Jeanna's foot, then jumped off. She walked Mabel off the grass and back to the paved parking lot. "Forget about Nurse Wilder, Mabel. You can't stay out here any longer. Please, let me help you back inside."

Mabel hesitated, her eyes watchful. A fly buzzed around her head and she swatted it away with a wrinkled hand. A car on the street honked. An airplane flew overhead across the bright summer sky.

"You're tired, Mabel. You must rest."

Mabel nodded. "I am tired," she said in a weak voice. "I'll go inside if you promise to help me, to keep me safe from Nurse Wilder."

Jeanna hesitated, then nodded. "I promise."

"I really don't want to go inside."

"I'm right beside you." Jeanna forced back the prick of fear as she walked toward the wide front doors. She

didn't want to face Nurse Wilder just yet. It would be
better to speak to Dr. Browne first, or even Mrs. Dillen.
"We have to get you back."

"But Nurse Wilder might see me."

"I'll make sure she doesn't." Jeanna looked around,
her heart hammering. No one was in sight. "The coast
is clear. Do you think you can hurry?"

Mabel pressed her hand to her heart. "I'll try."

Jeanna gripped Mabel's pillow-soft arm and walked
her into the front door. Several patients sat in the
lounge. Sue Gaylord had her back to the door. No one
noticed them as they walked through the reception area
and into the hall that led to Mabel's room. Nurse Wilder
wasn't in sight. The antiseptic smell stung Jeanna's nose.
The sound of sobbing echoed through the halls. Finally
they reached Mabel's room and Jeanna closed the door
and leaned weakly against it. The room smelled closed
in and musty.

"I do think I'll lie down awhile," Mabel said weakly
as she kicked off her slippers. "You won't leave even
if I fall asleep, will you?" She lifted wide, brown eyes
to Jeanna. "You promise!"

"I won't leave." Jeanna helped Mabel get into bed and
pulled a blanket over her. Jeanna sank to the chair near
the bed and watched Mabel wearily close her eyes. She
was asleep in seconds.

Restlessly Jeanna walked around the small room. She
picked up a book to read the title, touched a plastic rose
that Mabel especially liked, and rubbed the dust off the
small table. Why had she promised to stay? She had
to find Dr. Browne and talk to him and tell him what

she had seen Nurse Wilder do.

Jeanna stood at Mabel's side and listened to her deep, even breathing. "She won't know if I'm not here." Jeanna opened the door a crack and peeked into the hallway, then jerked back in alarm. Nurse Wilder was walking toward Mabel's room with an angry look on her thin face.

Frantically Jeanna looked around for a place to hide, but the room was too small. Maybe she could make it to the tiny bathroom. She moved and the doorknob turned. In a flash she jumped behind the door and flattened herself against the wall. Perspiration dotted her face and hot needles of fear pricked her skin.

The door swung open and she caught it to keep it from closing by itself. She held her breath and waited.

"So, you're back, Mrs. Pranger," Nurse Wilder said grimly. "Don't pretend to be asleep! It won't do you any good." There was no sound and Jeanna wanted to peek around the door, but she didn't move even a muscle.

"You're lucky that you're asleep," Nurse Wilder hissed. "That gives you a little more time. But you just wait! I'll be back soon with something special for you." She hurried out, leaving the door open.

Jeanna waited and finally pushed the door closed. Her heart hammered so loud she was sure everyone could hear it. How could she face Nurse Wilder? It was too frightening to think about.

Just then the door opened and before Jeanna could move Dr. Browne stepped in. He stopped short when he saw Jeanna. The color drained from her face and her tongue clung to the roof of her mouth.

"Dr. Browne, I must speak to you!" She stood before him, her hands clenched in front of her, her chest heaving.

"I thought you didn't work here, Jeanna."

"I came to talk to you, and then I saw Mabel and visited with her. She's asleep now. If you have the time I'd like to tell you something." Why couldn't she tell him? She sounded like a babbling toddler who couldn't find real words to say.

He shot back the white cuff of his jacket and glanced at his watch. "I suppose I can take a few minutes to listen to you."

Jeanna rubbed her hands down her jeans. "It has taken me a long time to get up my courage, but I finally did."

He glanced toward the sleeping Mabel, then looked impatiently at Jeanna. His white coat hung open to reveal a white shirt and gray slacks.

Jeanna moved restlessly. Could she really go through with this? "I know the truth about Grace Meeker's death."

Dr. Browne's eyes widened behind his glasses and the color drained from his face. "The devil you say! Explain yourself!"

"You remember I was there just after she died."

He nodded.

She licked her dry lips. "I know why she died." Her voice broke.

Dr. Browne rubbed his balding head. "I don't know what you think you know, but she was old and she died. Her heart stopped."

Jeanna shook her head, her face pale and her eyes wide. Nervously she twisted a curl around her icy finger. "I tell you I know the truth!"

Dr. Browne stepped toward her, his eyes narrowed into dark slits. "That's too bad, Jeanna."

Mabel groaned and sat up.

Dr. Browne sputtered and backed away from Jeanna.

Mabel waved a lined hand at Dr. Browne. "Oh, Dr. Browne, you must help me and Jeanna. Nurse Wilder is after us." Mabel awkwardly pushed herself up and clung to Jeanna's arm. "She's trying to kill me!"

"Now, now." Dr. Browne patted Mabel's shoulder. "You don't know what you're saying."

"But I do."

"Lie back down, Mabel," Jeanna said softly. "You're getting too excited again and it's not good for you."

"She's right, Mabel." Dr. Browne gripped the frail arm. "I don't know what makes you think Nurse Wilder is after you. She works here and she wouldn't harm you in any way."

"She killed Grace and now she's trying to kill me."

The color drained from Dr. Browne's face.

Jeanna caught Mabel's thin hand and held it. "What do you mean, Mabel?"

"I found out that Nurse Wilder gave Grace the wrong medication and now that she knows I know what she did, she plans to force me to take something that I'm not supposed to take. She thinks I took it today, but I fooled her and dumped it in my new plant."

"Are you sure of this, Mabel?" Jeanna wanted desperately to believe Mabel so that she could be rid of the guilt she'd carried.

"I'm quite sure, Jeanna. Just ask Dr. Browne." Mabel looked up into the doctor's strained face. "You told me not to take that medication, didn't you? You said it was wrong for me. Didn't you?"

He nodded, looking suddenly old and haggard.

"See, Jeanna! I am right! He said I shouldn't take it and Nurse Wilder is trying to force me to just the way she did Grace! She wants me dead, too."

Dr. Browne jerked the door wide. "I'll see about this. You two stay right here while I get to the bottom of this. Remember! Don't leave here and don't speak to anyone about this. You never can tell who might be a friend to Nurse Wilder and warn her that I'm on to her."

"We'll stay right here," Mabel said eagerly, shaking her head. "And I won't take anything she tries to give me. I won't!"

"I'll be back soon." Dr. Browne closed the door.

Jeanna rushed to it and peeked out. Two patients shuffled down the hall, but there was no sign of Nurse Wilder.

"This is too exciting for me." Mabel sank to her pillow with a tired sigh. "I'm too old for this."

Jeanna chuckled. "Me too, Mabel." Oh, was it possible that Nurse Wilder had caused Grace's death just as she'd suspected? If so, maybe she could start to live again. Soon everything would be in the open. Tears stung her eyes. For weeks now she'd believed that she was guilty of someone's death. And now it looked as if it wasn't true. Why had she waited so long to deal with the mess?

"She really was going to kill me." Mabel bobbed her gray head. "Dr. Browne said not to take the medication and then the nurse waltzed right in and said I had to. Well, I fooled her. I took the little plastic cup. When she turned her back, as fast as a mouse zips into his hole, I poured it in that planter. And then I snuggled down against my pillow and closed my eyes and I played dead the best I could. She walked out of here as if she owned the place. I had to force back a giggle. She'll have to get up pretty early to fool Mabel Pranger!"

Jeanna smiled stiffly and patted Mabel's arm. Hopefully Dr. Browne would return before Nurse Wilder did.

"We better see if that woman is coming. She's stronger than she looks and if she's desperate, she could get us both down." Mabel pushed her feet into the fuzzy pink slippers, then crept to the closed door, inched it open, and peeked out.

Jeanna stood on tiptoes and peered into the hallway over the top of Mabel's head. Nurse Wilder turned the corner and headed toward them. Jeanna's heart dropped to her feet and she jumped back just as Mabel did.

"What're we going to do now?" Mabel whispered, plucking at Jeanna's arm.

"We'll have to hide." Jeanna looked around in desperation, then grabbed Mabel and half-dragged her to the tiny bathroom. She pushed her inside, then squeezed in after her, closing the door quietly and carefully.

The rank odor rose around Jeanna and she pressed

her hand over her mouth and nose. Mabel huddled against the sink, her eyes wide and fearful and her hands locked over her heart.

No sounds came from the other room. Maybe Nurse Wilder hadn't come to the room after all.

Finally Jeanna slowly opened the door and looked out, her heart in her mouth. The room was empty. With a sigh of relief she opened the door wide and motioned for Mabel to follow her. "We must not stay here!" Maybe she should take Mabel home with her until everything was settled. But would it be safe? Mabel wasn't strong at all. Jeanna reluctantly abandoned the idea. "We'll go find Dr. Browne and he'll keep us safe from Nurse Wilder."

"Maybe we should call the cops." Mabel's eyes sparkled and she clasped her hands together. "I can sure tell them some stories!"

"They might not believe you."

"You're probably right."

"Let's go. Are you sure you can make it?"

Mabel nodded, her eyes sparkling. "I can do anything I set my mind to."

Jeanna chuckled. "Good for you."

Stealthily Jeanna crept down the hall with Mabel beside her. A radio played loudly from a room beside them. At the end of the hall she stopped and peeked around the corner. She stiffened and gripped Mabel's arm. Dr. Browne stood near the front door deep in conversation with Nurse Wilder. They were too far away for Jeanna to hear what they were saying. It didn't look good and she dodged back and pressed against the wall. "Mabel, I think it would be a good idea to get out of here. I have Dad's car. We'll go find help. Maybe Kip."

"Kip would help." Mabel nodded. "He's a fine boy. He'll know what to do. One day he stopped Nurse Wilder from yelling at me."

"Let's go. If I walk too fast for you, tell me." Jeanna didn't like the way Dr. Browne and Nurse Wilder had looked as they talked. Maybe the nurse had convinced him that she hadn't given Grace or Mabel the wrong medication. Butterflies fluttered in Jeanna's stomach. They had to find help. Kip would be glad to help. Just thinking about him warmed her heart and then brought tears to her eyes. But he might not want to see her or talk to her again.

They reached the back exit and Mabel pulled on the door. It was locked and she looked frantically at Jeanna. "What'll we do now?"

"We'll find a way to get out." Jeanna sounded surer than she felt. Maybe they were worrying over nothing. Dr. Browne might not take Nurse Wilder's word over theirs.

"We could climb out the window in my room."

"They're barred."

"So they are." Mabel nodded her head. "Might be that's why they are. I say a person shouldn't ought to have to stay in a place with bars on the windows. Seems like prison, don't you think?"

Jeanna didn't answer as she crept along the hall. An old man shuffled by, ignoring them. Two women wearing faded bathrobes stood in a doorway and watched them without speaking.

Just then Nurse Wilder turned the corner, a tray in her hand. "Jeanna Shaneck, what are you doing here!"

Jeanna stopped dead.

Mabel shrieked and grabbed Jeanna's arm. "We're goners for sure!" Mabel cried. "We're goners!"

Nurse Wilder's blue eyes stabbed into Jeanna. "I asked you, what are you doing here?" Nurse Wilder's brown hair was almost hidden under a white nurse's cap. Her face darkened with anger. "Answer me this minute!"

Jeanna forced back the fear that threatened to immobilize her. She squared her shoulders and lifted her chin. "I have learned the truth about Grace Meeker's death! I am no longer afraid of you or of what you said that I did. *You* caused Grace's death with the wrong medication. *I* didn't! And *you* are trying to give Mabel the wrong medication."

Mabel nodded. "Yes, you are. Yes, you are! But I didn't take it and I won't take it. I am not going to die like Grace did."

Nurse Wilder shifted the small tray from one hand to the other as she strode toward them, cutting away the distance quickly. "You don't know what you're talking about! I did not give the wrong medication! I never have and I never will!" She gripped Mabel's arm and Mabel screamed.

Jeanna grabbed the nurse's wrist and squeezed. "Release her this instant! I'm taking her out of here."

"We'll see about that! I'll call the orderlies and they'll put you right out of here and Mrs. Pranger will be forced to do what we say." Nurse Wilder's cheeks flamed red and sharp darts of anger shot from her eyes. "Jeanna, release me instantly, or you'll be very, very sorry!"

Jeanna hesitated, then dropped her hand to her side. She wasn't strong enough to forcibly take Mabel away.

Nurse Wilder caught Mabel's wrist.

"Let me go!" Mabel shouted, struggling weakly against the nurse's strong grip. "You can't kill me like you did Grace! I'm too young to die!"

"I'm not going to kill you, you silly old woman! Get to your room where you belong!"

Jeanna looked around wildly for help. Several patients poked their heads out the doors, but didn't move to help. She'd have to find Kip or Dr. Browne or someone else that might help. Even if Dr. Browne didn't believe her story, he'd check on Mabel to see that she was all right.

In a flash Jeanna ran down the hall, her shoes slapping against the tile floor and her heart drumming painfully against her rib cage. Where was help when she needed it badly? Silently she cried out to God.

The smell of coffee drifted from the kitchen. Someone screamed and she wondered if it was Mabel. A bitter taste filled Jeanna's mouth. She knocked on Mrs. Dillen's office door, then tried to open it. It was locked and her heart sank. Wildly she looked up and down the hall. Just then Dr. Browne stepped out of his office and she ran to him calling, "Dr. Browne!"

He stopped short and turned to her with a frown. "I told you to stay with Mrs. Pranger in her room. What are you doing here?"

Jeanna swallowed hard and tried to steady her racing heart. "Nurse Wilder is with Mabel right now and she's going to force her to take something she shouldn't take and I said I'd get help." Jeanna grabbed his arm. "Please, help her! I know Nurse Wilder gave Grace Meeker the wrong medicine and now she wants to do the same with Mabel Pranger!"

Dr. Browne unhooked her fingers and moved back. "My dear, you are entirely too emotional about this. Wait in my office while I check on Mrs. Pranger."

Jeanna shook her head and her curls bounced. "I'm going with you! Mabel needs me!"

Dr. Browne sprang forward and gripped Jeanna's arm and forced her into his office. "I said to wait here and that's just what you're going to do." He pushed her into a chair and she stared up at him with wide, startled eyes. "I want you to stay here! I'll take care of this matter!" He slammed out of his office and she sagged weakly in the chair beside a cluttered desk. Files lined the walls and a Christmas cactus stood on a book-lined bookcase. A diploma hung on the wall behind the desk with a large photograph of a graduating class.

Jeanna wrapped her arms around herself and fought back the chills that shook her body. She had to go to Mabel to reassure her that everything was going to be all right. With trembling legs she walked to the door and grabbed the knob. It wouldn't turn and she tried again. How could it be locked? And why?

She stumbled back from the door and looked around for another exit. The office window was covered with bars and her heart sank. She spotted a closed door next to the files. She ran to it and opened it. The room was small, but pleasant with a sofa, a desk, and two chairs. Several plants hung at the two windows. Bright sunlight filled the room. She ran to the door and it opened easily into a small hallway that led to a back door. Someone stood beside the door. The woman turned and Jeanna stopped dead in surprise.

"Grandma? What're you doing here?"

Carolynn hurried to Jeanna. "I've been looking for you. I saw your car out front, but nobody knew where you were."

"I came to tell the truth, only to find Mabel Pranger in trouble. We have to help her, Grandma! Nurse Wilder is trying to kill her!"

Carolynn frowned. She'd made arrangements to meet with Gil to introduce him to his birth mother. When he didn't show up, she'd gone looking for Jeanna. "Are you sure?"

"There's no time to explain. Dr. Browne went to see what he could do. He told me to wait in his office, but I couldn't."

Carolynn's eyes widened. "Dr. Browne? Let's go!" Carolynn opened the outside door and she ran through into the bright sunlight with Jeanna beside her.

Two minutes later they stood outside Mabel's closed door. Just as Jeanna reached to open it, Nurse Wilder stepped out. Jeanna jumped back with a shriek. Carolynn stood her ground.

"You can't go in. Dr. Browne is with the patient." Nurse Wilder's eyes darkened with rage and she clenched her fists at her sides. "Thanks to you, Jeanna

Shaneck, I lost my job. And I need this job! You and your accusations!"

Jeanna lifted her chin. "You wanted me to think that I was to blame for Grace's death, and all the time it was you. Well, you can't keep me a prisoner of fear any longer!"

"She's right," Carolynn said crisply.

Nurse Wilder ignored Carolynn and faced Jeanna squarely. "Maybe I was wrong to blame you for Mrs. Meeker's death, but you're wrong to accuse me. I gave her the right medication. Dr. Browne told me what to give her, and I did. Just like he did with Mrs. Pranger. Only I wasn't strong enough to hold the feisty woman down and give her anything. Dr. Browne is giving it to her now."

From inside Mabel screamed and the sound ripped through Jeanna. She pushed Nurse Wilder aside and opened the door with a loud crash.

Carolynn ran into the room, caught Dr. Browne's arm just as he was ready to inject Mabel with a needle, and wrested it from him. "No, you don't, doctor!"

Dr. Browne jumped back from Carolynn, a wild look on his face. "Who're you?" He didn't wait for an answer, but turned to Jeanna, his face dark with rage. "How did you get out of my office? I locked you in!"

Mabel cringed in the corner of her small bed. "He tried to kill me, Jeanna. He said I know too much to stay alive. It was him and not Nurse Wilder that killed Grace. He ordered the nurse to give the medicine to Grace. He told me!"

Dr. Browne turned with a growl. "Shut your mouth!

You stupid fool!"

Jeanna gasped and shook her head in disbelief. He was a doctor! How could he do such a terrible thing?

Carolynn stepped forward. "I think you have some explaining to do, doctor."

The man sank back. "Both of you leave immediately!"

Carolynn shook her head. "It's too late for that. I know what's been going on here."

Puzzled, Jeanna looked at her grandmother.

Dr. Browne groaned. "What have I done? How can I keep my terrible secret?"

"You can't!" Carolynn snapped. She looked out into the hallway and motioned to Nurse Wilder. "Come in here. You'll want to hear this."

Nurse Wilder walked hesitantly into the room, looking questioningly at Dr. Browne.

Mabel pushed out of bed and huddled beside Jeanna. "It wasn't her after all. It was him! He found out Grace left him some money and he said he couldn't wait for it. And then after she died and I found out that she'd been given the wrong medication, and then found out that you knew too, he said he had to get rid of me and you."

"Oh, my!" Jeanna shivered and clung to Mabel.

"Is this woman crazy, doctor?" Nurse Wilder asked sharply.

"Of course she is," he said in a weak voice.

"She's absolutely correct," Carolynn said briskly. She had to be careful not to say too much or she'd give herself away to Jeanna. "I think it's time to call the police." Carolynn picked up the phone, pushed nine for an outside line, then Farley's office number. As quickly as she could she told him what had transpired.

Several minutes later the sheriff and his deputy walked out with Dr. Browne.

Carolynn stood in the doorway while Nurse Wilder tucked Mabel safely in bed.

Jeanna kissed Mabel's wrinkled cheek. "I'll come see you tomorrow, Mabel. Rest now."

"I will. We had quite an adventure, didn't we?"

Jeanna nodded, then turned stiffly to Nurse Wilder. "I am sorry for making trouble for you."

Nurse Wilder lifted her chin. "I honestly thought you had caused Mrs. Meeker's death. I was wrong. I had no business trying to keep you away from here. You're welcome to come back to work when you want."

Jeanna nodded with a slight smile.

Nurse Wilder smiled stiffly at Carolynn. "I suppose I should say thank you for being here when we needed you."

"I suppose so," Carolynn said with a grin.

Nurse Wilder frowned and hurried away.

"I'll walk you to your car, Jeanna," Carolynn said.

"Thanks, Grandma."

Carolynn laid an arm across Jeanna's shoulders. "I saw a young man in the front looking for you."

Jeanna's pulse quickened. "Kip?"

"Yes. I think it's time you told him what's been going on here."

"He might not want to talk to me."

"He will." Carolynn kissed Jeanna's cheek. "It's always better to face the situation head-on."

"I'll try."

In the reception area Jeanna glanced around for Kip. "I don't see him."

"Maybe he went home. Find him, Jeanna, and talk to him."

Jeanna smiled. "I will, Grandma."

Carolynn hurried outdoors to her car. She'd track down Gil Oakes and see why he hadn't kept his appointment.

Jeanna turned to look one more time just in case Kip was sitting behind a big plant. As she turned back she caught sight of him walking down the hall. He wore jeans and a white tee shirt. He saw her and his eyes lit up.

She waited for him. "Can we talk?"

"Where were you? I looked all over!"

"Come with me, please." She led him to two chairs in a private corner. "Now I can tell you the truth."

He frowned. "About what?"

"Why I couldn't come back here." Jeanna turned so she could look into his face. He looked as if he was wearing an ice mask. She stumbled over the first words, then quickly told him everything. "I hope you understand why I couldn't come here before today," she said stiffly.

"You don't have to say another word about it. I've heard enough."

"What's wrong with you?"

He turned hard, brown eyes on her. "Should there be something wrong, Jeanna?"

She swallowed. "Not any more."

"Fine." He turned away from her.

"I don't understand you, Kip! You've been after me to tell you what's been bothering me, and then when you finally know, you freeze me out."

"Drop it, Jeanna." He rushed outdoors toward his car. Jeanna ran after him. "Kip, wait! What's wrong?"

He faced her, his eyes blazing. "Why couldn't you trust me enough to tell me sooner?" He climbed in his car and roared away.

She slid into her car and leaned back weakly as a sick feeling churned in the pit of her stomach.

"I'll never see him again," she whispered. "He's done with me for sure." A feeling of devastation swept over her and she closed her eyes. Never again would she feel his arms around her, nor would she glory in his kisses. What was she going to do now?

Was it possible to win his love?

She jerked forward. "Yes, yes, it is! Kip, here I come! Be prepared!"

Chapter 11

Just as Carolynn started to pull out of the Provincial House parking lot, Gil drove in. She smiled and backed up, swung around and parked beside his blue two-door. She frowned. Two-door. The real estate woman had said the killer had driven a two-door car. "What a suspicious person you are, Carolynn Burgess," she muttered as she got out. Gil Oakes had absolutely no connection with Gwen Nichols. Not every man who drove a two-door car was under suspicion. Andy Nichols drove one. But then he had an alibi.

Carolynn smiled as she got out of her car and walked to Gil who was standing by his car. He wore a lightweight, gray suit with a pink shirt and a flowered tie. A warm breeze tugged at his brown hair. "Hi, Gil. I was ready to give up on you."

He ducked his head. "I got scared."

"I'm glad you finally came. Let's go inside and meet your mother."

Gil trembled. "What's she like?"

Carolynn wanted to say, "Don't ask," but she said, "Wait and see."

"Will she hate me?"

Carolynn rested her hand on Gil's arm. "Don't be frightened, Gil. Do you want me to pray for you before we go in?"

He stiffened. Pray? Right out here in the open? "I guess I can make it. Thanks anyway."

Carolynn tucked her hand in his arm and walked inside with him and up to Sue. The roses on the counter filled the reception area with their aroma. "We came to see Nurse Wilder. Could you ring her, please?"

"Sure, Mrs. Burgess." Sue looked curiously at Gil, but didn't ask about him. She spoke into the phone, then hung it up again. Smiling, she said, "She's in her office. She said to tell you she has only a few minutes."

"Thanks, Sue." Carolynn walked with Gil to Nurse Wilder's office. Carolynn wondered if the nurse had collected herself since the upsetting incident with Dr. Browne. Knowing Nurse Wilder, she was probably already running the place.

Gil shivered. "I don't know if I can do this."

"Sure you can." Carolynn knocked, then walked in. She tugged gently on Gil's arm.

Frowning, Nurse Wilder stood behind her desk. "I hope you're not bringing the press for a juicy story, Mrs. Burgess."

"Not at all." Carolynn stepped away from Gil. "Bess Wilder, this is Gil Oakes."

Bess frowned at Gil. "Do I know you? You look familiar."

Gil balled his hands at his sides. In an unsteady voice he told her when and where he was born. "Does that mean anything to you?"

Bess sank weakly to her chair. "Should it?"

Carolynn tried to excuse herself, but Gil begged with his eyes for her to stay. She tipped her head in agreement. She sat on a chair against the wall and crossed her legs. The room seemed small and crowded because of the high tension. The sun shone in streaks through the white vertical blinds.

Gil repeated the date and place of his birth. With his hands on the desk, Gil leaned down toward Bess. "You gave birth to me."

Bess's eyes widened and she looked as if she was ready to faint.

"I'm the infant son you put up for adoption."

"It can't be," Bess whispered.

Carolynn felt sorry for her.

"I'm Gil Oakes. I went to my adoptive parents without a name and they named me."

Ashen, Bess groaned.

"My adoptive father left when I was six. My adoptive mother, Alma Carter, raised me."

Bess moistened her dry lips with the tip of her tongue. "I don't know what to say."

"Aren't you glad to see me?" Gil whispered. She had to be glad! It was supposed to work that way. She was supposed to take him in her arms, kiss him all over his face, bake chocolate chip cookies for him and read him bedtime stories at night.

"It's such a surprise. I don't know how I feel." Bess pushed herself up. "I don't have time for this. I have work to do."

Gil felt as if he'd been kicked in the gut. She didn't want him!

Carolynn saw the anguish on Gil's face and felt his pain. "Perhaps you could set up another time to meet," Carolynn said softly as she stood beside Gil to give him support.

Bess nodded. "Yes. I'd like to do that."

Carolynn patted Gil's arm. How had it happened that she'd become such a mother to him? Well, she couldn't think about that now. "Gil?"

He cleared his throat. "Maybe we could have dinner together."

"Yes," Bess said weakly.

Gil looked at her locked hands. "Tonight?"

Bess hesitated. "Yes. Tonight. At the Checkered Cloth Cafe?"

"That's a nice, homey place," Carolynn said. That's where she and Gil had had their first meeting. But she didn't say that.

"At six?" Gil asked.

"At six," Bess said. She opened the door and motioned for them to leave.

Carolynn smiled and walked out. Once again she slipped her hand through Gil's arm. She felt him tremble and she knew he was struggling to hold back tears.

In the parking lot Carolynn stopped and patted Gil's shoulder. "It'll take her time to get used to having her son. Be patient with her."

"She doesn't want me," he whispered.

"Let her get to know you. She'll learn to love you."

Gil caught Carolynn's hand. "Why can't *you* be my mother? You would never have given me away!"

"No. I never would have." Carolynn's eyes filled with tears. "Give Bess Wilder time to sort out her feelings. I'll be praying for you both."

Gil's heart jerked. Praying for them! Would it make

a difference? He cleared his throat. "Thank you."

"Talk to you later." Carolynn walked toward her car, turned and waved. He looked lonely and sad and her heart went out to him. "Are you going to work?" she called.

"Maybe later."

"I have errands to run, but Robert would enjoy having you drop in on him. He could show you his birdhouses."

Gil almost choked on a sob. Was Carolynn for real? Would Robert really be happy to see him? "I really should go to work."

"Remember what I said. Jesus loves you." Carolynn waved again, then drove away.

Gil sat in his car a long time. Life was so unfair! He wanted a mother to love him — a mother like Carolynn Burgess.

Much later, he drove out of the parking lot and pulled off to the side of the street. He stayed there until Bess Wilder drove out, then he followed her. He wanted to know where she lived and what she did with her time away from work.

He followed her to a small, green house on Pine. She parked outside the garage, then hurried to a side door and let herself in. The front yard was neatly mowed but there weren't any flowers or shrubs like at the Burgess house. White blinds covered all the windows so he couldn't see Bess Wilder walking around inside.

He glanced at his watch, sighed, then drove to work. He'd meet with his birth mother at six to talk. Maybe when she got used to having him around, she'd learn to love him.

*   *   *

Her mouth set stubbornly, Silver Rawlings unlocked the front door of her house. Cool air rushed out to meet the warm air. Behind her, Brittany gurgled and giggled in Holly's arms. Silver glanced back. She knew Holly wouldn't approve of her plan, so she hadn't told her the decision she'd come to during the middle of a long, sleepless night. Silver pushed the door wide and waited until Holly walked through with Brittany. The house was pleasantly cool and still tidy. Silver set her bags inside and closed the door again.

"Silver, are you sure you want to come home so soon?" Holly asked as she set Brittany on the carpet beside the couch.

Silver nodded. "Why should I give up my home because of what Tim did? He should be the one to move out."

Holly helplessly shook her head. Dark rings circled Silver's eyes. Her hair hung limply on her shoulders. She wore the same jeans and shirt as yesterday. "Silver, talk to him. Give him a chance to explain, to make things right with you."

Silver squared her shoulders. "I don't want to hear what he has to say. He ruined our lives." And he'll pay! But she kept that to herself.

Holly talked a few more minutes, then left for work.

Silver took a deep breath, then picked up the phone and called Sheriff Farley Cobb. It took awhile to get through to him, but she waited patiently, her heart frozen forever.

"What can I do for you, Mrs. Rawlings?"

"Call me Silver." She would never, never be called Mrs. Rawlings again!

"Silver."

She watched Brittany smear the picture window with two little handprints, then turned away from her. She couldn't do what she'd planned if she looked at Brittany. "I know who killed Gwen Nichols."

Farley sucked in air. He wanted to sound calm, but it was going to be hard. "Who did?"

"Tim."

"Your husband?"

He wouldn't be her husband for long! "Tim Rawlings. I saw him do it, but I didn't want to say."

"Does Carolynn Burgess know this?"

Silver frowned. "Why should she?"

"You should've called her."

"There's no need."

"Are you home?"

"Yes."

"Is Tim with you?"

"No."

"I'll be right there." Farley hung up and immediately called Carolynn. She wasn't in and Robert didn't know when she'd be back. "When you hear from her, have her go right over to the Rawlings' house, will you?"

Silver turned from the phone, picked Brittany up, and carried her to the kitchen. "Are you hungry, Brittany?" Silver put the baby in the high chair. "I'll make you a peanut butter and grape jelly sandwich.

You can eat that and drink milk from your sippy cup. Won't that be nice?"

Later she tucked Brittany in her crib for a nap, changed into white slacks and a white blouse. She brushed her hair, pulled it back into a pony tail, then ran downstairs to let the sheriff in.

He fingered the brim of his hat and studied her. Her eyes looked glazed, but other than that she looked fine.

"Shall we sit down?" she asked.

"Sure." He sat on the flowered chair and pulled out his notebook. "Tell me why you think Tim killed Gwen Nichols."

Silver perched on the very edge of the couch and locked her icy hands together. "Gwen wanted to see Brittany and I didn't want her to. I drove to the church and when I got there Tim was there on his bike. He yelled at Gwen, then he hit her hard with the tire iron. I tried to stop him, but he was like a crazy man. He stuck the tire iron in my car, then came back home on the bike. I drove home."

"Did you have the baby?"

Silver frowned. "No."

"Did he?"

"Well, of course. He wouldn't leave her home alone. She's a baby."

"Where's Tim now?"

"At the church I suppose."

"Does he know you planned to tell me this?"

She shrugged. "It really doesn't matter, does it?" She twisted the ring on her finger. "Could I get you something? A glass of water? Soda?"

"No thanks. I'm fine." He couldn't understand her. She seemed like a different person. "Did something happen?"

"Happen?"

"To make you tell."

"I just thought it was the right thing to do." The lies burned her tongue, but she wasn't about to back down. Tim deserved to die for what he'd done.

Farley glanced toward the door, hoping Carolynn would show up. He turned back to Silver. "Why'd he kill Gwen Nichols?"

"Why?"

"What was his motive?"

It was fuzzy to her. She hadn't thought of motive. Suddenly she remembered what Andy Nichols had said. "Gwen wanted the baby back. She was going to take me to court and get the baby back."

"But the adoption papers are legal. She would've lost the case. Tim would know that."

Silver spread her hands. "I suppose you'll have to ask Tim. He'd know his motive."

Farley didn't believe a word she said, but he couldn't just let it go. Where in the world was Carolynn Burgess when he needed her?

At that moment Carolynn pulled her car up behind Farley's. She stepped out of it just as Lavery stopped at the curb.

"Snooping again, Carolynn Burgess?"

Carolynn managed a smile. "Visiting a friend. And you?"

"Investigating a murder." Lavery flipped back her

black hair. "I think you're doing the same."

"How's Andy Nichols?"

"Why don't you ask him? I understand you've been snooping around."

"Just curious." Carolynn pushed a strand of hair off her cheek. "I hear you're going on vacation."

"Not until this case is solved. Dud tried to get me to go early, but I refused." Lavery narrowed her eyes. "Were you behind that? Were you afraid I'd finally learn the truth about you?"

Carolynn sighed. "Lavery, don't waste your time on me. Please excuse me. I'm on my way in to see Silver Rawlings."

"And Sheriff Cobb."

"Yes."

"I want to see him too. I want to know why he hasn't arrested Silver Rawlings. He's been negligent long enough."

"Negligent? That's a pretty strong word."

"But a correct one." Lavery brushed past Carolynn and rang the doorbell.

Carolynn wanted to send Lavery flying, but she stood beside her with a smile on her lips.

Silver opened the door, then frowned. "Carolynn, I wasn't expecting you."

"Is it a bad time?"

"I suppose it's not. Come in. You too, Lavery."

Lavery looked triumphantly at Carolynn, then sailed in.

Farley scowled at Lavery, then lifted a brow questioningly at Carolynn.

She shrugged slightly.

Farley turned to Lavery. "Suppose we go in the kitchen and have a cup of coffee or something and let these two friends talk in private."

"That's not necessary," Silver said briskly. "I want everyone to know Tim killed Gwen."

Carolynn gasped.

Lavery looked puzzled, then pleased. "I'm not a bit surprised. Not after hearing Andy's story."

Carolynn took Silver's arm. "Let's talk, shall we?"

Silver jerked away from Carolynn. "We have nothing to say."

Carolynn's nerves tightened. Silver must've learned about Tim's affair. "We need to talk privately, Silver. Right now!" Carolynn's command took Silver by surprise and she reluctantly agreed. "We'll go to the kitchen." Carolynn gave Farley a look that said, "Keep Lavery out."

He grinned and nodded.

Carolynn caught Silver's arm and led her to the kitchen, then outside to the deck where Lavery couldn't possibly overhear them. "All right, Silver, what's going on?"

Silver felt like a child again. She sank to a deck chair and whimpered.

"Why would you lie about Tim?"

"Because of what he did to me," Silver whispered in anguish. "Carolynn, he had an affair with Gwen Nichols! Brittany is his natural child!"

Pulling a chair close to Silver, Carolynn sat down and took Silver's icy hands in hers. "I'm sorry to hear that. I know it must be devastating. But, Silver, you know he didn't murder Gwen. He couldn't any more than you could."

"He deserves to go to prison! He deserves to die for what he did to me!"

"Silver, look in your heart. Jesus loves you. And Tim. Jesus says to love. Tim sinned. But, Silver, that doesn't give you the right to sin too. Does it?"

Tears filled her eyes. "I can't let him get away with what he did."

"He's not getting away with it. Think of the turmoil in his heart. Think of the guilt he feels."

"Why are you siding with him?"

"I'm not! I want you both to work through this horrible thing. I want you to be a happy family — you, Tim and Brittany. You can't be if you take revenge."

Silver's jaw tightened. "We can't be anyway. Tim ruined everything."

"You can get help to get through this. You can forgive Tim."

"No way!" Silver jumped up. "I can't listen any more, Carolynn! I want Tim to pay."

"Silver!" Carolynn snapped, leaping to her feet. "I won't let the sheriff arrest Tim. It would give the real killer a chance to escape — to get away with murder. It would ruin Tim. And the sheriff too. I won't let that happen!"

Silver crumbled and burst into tears. "What can I do? I hate Tim for what he did!"

Carolynn pulled Silver close and patted her back. "Let God take away the pain and the hatred."

"I can't. I just can't. I'm too angry."

Carolynn silently prayed for Silver. "This is one of the greatest tests in life you'll ever have, Silver. Will you let God rule you or will you give the devil place in your life? It's your choice."

Several minutes later Carolynn walked back inside, leaving Silver alone on the deck. Lavery and Farley were sitting in the living room talking about the weather.

"Sheriff, I'm sure you know Silver was under a great deal of pressure and didn't mean what she said." Carolynn sank to the edge of the couch as far away from Lavery as she could sit. "She's upset with Tim and wanted to hurt him. Sheriff, you know he's innocent, don't you?"

"Since when are you the judge and jury?" Lavery snapped. "I want to see the man jailed!"

"You want to be able to say your case is closed," Carolynn said sharply. "It's not closed at all!"

Farley sighed heavily as he pushed himself up. "I hate things like this. See you ladies later."

Lavery hurried after Farley. "You can't just ignore what Mrs. Rawlings said."

"Sure can." Farley looked back and gave Carolynn a wink, then hurried out.

★   ★   ★

Her stomach fluttering, Carolynn sat in her den and scanned the print-out Jay Sommers had put together for her of murders similar to Gwen's in the past year. There were three of them — one in Belding, one in

Kalamazoo and another in Grand Ledge — all within forty miles of Middle Lake. All three women had given birth to a child she put up for adoption through Children's Services. Carolynn sat back, her eyes wide. Meg Butterworth had gone to Children's Services to put her unborn baby up for adoption. She'd been attacked. "Is there a connection?" Carolynn whispered. A shiver trickled down her spine.

Gil Oakes worked at Children's Services. Carolynn frowned at where her thoughts were taking her. There were other men who worked at Children's Services also. Like Andy Nichols. He worked for a cleaning crew who cleaned the offices of the Children's Services. Another man worked with him — Mike Russo. She'd met him when she'd gone to talk to Andy at work. Mike had said Andy missed work more than he should, and if he missed any more he'd be fired.

Carolynn leaned back in her rocking chair and looked unseeingly at the plants on the table in front of the window. Gil Oakes had been adopted and he now worked at Children's Services. Andy Nichols felt very strongly about birth mothers keeping their babies. Mike Russo had been raised in a foster home. Andy had a connection with Gwen. The others didn't to her knowledge. Was there a connection she didn't know about? To top it off, all three drove two-door cars. She'd checked even though she'd felt terrible doing it. She didn't like being suspicious of everyone.

She tapped her leg with the print-out. What about the tire iron planted in Silver's car to make her look guilty? Andy knew about Silver. But what about Gil and Mike? What about a million other men it could be? The tire iron didn't fit any of their cars, but that would make it too easy.

Carolynn brushed her hair back. Children's Services would have the addresses of the adoptive parents. She'd thought it always came back to the tire iron, but it really always came back to Children's Services. That was the connection of four deaths and attempted murder — where Meg Butterworth was concerned.

Robert walked in with a dish of chocolate ice cream in his hand. "There you are." He held out the dish. "Want some?"

"No thanks." Carolynn held up the print-out. "Can you listen a minute?"

"Sure." Robert sat on his recliner and took a spoonful of ice cream.

She told him what she'd been thinking. "Any holes in it?"

"You've made a pretty big leap I'd say."

"It's just that the three of them have access to records. Or could have if they wanted to." Carolynn moved restlessly. Lately she'd been wrong in some of her deductions. Maybe she was again. It felt strange to feel unsure of herself when it came to this kind of thing.

"I guess you'll have to check into it further. You might find somebody else who has motive and opportunity."

Carolynn giggled. "I love it when you talk like that."

Robert chuckled. "Motive. Opportunity. Deductive reasoning. Alibis. Suspects. Is it working?"

Carolynn ran to him and hugged him, then kissed

him. His lips were cold from the ice cream. "I love you, Robert."

"I love you, you little detective, you."

★　　★　　★

Fighting back tears, Jeanna stood at her back door. Kip had gone away — probably to keep from seeing her. His parents wouldn't tell her where he'd gone. Mick had said he'd promised not to tell.

Blacky whined at Jeanna.

She bent down and scratched around his ears. "We're alone, Blacky. Mom and Dad went out on a date. Mick and Adrial went to the lake with the church youth group." Jeanna sank to the grass and pulled Blacky close. "I wish I would've believed Kip when he said he loved me." Just how long would it take him to fall out of love? He'd done it often enough with other girls. Jeanna looked up at the bright, blue sky. "Heavenly Father, give me strength to stand. I don't want to give up on Kip. Take care of him wherever he is. Comfort him and fill him with peace."

★　　★　　★

Tim walked in the front door and stopped in surprise. Silver was home! With a glad cry he ran through the house until he found her in their bedroom. "I've been so worried!" The words died in his throat when he saw his clothes piled on the bed with luggage opened nearby. "What's this?"

Silver turned; her eyes had a hard and angry look. "You're leaving."

Helplessly he shook his head. "I can't. I won't. Don't ask me to."

"You ruined any chance for us, Tim. Now, get out!"

"Please listen to me, Silver. Honey, I love you!"

"Don't even say the word! You don't know what love is or you would've stayed faithful to me."

He hung his head. "I know. Don't you think I've kicked myself over and over for what I did?"

"Does Al know? Did he ask you to be his assistant pastor knowing what you did?"

"I didn't tell him. It was in the past. I'd repented of it."

"I'm going to tell him. The whole miserable story!"

"Don't! Don't do it, Silver. I'm too ashamed to let anyone know."

"Too bad!" Silver flung a shirt on the pile of clothes. "I told the sheriff you killed Gwen. I wanted him to arrest you!"

Tim blanched. "How could you do that?" he whispered.

"Because I want to get even."

"I don't blame you. So, why didn't he arrest me?"

"Carolynn Burgess stopped him. She tried to convince me to forgive you." Silver's chest rose and fell. "I told her I couldn't and I wouldn't!"

In defeat, Tim tossed his clothes in the luggage. The closets looked bare without his things hanging beside hers. "I won't leave. I'll sleep in the guest room. I don't want you to be alone. What if the killer comes for you?"

Silver trembled. She'd been too angry to think of that. "You can stay in the spare room."

Tim wearily picked up the messy luggage.

"And the minute the case is solved, you're leaving. We're getting a divorce and I'm keeping Brittany."

Tim slowly walked out. He was getting just what he deserved.

Deep in his heart he heard, *"What about My grace?"*

"I don't deserve your grace," Tim whispered as tears spilled down his cheeks.

"Grace is not earned. It's a gift."

Tim dropped to the edge of the bed and covered his face with trembling hands.

★   ★   ★

The man sat in his car, down the street from Meg's house. His stomach was knotted and he drummed the steering wheel to release his mounting tension. If he couldn't kill Meg before she delivered, he'd count himself the failure his mother had always said he was.

He'd watched the police car cruise past and had learned they did it every hour. He could easily kill Meg while they were cruising another street.

Suddenly he had another idea, one more brilliant than the last. Why not kill Meg in the hospital when she went in to deliver the baby? She'd be alone in her room some of the time. He could put on hospital gear and no one would even question his presence. He could slip right into her room, say a few comforting things to her, then kill her. He touched the knife on the seat beside him. A knife would be so perfect — quiet and easy to hide as he made his getaway.

"Now I won't have to watch her house," he muttered as he drove away. He'd know when she went into labor.

He chuckled. "You're an absolute genius!" No matter what Mother had said. "I am brilliant!"

He stopped at a red light, then another thought hit him. What if Meg started labor in the middle of the night and delivered quicker than they expected?

Impatiently he shook his head. "You think too much. Take it easy. You'll be able to accomplish your great plan." He smiled and nodded. He deserved to feel good. He deserved to be proud of himself. He laughed and drove a little faster.

Chapter 12

In the Checkered Cloth Cafe Gil fumbled with his fork and almost dropped it. He set it carefully on his salad bowl and managed to smile at Bess Wilder. She looked different in her pale-yellow suit with shoes to match and a deeper-yellow blouse. Her eye makeup made her eyes appear wider than they actually were. Her lips were bright-red. She looked younger than she had at her office in her white uniform. He glanced down at himself and barely managed not to make a face. He wore the same suit, but had put on a clean white shirt. He had only one suit. Would she notice? Did she think he looked all right?

Gil darted a look around the cafe. Country music was playing in the background. The other customers talked and laughed as they ate at the round tables covered with various colors of checkered table cloths. Gil turned back and watched Bess eat a tomato from her salad.

She felt his eyes on her and the tomato lost its flavor.

"What shall I call you?" Gil asked, trying to keep his voice normal.

Bess shrugged. She struggled with what to say and how to act toward the man who claimed to be her son. Her son! "I hadn't thought of it. What do you want to call me?"

Mom or Mommy, but never Mother. Mother had raised him, had beaten him, locked him in his room, made him go without food. No, not Mother. "How about — Melanie?"

"I haven't been called that in years."

Gil balled his napkin in his lap. This wasn't going like he'd planned. When he was alone he'd said her name aloud over and over — Melanie Reeve, Melanie Reeve, Melanie Reeve. In his mind he always called her Mommy. "Don't make me call you Mrs. Wilder, please."

She wasn't Mrs. Wilder anymore anyway. The divorce had gone through a couple of days ago. "Make it Bess." She moved restlessly.

He tipped his head slightly. "I can do that."

She tried to eat a slice of radish, but it stuck in her throat. She drank a swallow of water and finally washed it down. She lifted her eyes to his. "How did you find me?"

"It took me a long time." He watched a family at a nearby table eating and laughing. That's what he wanted. What did a family even find to laugh about? He turned back to Bess and wanted to ask her about families, but he didn't. "I asked questions. Wrote letters."

"Oh."

"Did you ever — think about me?"

Feeling as limp as an old dishrag, Bess took another drink of ice water, then dabbed her mouth with her red checkered napkin. How could she answer his question? It would sound so heartless. But then she'd been without a heart for years. "I did at first, then I trained myself not to."

He leaned eagerly toward her. "I always thought about you! I wanted to know what you looked like." Mother had been of a medium build with dyed blonde hair and blue eyes that never looked into his heart. "And what you smelled like!" Mother had smelled as if she never took a bath. "I wanted to know what your voice sounded like." Mother's had been harsh and shrill.

Bess chewed a bite of lettuce, but barely swallowed it around the lump in her throat.

Gil ate a few bites of the yeast roll without tasting its delicious flavor. He rubbed butter off his fingers with his napkin. "Why'd you give me away?"

"Because I couldn't keep you," Bess snapped. She lowered her voice and leaned toward him, her eyes bright with unshed tears. "I was seventeen. Unmarried. And my parents kicked me out."

He tried to understand, but he couldn't. If he had a baby, he'd never give him away. "Did you ever look for me?"

"No!" She'd studied faces of little boys for years, wondering if he was one of them. "I signed a paper saying I wouldn't try to see you or talk to you or contact you in any way."

"I'd never do that to my baby."

"I did what I had to do!" Color blazed in her cheeks and she wanted to run away from his accusing look.

A man stopped at the table with a questioning look at Gil and a smile for Bess. "Hi, Bess."

She almost dropped her napkin. Sherard Roscoe of all people! He wore jeans, a plaid shirt and wide red suspenders. "Hello, Sherard." She struggled to sound normal. "Sherard, this is Gil Oakes. My — a young man I've just met."

A sharp pain pierced Gil's heart. She couldn't claim him as her son! She was embarrassed of him! "Hello," Gil mumbled.

"Glad to meet you, Gil." Sherard smiled, then looked closer at Gil. "Do I know you? You look familiar to me."

"You don't know him," Bess said sharply. If only he knew!

"Bess and I are old friends. We go way back when she was still known as Melanie Reeve. I've been trying to get her to have dinner with me for a long time."

"Don't, Sherard." Bess felt at a loss for words. She couldn't let Gil or Sherard know they were father and son. She'd never told Sherard she was pregnant. She frantically searched for something to say. "Sherard is the janitor at Middle Lake Christian Center — the church where that young woman was murdered the other day."

"Is that right?" Gil was too upset to get pulled into a conversation with Bess and the man.

Sherard pulled up a chair and sat down. "It was bad news all right — a murder in a parking lot. I was working late that night. I probably left just before it happened. I even saw the murdered girl. She came into the church looking for somebody." Sherard shook his head and clicked his tongue. "Sad thing, all right."

Gil took a bite of fish and searched his mind for a way to tell the man to get lost. Why didn't Bess send him away? Did she like the guy?

"I know who you look like!" Sherard laughed as he wagged his finger at Gil. "My nephew Paul. You look like my nephew Paul Roscoe. Do you know him?"

Gil shook his head. Why didn't the man leave them alone?

Bess sat very still, her stomach a ball of ice. "Sherard, give me a call tomorrow about dinner, will you?"

He smiled and nodded, then finally put the chair back at the neighboring table, and walked away.

"I thought you were married," Gil said impatiently.

"Divorced."

"Children?"

Just you, she thought. "No."

"How come?"

Bess shrugged. They'd wanted children, but had never had any.

He ate without speaking and listened to others around him having a good time. He'd expected tonight to be different — to be wonderful. He noticed she'd eaten most of her chicken and potato. "Do you want dessert?"

"No thanks." She knew she was too tense to eat another bite. "I have to go home. I have to go to work early."

He wanted to hold on to her, keep her with him forever, but he knew where she lived. He could go to see her anytime he wanted. He would let her go right now. He nodded. "I'll walk you to your car."

"It's not necessary." Were her legs strong enough to carry her to the car?

He peered closely at her. She looked pale and shaken.

"Are you all right?"

"Of course!" She lifted her chin. "You don't have to start watching out for me."

"But I want to!"

She frowned. "How do I know you're really — who you say you are?" She couldn't make herself say the words — my son.

Gil felt a sob rise and he forced it back. It wouldn't look right to cry in the cafe where others could see him. Hadn't Mother said over and over, "Sissy tears! You always are crying those sissy tears! You are a sissy!" Gil cleared his throat. "I have proof. The records from the adoption agency. My birth certificate."

"Why didn't you hunt down your birth father instead of me?"

"His name's not on the certificate. What's his name?"

"I've forgotten," she said gruffly. Abruptly she stood and picked up her purse. "I don't have time to stay here like this."

Gil jumped up. "Can we get together again?"

"I don't know if we should."

"For breakfast?"

She frowned. "No! I'll think about it and give you a call."

"I'll call you. Or stop in and see you."

"Don't you dare make me lose my job! I need that job." She started for the door, but he caught her arm. His touch sent a shiver through her. She looked at him and saw the same expression she'd often seen on Sherard's face years ago. "What'd you want?"

"I'm glad we finally met," Gil said softly. "I want to

get to know you better."

Tears stung her eyes. Abruptly she pulled away and ran to her car.

Gil paid the check and walked to the sidewalk in front of the cafe. He watched Bess drive away and he smiled. If he wanted, he could drive right to her house to see her. Maybe she'd invite him in for a cup of cocoa. She would learn to love him. It'd just take time.

★   ★   ★

Carolynn walked slowly out of the library where she'd read the microfilms of newspapers of the murders Jay Sommers had given her reports on. In each case the adoptive parent or parents were suspects because the murder weapons were found in their possession. Had the same man killed all three of the women as well as Gwen, and had he tried to kill Meg Butterworth?

A bitter taste filled Carolynn's mouth. Was this case bigger than she'd thought? Farley would certainly be interested in what she'd learned.

Carolynn drove past the Checkered Cloth Cafe. Gil's car was parked across the street from the cafe. He was inside right now with Bess Wilder. Carolynn bit her lip. Should she stop in and see how the meeting was going? She shook her head. It wasn't her place to do that. Robert always told her she tried to solve the problems of the world and get involved in lives she shouldn't get involved in. But she couldn't help it. She wanted to right wrongs, help heal broken hearts.

She thought of Meg Butterworth again. Thankfully Christa was helping Meg. Carolynn slowed for a car

pulling out of a parking lot. Yesterday she'd talked to
Logan Dimarco, the boy who got Meg pregnant. He
was frightened and didn't want to take any
responsibility for Meg or the baby. After talking to
Logan, Carolynn had crossed him off as a murder
suspect. He was too busy thinking of himself and how
much fun he could have. He wouldn't give Meg or the
baby enough thought to consider murdering her. And
he didn't have any connections with the other women.
He'd been a long shot, but Carolynn had checked him
out anyway.

She frowned thoughtfully. What was keeping her
from finding the killer? Was it because she was afraid
who it might be? What if it was Tim Rawlings? What
if Silver was telling the truth, but telling it in such a
way that no one would believe her?

"Stop it, Carolynn! Your thinking is all twisted up."
She wrinkled her nose. Somehow she had to get back
on track. It wasn't like her to reach a wrong conclusion.
And now that she was afraid she might, it made things
even worse. She wouldn't let that happen! "God gave
me a strong mind," she said loudly. "I won't accept
anything else!"

★   ★   ★

Tim finished the hamburger he'd fried for himself
just as Silver walked in the kitchen wearing her apricot-
colored nightgown and blue bathrobe.

"Brittany's hungry," Silver said defensively. "Or I'd
never step foot in here while you're here."

"Don't do this, Silver. We can share the house." He

wanted to beg her to listen to him, but he'd already said it too many times. She was too hurt and too angry. He didn't blame her a bit. "I want to talk to you after Brittany's asleep."

"We have nothing to say to each other!"

★   ★   ★

Andy Nichols stood outside the Rawlings' house, his face dark with anger. Lavery had told him what Silver had said. He'd suspected all along that one or both of them had killed Gwen. "They'll pay for Gwen's death!" Andy muttered. He crept to the side window and looked in. The room was dark and no one was in it. He inched his way to the kitchen window. Silver and Tim were standing on either side of the square table. They looked angry and they were talking, but he couldn't hear what they were saying. If he could get inside, he could take Brittany and drive away with her. He had every right to her. He was her uncle! Gwen had been wrong to give Brittany up without discussing it with him or Mom and Dad. They probably would've agreed with her. Andy's jaw tightened. They always took her side over his. All his life he'd wondered why, then when he was sixteen, he'd learned he was adopted. No wonder they loved her more! She had been born to them.

He walked to the front door and stealthily tried the door handle. It was locked. He doubled his fists and lifted them to hammer on the door, then dropped his arms to his sides. He didn't dare warn them of his plan like he had when he said he'd take them to court and take Brittany away from them.

Slowly he walked to his car, watched the house awhile longer, then drove away. He was sleepy, too sleepy to wait around for a chance to steal Brittany.

* * *

Tim took a deep breath and tried to keep calm. "It's not about what I did."

Silver stiffened. "What else is there?"

He set the catsup and mustard in the refrigerator and closed the door. "I don't want us to reject God's promises because of how we're feeling."

"Always the minister," she said mockingly. She took a graham cracker out of the box and filled the sippy cup with milk.

His heart tight with pain, Tim leaned against the counter. "Will you come back downstairs to talk to me?"

She wanted to say no, but she found herself agreeing. She thought of what Carolynn had said about this being the biggest battle she'd ever have to fight. It was! Just because she listened to Tim didn't mean she had to stay married to him. "I shouldn't be more than half an hour."

"Fine." He watched her walk away and he groaned. How could he be so stupid to ruin his life with Silver for a moment of pleasure with Gwen?

Later in the living room Tim sat in the flowered chair, gripping the arms. Silver curled on the couch with her legs tucked up under her, hugging a throw pillow. A lamp cast a soft glow in the room. The blinds were closed, shutting out the world.

"Well? What'd you want to say, Tim?"

He took a deep breath. How could he say anything when Silver was acting so hard-hearted? Silently he asked the Lord for just the right words. "In my deep despair earlier today God spoke to me about His grace. He forgave me for what I did because I repented and asked Him to. But I couldn't forgive myself — not without His grace. Grace is God giving me the ability to do something that I can't do on my own. Of course, grace is much more than that. But I needed that facet of His grace to be able to forgive myself."

She frowned.

"It doesn't mean I was right in what I did. I sinned! I know that more than anybody. I deserve to die for it, but God's grace is there for me." Tim leaned forward. "And there for you, Silver. God can help you forgive me even though I don't deserve it."

Silver wanted to run away, but she couldn't. She listened to him as he continued talking. Tears filled her eyes and she tried to blink them away. She jumped up, but before she could run away, he caught her.

"Please don't go." He wiped her tears away, then pulled her close. "Oh, Silver, I love you so much! I'm sorry, so sorry for what I did to you."

She tried to push away, but it felt good to be in his arms again. Slowly she wrapped her arms around him.

He held her a long time, then lifted her face and kissed her as if he'd never let her go.

Hungrily she returned his kisses. Suddenly a picture of him with Gwen flashed across her mind and she pulled away with a cry. She pushed his hands off her and ran to the stairs. Her eyes blazing, she looked over her shoulder. "Don't you ever do that again!"

He sank to the edge of the couch and buried his face in his hands.

★   ★   ★

Sweat popping out on her face, Meg felt another contraction filling her with pain. She couldn't stand yet another one! She'd checked into the hospital just after midnight, but now she wanted to run away and not face what was coming.

"Relax, Meg," Sarah said frantically. "The nurse said it's important to relax."

"It — hurts too much," Meg gasped. The contraction subsided and she was without pain again. She turned to Sarah on a chair beside the hospital bed. "I want to go home! I don't want to have this baby."

Sarah felt the same way, but she didn't say so. Mom should be at Meg's side, not off drinking again. Sarah had called Jeanna and she was coming even though it was so late. It'd help to have Jeanna there even if she couldn't be in Meg's room. Sarah tried to smile at Meg. "Labor won't last much longer, then it'll all be over."

"It's taking too long!" Meg cried.

Just then Carolynn Burgess peeked her head in, smiled and said, "Hi, girls."

"Hi!" they said happily.

"Jeanna called me."

"We're glad," Sarah said in relief.

Carolynn walked to Meg. "How's it going?"

"Not very well."

Carolynn patted Meg's arm. "I came to pray with you. Is that all right?"

Meg nodded. Just having an adult with her who cared helped.

Carolynn turned to Sarah. "Jeanna's out in the hall. Go out with her if you want and I'll stay with Meg."

"Is that okay, Meg?" Sarah asked, willing her to agree.

"Sure." Meg was thankful for Sarah, but she was too tense and worried. It was easier to have Carolynn Burgess with her.

Sarah smiled. "See you later."

"We'll call you if Meg needs you." Taking the chair Sarah had vacated, Carolynn leaned close to Meg. "Giving birth is a natural process, Meg. Your baby knows it's time to come out and see the world. And he's fighting to do it. As you relax and help him, it makes it easier for him."

"But it hurts so much!"

"It'll hurt less when you relax." Carolynn held Meg's hand. "I'm going to pray for you and for your baby."

"Okay," Meg said in a little-girl voice.

"Heavenly Father, you're with Meg and her baby right now. In Jesus' name, fill her with peace. Comfort her. Help her relax. Relieve the pain and help her deliver quickly and easily. We love you and thank you. Amen."

Meg smiled. "Thanks." She gripped Carolynn's hand. "Here comes another one."

Carolynn stroked Meg's head and talked soothingly to her until the contraction was over.

"Will you stay with me until the baby is born?" Meg whispered.

Carolynn hesitated a second, then nodded. "I'll have to get the doctor to agree, though."

"She will." Meg groaned. "Another one!"

Carolynn once again stroked Meg's head and quietly prayed for her. The soft murmur of voices drifted in from the hall.

Meg closed her eyes and moaned. "I don't like this. I don't like it at all!"

"If it hurts to stay on your back, turn on your side, Meg. If that doesn't work, sit up."

Meg looked at Carolynn in horror. "But the nurse said to stay in bed."

"She won't mind a bit if you get up since I'm with you."

"If you're sure."

"I am." Carolynn helped Meg try different positions. She settled on sitting in a chair.

"It feels better," Meg said in relief. She laid her hands on her swollen stomach. "Why did you come, Mrs. Burgess?"

"To be with you." Carolynn couldn't tell her that she was afraid for Meg's life. "This is not the time for you to be alone."

"Logan should be here. I called him, but he hung up on me." Tears filled Meg's eyes. "He says this is probably not even his baby. But it is! He's the only boy I've ever been with." Meg rubbed at her tears. "It's not fair, is it? That I should go through all this pain and Logan doesn't suffer at all."

"One of these days he'll have to deal with having a baby somewhere out there. He might try to forget this baby is his, but he won't be able to. When he's older and married and has a family, he'll remember this first baby of his. Only with God's help will he be able to forgive himself and let the baby go."

Meg didn't know if she believed Carolynn, but she nodded anyway. Just then another contraction began. She gripped the arms of the chair and closed her eyes. She thought of the baby pushing into the birth canal to get out and she smiled.

A few minutes later Dr. Leigh Meadows walked in, a stethoscope around her neck. She wore red slacks and a red jacket with a white blouse. "I thought I'd find you in bed, Meg."

"It's easier here." Meg introduced Dr. Meadows to Carolynn. "I'd like her to stay with me until after the birth."

"Are you family?"

"No. A friend. Meg doesn't have anyone else except her sister to stay with her. Her sister is too young."

Dr. Meadows nodded. "You may stay with her. I'll ask someone to get you a gown." She turned to Meg. "I'll have to have you get back on the bed so I can see how you're coming."

Several minutes later, Carolynn stood at Meg's side in the delivery room. Meg sat on a special delivery chair instead of lying down with her knees up.

"One more push and the baby will be here," Dr. Meadows said cheerfully. "Keep up the good work, Meg."

"I'm trying," Meg said weakly.

Carolynn wiped sweat from Meg's forehead. "You're

doing a fine job."

Soon the baby was in the doctor's hands, crying at the top of his lungs. "A healthy baby boy, Meg."

"A boy?" Meg smiled at the baby, then with a surprised look on her face turned to Carolynn. "It's a boy, Mrs. Burgess."

"How wonderful!" Carolynn kissed Meg's cheek. "Congratulations."

"I never thought about it being a boy or girl. It was only the baby."

Dr. Meadows handed the baby to Meg. "Seven pounds even and nineteen inches long."

Meg held the baby to her. "Seven pounds. He looks so tiny. It's a boy! And he's really cute. Don't you think he's cute, Mrs. Burgess?"

"He's beautiful, all right!" Tears shining in her eyes, Carolynn remembered the birth of her four children. She touched the baby's soft cheek with her fingertip. "He really is beautiful!"

"A boy," Meg whispered, looking in awe at the newborn in her arms.

Later Carolynn stood at the nursery window with Jeanna and Sarah. There were five babies in the nursery. Meg's baby was in a clear plastic crib pushed close to the window. His eyes were dark slits in his round, red face. He moved his head and fists and made sucking noises with his mouth.

Sarah finally turned away. "He's real, Jeanna. A real baby."

"I know," Jeanna whispered. She moved close to Carolynn. "I'm glad you're here, Grandma."

"Me too."

"The adoptive parents are coming tomorrow. Children's Services already called them." Sarah's voice broke. "I don't know if I can let him go. He's my nephew and I'll never get to see him again."

Jeanna slipped an arm around Sarah to comfort her.

Carolynn laid her hand on Sarah's thin shoulder. "God's peace is yours, Sarah. He'll help you let the baby go because it's for the baby's good. The parents will love him and care for him better than Meg or your family could."

"I know," Sarah whispered. "But it's still hard."

Carolynn talked a few minutes more, then walked to Meg's room. She felt uneasy about leaving Meg alone. Carolynn sat on a chair near the bed and watched Meg sleep. Farley had said he'd send a policewoman to guard Meg. He'd promised to play it low key.

With a long sigh Carolynn leaned her head back and closed her eyes. Today had seemed like five days.

The next morning before seven Carolynn covered a yawn as she walked into Meg's room. She'd felt an urgent need to be with Meg until she checked out to go home.

Meg sat on the edge of her bed, sobbing as if her heart would break.

Carolynn took her in her arms. "There, there."

Meg lifted a tear-wet face. "I don't want to give my baby boy away. I want to keep him."

"I know you do. You love him. But think about your home life, your age. Your baby will need a lot of attention and love and care. How can you give him what he needs? Right now you must think about the baby."

Just then the man started to walk into Meg's room, then stopped. She wasn't alone! Would he ever find the perfect time to kill her? Frustrated, he eased out and stood just outside the door where he could hear the conversation between Carolynn Burgess and Meg Butterworth.

"Mother-love is a strong love, Meg," Carolynn said. "Mother-love thinks of the baby first. What would be better for him? A home with parents able to care for him? Parents who'd prayed for him to be their own baby? Through Children's Services you were able to say you wanted Christian parents. The couple who want to adopt him are Christians."

The man knotted his fists and his heart thundered. He was too late! The baby was born and ready to be given away! Meg wasn't alone and probably wouldn't be.

"Mrs. Burgess, how will I survive without my baby?" Meg asked tearfully.

"With help from God."

The man crept away from the door and hurried out to his car. Maybe he could wait by Meg's house and kill her when she got home. He whimpered. He'd failed. Now the baby would have to endure years of living with adoptive parents. But Carolynn Burgess had said that was better for the baby. Could that be true? He shook his head. It wasn't true! He knew it for a fact.

In the hospital room Meg dried her tears. "I want to keep my baby. I never thought I would, but I do."

"Think about the baby, Meg. Think of his needs."

"He's so adorable!"

"I know." Carolynn squeezed Meg's shoulder. "Why don't you write a long letter to your baby? Tell him who you are and why you must give him to someone else — parents who'll love him and raise him right. Tell him how you feel and how much you love him. Someday he'll want to know that so he doesn't feel rejected by you."

"Why can't I keep him?"

"Because of your circumstances and your age. Because of your baby's needs."

Just then Mrs. Breech from Children's Services walked in carrying the baby. "I brought him in to you one last time, Meg. I want you to make sure you really want to sign the papers to give him up."

Carolynn saw the pain flash across Meg's face, then the joy when she took the baby in her arms.

Meg kissed the baby's fuzzy head, then nuzzled his fat cheeks. "I love you, baby boy. I'll always love you and remember you." At long last, Meg held the baby out to Mrs. Breech. "I'll sign the papers."

"The adoptive parents will take very good care of him. They're waiting for him to take him home. He'll have a fine Christian home."

"She wants to write a letter for them to give to the baby when he's old enough to understand," Carolynn said softly. "Will you take care of it?"

Mrs. Breech nodded. "The adoptive parents will understand and will keep the letter for the baby."

"Did they choose a name for him?" Meg asked

tearfully.

"Yes. But I can't tell you what it is." Mrs. Breech held the papers out to Meg. "Please sign them."

Meg sobbed as she took the papers.

Carolynn held her hands out to the baby. "May I hold him?"

Mrs. Breech hesitated, then gave her the baby.

Carolynn held him close and silently prayed a blessing over him. When the paperwork was finished, she held the baby out for Meg to kiss him one last time, then handed him to Mrs. Breech.

Sobbing, Meg reached for Carolynn's hand and clung to it as Mrs. Breech walked out.

After a long time, Carolynn opened her purse and pulled out a notebook and ballpoint pen. "Write him a letter, Meg." Carolynn laid an envelope on the stand. "Seal it in here when you're finished. I'll see that Mrs. Breech gets it and sends it on to the adoptive parents."

"Thank you," Meg whispered. She bent over the notebook and started to write.

Chapter 13

Smiling, Gil knocked on the door of the green house on Pine Street. He held a bouquet of summer flowers behind his back.

Frowning at being interrupted so early in the morning, Bess opened the door. Her heart plunged to her feet. "Gil! What're you doing here?"

"I came for breakfast." He thrust the bright bouquet toward her. "These are for you."

"Thank you." Bess took them reluctantly, then motioned for him to come in.

"What's for breakfast?"

"I already ate."

"Will you cook breakfast for me? Just like a mommy does for her little boy?"

Pain wrapped around Bess. "Come to the kitchen."

Gil followed Bess through the sparsely furnished living room into the small kitchen. The aromas of coffee and toast hung in the air. The table was big enough for only two people. The walls and cupboards were white. A bright-yellow cup stood upside down in the white dish drainer. A bright-yellow tea kettle rested on the gas stove.

Bess stuck the flowers in a vase and filled it with water. The red, gold, yellow, orange and pink flowers looked bright and bold against all the white. She touched the flowers gently, then turned to Gil. "I can make you some toast and coffee. Or tea. I have milk too." She felt nervous with him in her house.

"Milk. Milk and toast." He sat at the table and smiled at her. "Two pieces of toast. With jelly. You got any jelly?"

"Grape jam."

"I like that. Grape jam." He chuckled, crossed his arms, leaned contentedly back in the chair, and watched her drop two pieces of whole wheat bread in the toaster, then fill a glass with milk from a half-gallon jug.

"I have to hurry to work."

He caught her wrist. "Not until you bake me a batch of cookies!"

She twisted free and rubbed where he'd touched. "I don't have time."

His face hardened. "Then take time. You're not leaving until you bake me cookies!"

Her heart lurched at the look on his face and the tone of his voice. Was he going to get mean? "What kind of cookies do you want?"

He laughed and shrugged. "I don't care."

She looked in the cupboard. "Oatmeal cookies?"

"I guess that's okay. Thanks, Mommy."

★   ★   ★

Jeanna walked wearily across the yard toward the Jennings' swimming pool. Shouts and laughter met her, but she couldn't force even a smile to her wide lips. She'd begged Mom to let her work long hours the past few days so she wouldn't have time to miss Kip. A tear slipped down her cheek and she flicked it away.

"Hi, Jae. Come on in!" Adrial shouted with a wave where she stood with Mick in shoulder-high water.

"It's too hot to stand out there," Mick said with a grin.

"I'll be in soon." Jeanna spotted Sarah, hesitated, then walked toward her.

"Hi, Sarah. How's Meg?"

Sarah stood alone near a lounge chair draped with several towels of bright shades. "She's all right, I guess. She cries a lot."

"I'm glad you could come today."

"Me, too."

"Mom told me Meg's going to go to camp in a couple of weeks where she'll have special attention and help."

Sarah nodded. "She's afraid to go, but I know she'll love it." Sarah bit her lip. "I feel terrible that I couldn't help her. I should have been able to." Sarah bowed her head and the bright sunlight turned her hair into spun gold.

Jeanna reached out and touched Sarah's arm. "There are some things that we can't do, Sarah. It isn't your fault that you couldn't help Meg. She needed something that you couldn't give her."

Sarah lifted her head. "Do you really believe that?"

"Yes."

"I feel so guilty because it feels good not to have to watch her constantly. Am I terrible?"

"Never! You're wonderful. You've always been there for Meg. I'm sorry I wasn't always there for you. You are my best friend and I'll never forget it again."

"Thanks." Sarah smiled through sudden tears, then hugged Jeanna.

She smelled the chlorine on Sarah's damp skin. "Best friends always, Sarah?"

"Yes. Best friends always."

Jeanna smiled, but her eyes were still filled with a great sadness. "I wish I could settle things with Kip."

"Is he coming today?"

"Probably not. He's staying as far away from me as he can get."

"I really thought he loved you."

Jeanna's heart leaped at the thought, then sank. "I wish he did, but he doesn't."

Sarah caught Jeanna's arm. "Look! There's Kip now. He has a girl with him."

Jeanna clutched her belt ties and slowly turned. Kip! He looked wonderful! Her legs trembled as she looked at the blonde girl walking beside Kip. It was Sheila Montcalm and she'd been after Kip for a long time. Her figure equaled Adrial's and her long hair hung in two beautiful blonde braids. She was devouring Kip with her large brown eyes. Jeanna wanted to shove her into the pool. Kip's arm circled Sheila's narrow waist and jealousy surged through Jeanna, taking her breath away.

"Don't faint, Jeanna," Sarah whispered.

Jeanna stiffened her spine, but inside she'd melted around her feet.

Kip walked right up to Jeanna and stopped in front of her. He smiled, but the smile didn't reach his eyes. "Jeanna, I believe you know Sheila Montcalm. Sheila, Jeanna Shaneck."

"It's a beautiful day for a party, Jeanna. I'm glad I could come."

"Have fun, Sheila." It was hard for Jeanna to push the words out. "You, too, Kip."

He turned from Jeanna to smile into Sheila's eyes. "I will have. Sheila, are you ready to swim now?"

"I'd like something to drink first, Kip."

"A Coke maybe?"

"Sounds good."

Without a look at Jeanna, he walked away with Sheila, his arm firm around her waist.

Jeanna dropped to a chair, the color drained from her face.

"Are you all right?" Sarah asked softly.

"No, but you go ahead. Jimmy wants you."

Sarah hesitated, then ran to the pool and jumped in beside Jimmy.

Jeanna shivered, even though the afternoon sun was hot. Water splashed on her and she jumped, then looked up to find Greg Malloy dripping water all over. He grinned and she managed to smile back. Water ran from his dark hair and over his face and down to the cleft of his chin. His eyes were as blue as the water in the pool.

"Hi," he said. "How would you like to get wet? This is a swim party, you know, but you don't seem to be joining in. So, I appointed myself your official dunker. If you're not in the water on your own steam within five seconds, I'll toss you in."

She laughed, a real laugh, and it felt good. "All right. I'll go in." She pulled off her cover-up and dropped it on the pile of towels.

"Your time is up." He grabbed her and she squealed,

then they jumped into the water together. Water closed over her head and it felt soft and cool against her hot skin. She swam the length with Greg beside her, then they played keep-away with a red-and-white beach ball. Twice she bumped into Kip and her body burned from the touch for several minutes after. He didn't seem to notice her and that hurt more than she cared to admit.

Finally she pushed herself out of the pool and sat on the edge with her feet dangling down. Greg pushed himself up beside her and leaned toward her with a smile.

"Now, you look alive again, Jae."

"Thanks to you, Greg." She smiled and before she knew what he was going to do, he leaned closer and kissed her damp lips. She jerked back with a quick look around. Her eyes clashed with Kip's steely eyes. Abruptly he turned away and she shivered.

"I'll get a towel for you." Greg grabbed an orange and green towel and draped it around her and she held it as if it was a lifeline.

"Thank you." Her throat felt too dry to speak clearly.

"Do you want something to eat? There are plenty of sandwiches and chips and cookies."

"Nothing, thanks, but you go ahead."

"Thanks. I am hungry. I'll be right back."

She looked around cautiously for Kip just as he popped up at her feet. Her stomach tightened.

"Looking for me?"

"Should I be?"

Water streaming off him, he levered himself out of the pool and sat beside her, the smell of chlorine strong.

"Where did the boyfriend go?"

"He's not my boyfriend," she said stiffly. Every fiber of her being was aware of Kip. Could he hear her heart hammering? "Your girl friend is probably looking for you."

"Probably."

"Not as hard as I am." The words hung between them. Had she really said that?

He tensed. "Why should you want to find me?"

"We have something to settle between us."

"You already settled it."

She shook her head and tried to stop trembling. "We need to talk."

"Kippy," called Sheila just then with a wave.

"Kippy?" Jeanna lifted her brows and Kip made a growling sound deep in his throat. "Run along and play, Kippy. Come see me when you're ready to talk."

He shot her a startled look, then slipped into the water and swam to join Sheila.

Jeanna weakly pushed herself up and walked away from the pool and away from the party. She couldn't stay and watch Kip with another girl. Her hand trembling, she opened the back door of her house. Her legs almost gave way as she walked inside.

★   ★   ★

From the chair on the deck, Silver watched Brittany fill the little blue-and-red pail with sand from the sandbox Tim had built for her a couple of months ago. He'd worked hard on the sandbox with the blue canopy over it and had been proud when he finally finished.

Tears filled Silver's eyes. Tim loved Brittany. Was it fair to separate them? Was it possible to stay married to him and become a family again? He'd said he'd see a counselor if she wanted.

"I don't know what I want," she whispered raggedly.

Just then she heard the gate creak and she jumped. Was the killer after her? Or maybe it was Andy Nichols coming to harrass her again. It was Tim and she sighed in relief.

"I asked for the day off." Pulling his tie off, Tim walked slowly up on the deck and sat in the chair beside Silver. "I wasn't able to do anything at the church. My mind was on you."

She didn't want to talk about that. "What will you do if Al asks you to resign?"

Tim shrugged. "I have no idea."

"How can you continue to be the assistant pastor after what you did?" she asked sharply.

He rubbed a hand over his face. "If people without sin worked in the church, there'd be nobody working. God's love and grace make me qualified to stay."

She didn't have an answer for that one.

The faint sound of the doorbell drifted out to them. Silver gripped the arms of the chair and looked fearfully at Tim.

"I'll get it," he said.

He hurried through the house, then stopped in alarm when he saw Silver's mother at the door. She looked like an older version of Silver. Tim wanted to send her packing because of her disapproval of them adopting Brittany, but he opened the door and even managed to smile. "Mrs. Terrill, what a surprise."

"I came to see Silver. I heard she's a suspect in a murder."

Tim bit back a cry of alarm. "Where'd you hear that?"

"Somebody called me and told me." Mrs. Terrill frowned. "Don't ask me who. I asked and she wouldn't give me her name. Where is Silver?"

"In the back yard with Brittany."

"I knew no good would come to you if you disobeyed God's laws and adopted that baby!"

Tim's temper flared, but he managed to control it. "We love our daughter. Whether you admit it or not, she's your grandchild. So, get used to it."

"I can't!"

"I don't want to say anything to upset Silver. She doesn't need her own mother to be against her."

Mrs. Terrill frowned. "I'm not *against* her. I just don't approve of adoption."

"Then keep it to yourself. Please." Tim smiled to soften his command. "I love my wife and I want to protect her."

In the kitchen Silver overheard the conversation. She shifted Brittany from one hip to the other. Tim was standing up to her mom to protect her! He'd never done that before. Her heart softened toward him, then she frowned. Not even that would make her open her heart to him again!

★   ★   ★

Carolynn stood in her kitchen and called Gil at work, but the woman who answered said he hadn't come in.

She sounded very upset. Carolynn called Gil's home number and let it ring ten times. He didn't answer. Carolynn thoughtfully tapped her lip with her finger. Maybe he was at the Provincial House to see Bess. Carolynn looked up the number, then called. Sue answered on the first ring.

"Sue, Carolynn Burgess here. May I speak to Nurse Wilder, please?"

"It's really strange, Mrs. Burgess, but she didn't come in. She didn't even call. That's not like her at all. She's always here on time."

"Could you give me her home number?"

"Sure, but I called and didn't get an answer."

Fear trickled down Carolynn's spine. "Give me her address, will you?"

"I wouldn't ordinarily, but since it's you, I will."

Carolynn jotted the address in her notebook, said a quick goodbye, and headed for the door. She had a few questions she wanted to ask Gil Oakes. Suddenly it seemed urgent that she see him.

★   ★   ★

Meg walked listlessly around the house, then stopped in the kitchen. She felt the baby in her arms and smelled his special odor. But of course he wasn't in her arms, he was with his adoptive parents. She moaned. Could she survive without her baby boy?

Sarah glanced into the kitchen and saw Meg staring out the window. "Are you hungry, Meg?"

She didn't turn around. "No."

"I just saw the police car cruise past again."

Meg turned, her eyes wide. "I've been thinking so much about the baby I forgot about somebody being after me." She shivered. "Why would anyone want to kill me?"

"I have no idea."

Meg sank to the edge of a kitchen chair. "What'll I do?"

"I'll stay with you every minute until you go to camp."

Meg nodded while she frantically searched for a way she could get away from Sarah long enough to go to Children's Services to see if she could learn who'd adopted her baby boy.

A couple of hours later, Meg peeked into the bedroom. Sarah was fast asleep. "Now's my chance," Meg whispered. She could easily catch a bus at the corner. If she wasn't so sore, she could walk to Children's Services. As tired as Sarah had been lately, she might sleep a long time. Meg nodded. She could be home before Sarah woke up.

Later Meg walked into Children's Services. She felt as if she'd collapse on the floor, but she managed to walk to the counter and lean heavily against it. The man she'd seen at the computer was there again today. She smiled and said, "Is Mrs. Breech in?"

The man could barely breathe. Here was his chance to kill Meg! But he had no weapon. He forced a smile. "She's having a coffee break, but she'll be right back."

Meg leaned over the counter and whispered, "I need some information. Please, will you help me?"

He heard her desperation and his heart softened. She

was so young! "How can I help you?"

"I was forced to put my baby boy up for adoption, but now I want him back. Will you give me the people's name and address? Please?"

He smiled. She wanted her baby back! Now he didn't have to kill her! He'd get her baby back for her and they'd live happily ever after. He pulled her file up on the computer, but before he could give her the information, Clara Breech walked in. He quickly flipped to another file.

"Meg! Is something wrong?" Mrs. Breech hurried around the counter and took Meg's hand. "You shouldn't be here."

"I want my baby boy back, Mrs. Breech," Meg said brokenly. "I was wrong to give him up."

"It's too late, Meg. He's with his adoptive family. They fixed a nursery for him and named him. They love him very much and are going to take good care of him."

Meg glanced toward the man at the computer, but he kept his face turned. Maybe she could come back later and get the information from him.

Mrs. Breech slipped her arm around Meg's shoulders. "Your feelings are normal, Meg. You miss the baby. I understand totally. Instead of thinking about how much you miss him, think about how happy and cared for you've made him. Because of your love for him, you've let him go to a better life."

The man wanted to leap up and shout for Meg not to listen to Clara Breech, but he sat still with his lips pressed tightly together.

Meg brushed at her tears. "I know you're right, Mrs. Breech. I'm sorry I bothered you. I won't try again to get my baby boy back. He is better where he's at."

The man froze inside. She'd changed her mind again! She deserved to die just for being so wishy-washy! He noticed the scissors nearby and he smiled. It was going to work out after all. When she left he'd follow her and stab her. She deserved the painful thrust of scissors in her heart.

Meg whispered goodbye and walked outdoors to catch the bus. She suddenly felt overwhelmingly tired. The corner where she was to catch the bus seemed a mile away instead of half a block. Hot wind whipped her hair in tangles. Her jeans felt heavy on her legs. A car honked and she jumped.

The scissors hidden at his side, the man ran out behind Meg. He'd get her behind the dumpster where nobody could see them, then he'd kill her.

Just then Carolynn Burgess pulled up at the curb and called, "Meg!"

The man turned, his face ashen, and ran back inside.

Meg blinked back tears as she walked to the car. "Hi, Mrs. Burgess."

"Sarah called me and said she couldn't find you. I told her I'd look for you." Carolynn smiled. She could understand a mother's love. "I knew right where to look. Let me take you home."

Meg slipped into the car and leaned wearily back. "I'm glad you came."

"Me too." Carolynn squeezed Meg's hand, then drove her home.

Chapter 14

The silence of her house soothed Jeanna as she padded upstairs to change from her swimsuit into jeans and a light-blue tee shirt. Her head whirling with thoughts of Kip, she quickly dried off and pulled on clean, dry clothes.

The bedroom door burst open and Adrial rushed in, her face red and her breathing ragged.

"What's wrong?" Jeanna caught Adrial's hand and led her to the chair at the desk. "Sit down before you fall down."

Adrial's eyes filled with tears. "Jeanna, I'm so awful!"

"Why? What happened, Addie? You're scaring me."

"I scared myself." Adrial bit her lip and looked imploringly at Jeanna. "I need you, Jeanna! You've got to help me!"

"How? I'll do anything."

Adrial pressed her hand to her throat. "Mick and I were kissing and I wanted it to go on and on. I wanted more than kissing. Oh, you know! Then I remembered what you'd said — God's strength is mine all the time and I don't have to sin. I knew I'd have to choose. Oh, but it was so hard to resist!"

Jeanna sank to the edge of her bed. "What about Mick?"

"He felt the same way." Adrial gripped Jeanna's hand.

"I don't know if I'll be strong enough to resist the next time. I love Mick so much!"

"And he loves you." Jeanna tried to remember the talks she'd had with her mom and with Sarah. "You both know if you really love each other, you won't have sex before marriage. God really is always with you to help you."

Adrial smiled weakly. "You know, Jeanna, you're different than when I first came. You were so wrapped up in yourself you wouldn't give me any time. I'm glad you got all that stuff settled."

"Me too. I'm really sorry I ignored you so much."

"That's all right." Adrial sighed. "Now if you and Kip could make up, things would be perfect."

"I'm praying," Jeanna said, trying to sound brave and strong.

"I'll be praying too." Adrial took a deep breath. "I don't know if I can go out for pizza with Mick and the others now. It'll be so awkward."

Jeanna shook her head. "It doesn't have to be. Talk it out with Mick and settle it. Then make sure you're never alone long enough to give in to temptation."

Adrial jumped up. "You're right! Thanks, cousin."

Jeanna smiled. Who had the perfect answer for her?

After Adrial left, Jeanna wearily stretched out on her bed and fell asleep. Later she awoke with a start to darkness around her. She rubbed her eyes and sat on the edge of the bed. The house was silent. The red numbers on her digital clock said ten-fifteen. Mom and Dad wouldn't be home until much later.

In the bathroom she splashed cold water on her face,

then patted it dry. The dark circles that had been under her eyes were gone, but she looked sad and lonely and pale. She shook her finger at herself. "I don't care how I look or how I feel, I know things will work out with Kip. They have to!"

Slowly she walked downstairs to the kitchen and clicked on the light. Her stomach growled and she peeked inside the refrigerator to find something to nibble on. She opened a bag of carrot sticks, took out two, and ate them while she fixed a peanut butter and jelly sandwich.

Was Kip sitting with Sheila, eating pizza and talking? Jeanna moaned and shook her head.

The back doorbell buzzed and she jumped. Had she locked out her parents? But they weren't due home yet. She rubbed her mouth and fingers with a napkin as she hurried to open the door. It was Kip. Was she dreaming? She couldn't move to let him in. Finally he nudged her aside and walked in, closing the door behind him.

"Kip?"

"It's me."

"It is! I was afraid it was a dream."

He folded his arms over his chest. He wore jeans and a white tee shirt. "You said you wanted to talk."

She nodded and tried to steady her racing heart. "I did?"

"I thought you did. If not, I'll leave." He turned to the door and she caught his arm.

"Wait! Don't go. Please. I do want to talk. Let's go to the kitchen. I could make you a sandwich."

"I'm not hungry."

In the kitchen she turned to face him, her eyes wide with wonder. "I hope I'm not dreaming, Kip. I've missed you so much!"

"Is that right?"

She nodded. "I was wrong to act the way I did. I should've trusted you."

"You should've."

"I wasn't thinking clearly." The excuse was lame and she knew it.

He stabbed his fingers through his hair. "I've wanted to believe that you love me as much as I love you, but I was wrong. You turned away from me time after time. You sent me out of your life! You didn't trust me enough to tell me what had happened at the Provincial House." His eyes were full of torment and she tried to reach out to him, but she couldn't move.

"Do you really love me, Kip?" she asked, her eyes wide, her heart leaping.

"I've been telling you for a long time."

"No. No, you haven't."

"But I have!"

"I never heard you."

"You were busy pushing me away."

"Oh, Kip, I thought you were just playing with me because you were bored with the girls around here."

"You don't trust me or believe me. You push me away, and still you say we have to talk! What are you doing to me, Jeanna?"

She slid her hands across his chest and around his neck and curled her fingers into his thick brown hair.

"I didn't mean to hurt you, Kip."

"You almost killed me!"

"I am so sorry! Forgive me. Please."

He clamped his hands to her waist and tried to push her away, but she clung tighter.

"I love you, Kip," she whispered.

He grew quiet.

"I love you!"

He studied her face and looked deep into her eyes. "I don't believe you."

She flinched. "I deserve that, Kip. Please don't push me away because I couldn't trust you or believe you. I do now. I do love you. With my whole heart."

"Jeanna, Jeanna."

She pulled his head down and touched her lips to his. He kissed her, his mouth warm on hers. Finally they drew apart. She looked at him, her eyes shining with love.

He smiled. "I love you, Jae."

The words warmed her heart and she kissed him again.

*   *   *

Frowning, Carolynn Burgess stopped outside Bess Wilder's house. The place looked as deserted as it had this morning when she'd stopped. Had Bess left town without notifying anyone at the Provincial House? Had meeting Gil Oakes frightened her away?

Carolynn walked briskly to the door and knocked. She waited and knocked again. She put her ear against the door, but couldn't hear a sound. Too bad all the windows were covered with blinds or she'd peek in. She'd tried to look in the garage this morning, but the windows were covered and the door locked.

Slowly she walked back to her car and drove away. Shivers ran up and down her back. Her hands felt icy-cold on the steering wheel. What was wrong with her? She slowed the car, then pulled to the curb. Maybe she should watch Bess Wilder's house to see if Gil Oakes came to visit. She'd gone to see him at work twice, but had missed him both times. They said if he didn't stay on the job like he was supposed to, he'd be out of a job.

She drove back toward Bess Wilder's house and parked in a secluded spot down the street. If no one showed up within half an hour, she'd go home. That's where she belonged anyway. She'd told Robert she'd be home to cook dinner. Holly and Stan were going to be there. Maybe they were ready to announce their wedding day. Carolynn smiled. She liked weddings.

Several minutes later she observed a car slowing down at Bess's driveway. Carolynn watched closely. It was Gil Oakes. He parked outside the garage, then ran to the front door. He unlocked the door and let himself in. "Interesting," Carolynn muttered.

She drove up the street and pulled behind Gil's car. She rubbed her hands down her gray slacks and fingered her necklace. Finally she walked to the house and knocked on the front door. Gil didn't answer. She knocked again, then called, "Gil, it's Carolynn Burgess. Could I talk to you please?"

After a long time Gil opened the door. He smiled and said, "Hello, Mrs. Burgess. What brings you here?"

"I wanted to speak to Bess Wilder, then I saw your car and thought it'd be nice to say hello to you."

"My mom is still at work."

It was an outright lie! "Can I come in?"

"Sure." He held the door wide open, and she stepped inside, directly into the living room. There was a small, plaid couch, one plaid, blue chair and a small, portable TV set on a small, round table.

"How'd your dinner go last night, Gil?"

He grinned as he closed the door. "Really well, thank you."

Carolynn felt tension in the air. Something wasn't right and she wanted to find out what it was. "Do you think you'll be able to have a mother-son relationship with Bess Wilder like you want?"

"Given time we will. She's a nice woman, but when she gave me up she got kind of hard. But she's getting nice again."

Carolynn cleared her throat. "Gil, could I have a drink of water please? My throat's dry."

"Sure! I'll get it for you. Just wait right here." Gil smiled again and hurried to the kitchen.

Carolynn quickly unlocked the front door so that when she went out it wouldn't lock behind her. She hated doing it, but she had to. Things weren't right and she wanted to find out why.

He brought her a full glass of water. She drank a few swallows and handed it back. "Thanks, Gil. How about coming for dinner again one of these days?"

"I'll be busy with my mom. Having dinner with her and things like that. Going to the movies. You know."

"Sure, I know." Carolynn smiled. Nurse Wilder really had to turn over a new leaf to change that much. "Tell your mom to call me when she gets home, will you?"

"Well, she'll be too busy to call tonight, but maybe tomorrow."

"That'll be fine. Thanks for the water." She opened the door, lifted her hand in a wave and walked out, closing the door. She hurried to her car and drove away. Once again she parked down the street. She waited almost an hour, but still Bess didn't drive in. "What do you think is wrong?" Carolynn whispered, frowning. She didn't want to say aloud what she was thinking. It was too terrible.

She walked up the street, then ran to the front door. She pressed her ear against the door, but couldn't hear anything. Slowly she turned the knob. It turned without a sound. She eased the door open and slipped inside, her stomach fluttering nervously. Voices drifted out from the kitchen. She crept across the room and pressed against the wall just outside the kitchen. Gil and Bess were together. Carolynn frowned. Gil had lied to her. Was it possible Bess had been here the entire day and hadn't answered the door?

"I brought the things you need so we can bake chocolate chip cookies, Mommy."

The sound of Gil's voice sent shivers down Carolynn's back.

"I get to lick the bowl. Do you know how many times I dreamed about us making cookies together? I always got to lick the bowl in my dreams."

"Gil, why are you doing this to me?"

"Doing what? You're my mommy and we're doing things together a son and a mommy should do."

"Just let me go, Gil."

"But if I do, you'll run away and leave me. I won't ever let you leave me again!"

Carolynn took a deep breath, then peeked around the doorway. "Hello, you two."

Gil turned with a startled cry.

Bess Wilder lunged forward, but couldn't reach Carolynn. A chain was locked around her ankle with the other end padlocked to the metal towel rack on the counter near the sink. "Help me, Mrs. Burgess!"

Carolynn's heart thundered in her ears. How could Gil do this to his own mother?

Gil scooped up a gun from the table and aimed it at Carolynn. "Don't come any closer, Mrs. Burgess. Me and Mommy are baking cookies. You can't talk to her until we're done."

Carolynn saw the wild light in Gil's eyes and she knew she'd have to be very careful. "Gil, put that gun down before you hurt someone! And let your mother go this minute!"

"She's not Mother! She's Mommy." Gil aimed the gun at Bess. "And as soon as we finish making cookies together I'm going to kill her."

"No, no, no," Bess said, sobbing and shaking her head.

"Don't cry, Mommy. It won't hurt for long."

Carolynn silently prayed for wisdom in dealing with Gil. If she did anything to upset him, she knew he'd kill her as well as Bess. "Since you and your mommy are busy I'll leave and come another time, Gil."

"Don't even think about it!" Gil turned the gun on her. "I think you're a wonderful woman and I know you don't deserve to die, but I'm not stupid. You'll call the sheriff and have him come and arrest me. He talked to me about that murder outside the church. He thought I did it."

"And did you do it?" Carolynn asked softly.

"Of course not!"

"He did!" Bess cried. "He told me! He killed her because she gave her baby up for adoption. He said she deserved to die like the others he killed! And he plans to kill a girl named Meg."

Gil clicked his tongue. "Mommy, I told you that was our secret. Shame on you for telling Mrs. Burgess. I didn't want her to know. She likes me. Now she won't."

"I still like you, Gil," Carolynn said gently.

"No, you don't. You're just saying that so I won't kill you."

"I'd like to help bake cookies with you. I've baked them lots of times with my kids. And with my grandchildren." Carolynn inched her way forward as she talked. If she could get within kicking distance, she could kick the gun from his hand. He had no idea she was trained in martial arts.

Gil shook his head. "I just decided what I'll have to do. I'll tie you to a chair so you can watch me and Mommy."

"Please don't, Gil," Carolynn said. She judged the distance as he walked toward her. Suddenly she kicked his wrist, sending the gun flying across the room. It crashed against the counter and slid close to Bess.

Gil lunged for the gun, but Bess scooped it up.

"Don't!" Carolynn cried. She knocked Bess's arm up just as she fired and the bullet tore through the ceiling. Carolynn wrested the gun from Bess just as Gil lunged forward with a butcher knife held high. Carolynn sidestepped, whirled and kicked Gil in the chin. He crumpled to the floor, dropping the knife. She scooped it up and tossed it in the sink. She emptied the chamber on the gun and dropped it and the bullets in her purse.

"Unlock the chain," Bess said hoarsely. "The key's in his shirt pocket."

Carolynn lifted Gil enough to get the key. His head rolled back, but she knew he wouldn't be out long. She quickly unlocked Bess. "Call Sheriff Farley Cobb at this number." Carolynn rattled it off as Bess picked up her phone.

Gil groaned and sat up. He watched Bess talking on the phone. Tears filled his eyes and slowly ran down his cheeks. "Don't, Mommy. Please don't let the police take me away."

Bess glared at Gil. "You shut up! You hear me? Just shut up!"

Gil covered his face and sobbed.

Carolynn lifted him to his feet and set him in a chair at the table.

"She hates me," Gil whispered.

Carolynn touched Gil's arm. "Everybody in the world could hate you, but Jesus would still love you."

"Do you hate me, Mrs. Burgess?"

"No, Gil."

He sighed in relief.

"And neither does God. He loves you." She told him of God's great sacrifice of sending Jesus to die in his place, then of rising again to live in heaven, always making intercession for him. "Jesus wants to be your friend and Savior. He wants to help you become a whole person full of love for others." She leaned closer to Gil. "Jesus wants to take away your pain and anguish."

Moaning, Gil shook his head. "No, no! I've done terrible things."

"Yes, you have. But Jesus loves *you*. When you turn your life over to Him and accept Him as your Savior, you become a new creation in Christ. Your old life is behind you. You begin a whole new life."

A ray of hope shone in Gil's eyes.

Carolynn said softly, "Gil, it's your decision. Would you accept Jesus as your Savior now?"

He nodded as tears filled his eyes.

Carolynn held his hand and prayed with him. Between sobs, he asked Jesus to forgive his sins and to be his Lord and Savior. He took a long, shuddering breath and said, "I don't feel scared and alone any more."

"That's because you're not alone. I'll give you a Bible to study. It's God's Word. You'll learn His promises to you as you read and study."

"Thank you, Mrs. Burgess." Gil smiled. "Maybe someday we could bake cookies together."

Struggling against tears, she squeezed his hand. "I'd like that."

$$\star \quad \star \quad \star$$

Much later Carolynn rang the Rawlings' doorbell. She'd asked Farley if she could tell them the killer was in custody.

Tim opened the door. "Carolynn, come in. We weren't expecting you."

Silver sat on the couch with her mother beside her. Brittany was in her pajamas playing with a pile of blocks. "Hello, Carolynn," Silver said, sounding nervous. "This is my mother, Mavis Terrill. Mom, Carolynn Burgess is a dear friend."

"It's nice to meet you, Mrs. Terrill." Carolynn shook hands with her, then picked up Brittany and kissed her soundly. "Oh, but you smell good! I bet you just had a bath, didn't you?"

Brittany chattered her baby talk and tried to pull Carolynn's necklace off.

"I have news." Carolynn put Brittany down and faced Tim and Silver with a wide smile. "The killer is in custody." She told them briefly about Gil Oakes. "He wanted to put the blame on you, Silver, because you adopted Brittany."

Silver shivered. "I'm glad it's all over."

"So this man Gil Oakes worked at Children's Services," Tim said, shaking his head. "He had access to all that information."

Carolynn nodded. "He didn't feel it was right for anyone to adopt."

Mrs. Terrill flushed. "I can understand that."

"It is better if the birth parents can keep their child, but if it's not possible, those precious babies need homes." Carolynn reached down and stroked Brittany's head. "Wouldn't it be terrible if a baby had to go through life without love just because someone didn't believe in adoption?"

"She's right, Mom," Silver said.

"I suppose I have taken a hard line about it." Mrs. Terrill patted Silver's leg. "I'll try to look at it differently."

Brittany toddled to her grandma and leaned against her leg, then smiled.

"Who can resist that?" Carolynn said softly.

Mrs. Terrill rested her hand on Brittany's shoulder. "Not me." She hesitated, then picked Brittany up and hugged her close.

Silver's eyes filled with tears. She turned to Tim. "Mom's not the only one who can change. We'll work things out."

Tim nodded. "Together," he whispered.

Carolynn walked to the door. "Now that all of this is settled we're going to have a wedding in our family. Holly and Stan."

Just as Carolynn reached the door someone rang the bell. "Shall I answer since I'm right here?"

"Sure," Tim said with a nod.

Carolynn swung the door open. Andy and Lavery stood there. Carolynn hid a grin. She should've known Lavery would show up again. "Come in. I assume you came because you heard the killer was arrested."

"What?" Lavery cried.

"Who was it?" Andy asked sharply.

Carolynn closed the door and once again told the story. She didn't say a word about the fight she'd had with Gil. It wouldn't do at all for Lavery to hear she knew martial arts.

Brittany walked to Andy and looked up at him with her wide smile and baby talk. He picked her up and held her without speaking.

"We'd be willing to let you be an uncle to her," Tim said gently.

Andy nodded. "Thanks. I'd like that."

Carolynn turned to Lavery. "Well, it looks like your case is solved and you can go on vacation with your husband."

Lavery scowled and slammed out the door.

"What's her problem?" Silver asked.

Carolynn shrugged.

★   ★   ★

Later at home Carolynn peered in the refrigerator while Robert sat at the kitchen table drinking diet Pepsi. As well as telling all the details of finding the killer, she'd already apologized five times for not making it home for dinner.

"We can't all have nice home-cooked meals," Robert said with a laugh.

She turned from the refrigerator. "Where are the leftovers?"

"There aren't any. We ate out."

She chuckled. "I guess I could scramble an egg. Or nibble on a piece of cheese."

"Or we could go to the Checkered Cloth Cafe for a late dinner."

"Are you serious?"

"Sure am."

She hugged him. "Would you really want to, Robert? You hate going out at night."

He shrugged. "I figure I gotta keep you fed or you won't be able to solve your next mystery."

She laughed, then kissed him.